Praise for SECRETS OF SIN

"The steamy sun of the Caribbean is nothing compared to the wicked heat between Emiline and Reinier. Submission, obsession, and passion sizzle on the pages of this mouthwatering debut."
—*Kate Douglas,* author of the Wolf Tales series

"Sensuality at its best!"
—*Diana Cosby,* author of *His Woman*

Secrets
of Sin

CHLOE HARRIS

APHRODISIA

KENSINGTON BOOKS
http://www.kensingtonbooks.com

APHRODISIA BOOKS are published by

Kensington Publishing Corp.
119 West 40th Street
New York, NY 10018

ISBN-13: 978-0-7582-3853-5
ISBN-10: 0-7582-3853-3

First Kensington Trade Paperback Printing: February 2010

10 9 8 7 6 5 4 3 2 1

Printed in the United States of America

To John Donne (1572-1631)
and
You, dear reader.

Acknowledgments

Chloe Harris would like to thank both her amazing agent, Emily Sylvan Kim, and her rock star editor, Amy Pyle. She could not have asked for better!

Barbra individually would like to thank:
My parents for their patience and support and Christine for believing in me even when I had my moments of doubt.

Noelle individually would like to thank:
The Carolina Romance Writers. Their support has been invaluable.

1

If a lady was thinking of doing the unthinkable, she should dress unobtrusively. That didn't include not looking one's best.

Emiline brushed a fold out of her skirts.

Raise your skirts for me. Are you naked underneath?

How she despised those haunting memories. She pressed her eyes closed. Sometimes darkness could scatter them. Reluctant silence spread in her mind and she opened her eyes again.

Emiline was thankful she'd chosen a simple, light turquoise linen gown for the journey. The flimsy lace around the short sleeves and her décolletage was just enough ornament. Too much to mistake her for a common lady and just a sufficient enough amount to show interested eyes how high her standing really was.

Sit. I want your legs spread, knees up by your ears. Show yourself to me.

Emiline tried to ban his words from her mind with a curt shake of her head. Her response to him had been disgusting. She'd let him humiliate her; she'd allowed him to make her beg for his touch. Emiline could still see his vivid green eyes, recalling that very special glitter when he heard her desperate plea. She thought she could even hear his virile, soft laugh in reply.

Arousal shivered through her when she saw him kneel down in front of her. His hands rose and he slowly ran them down the inner side of her thighs. With every inch they advanced toward her, she felt her core spasm just a little, pumping more of that inviting moistness out of her. She didn't dare move. Not because she was afraid to, but because she loved the eroticism of the moment. Each and every moment with him was wonderfully special, and she enjoyed it to the full, this whole new world he'd shown her.

Her breathing had almost stopped. He seemed so fascinated with her, watching his hands, his pale hands compared to her bronze-colored skin, wander lower. And they did, but his touch was light, too light. Just his thumbs brushed over her creamy folds; then suddenly he squeezed her erect, sensitized nub between the tips of them. Her head fell against the back of the chair. Sizzling sparks of longing shot through her body as violent as a bolt of lightning tearing a tree apart.

He looked up at her as he increased the pressure on her nub between his thumbs. His pale green eyes had darkened, yet they looked as if they shone with an inner light. It was just the afternoon sun, Emiline told herself. It bathed half of him in darkness.

"Tell me you want me."

Emiline was fighting for breath, gulping in just enough air to tell him that.

"Tell me."

She moaned as he increased the pressure even more until it would be almost painful if it weren't so sensual. Yes, yes. She nodded. She wanted him. She needed him. Her whole being existed just for him now. She loved him. They'd said the words, of course. But up to that moment she hadn't really known what they meant. She loved him with every fiber of her being.

Emiline never had the time to utter anything but soft, low moans because he'd wrapped her hair around his wrist. Twisting those long chocolate curls he'd said he liked so much, he forced her head back up to watch him as he ripped the fly of his breeches open. His hand was shaking with need as much as her body did.

Then his lips were on hers, taking her mouth with a greedy, hard kiss. If she didn't know better, she'd call it desperate. Oh, she was desperate too. She was sure she was going to burn alive if he didn't—

He stuffed her. She loved when he took her fast and seated himself in her with one hard thrust; but this time he took her slow, shivering with every inch he slid deeper. He even closed his eyes as if memorizing that very moment, then the next, and the next . . .

Emiline moaned helplessly into his mouth, her tongue swirling around his, chasing it back and forth. She quivered against him, her secret muscles sucking him in, recklessly commanding him to take her deeper, faster.

They broke their passionate kiss when he was finally seated to the hilt. A hairsbreadth apart, they moaned against each other's lips. His free hand came around to the small of her back to shove her closer to him. His other hand didn't lessen its tight grip on her hair. The linen of her dress chafed her erect, hard nipples. The back of the chair bit into her shoulders. Each spot where slight pinpricks spread added to the pleasure until her body roared with want.

With a quick flick of his tongue over her bottom lip, he drew her attention. When her eyes met his, her heart gave another stutter. He was so beautiful. And he was here in her arms.

He rolled his hips back and left her. The sudden emptiness made her want to cry. But the next instant, he thrust into her, hard and fast.

The chair squeaked. Her shoulders would be sore. They would be a constant, pleasant reminder for the next day or two. His torso rolled against hers, increasing the chafing sensation on her breasts. They, too, would sting in the days to come.

He drove his member in and out of her slick, clamping core. They'd shared many ardent moments in the last year, but each time it was more passionate. Burning waves of pleasure washed through her and rebounded from the contact points of his member in her, from his chest rubbing against her breasts. Her hips answered his every thrust, grinding against him, silently begging him for more.

He deepened his rolling thrusts. He pumped in and out of her, stroking her so deliciously that the hot friction they both created started that surge that flowed through her thighs and back and sides. Emiline knew she was going to come, sooner than she wanted or expected and fiercer than ever before.

She was marginally aware that her nails bit into his shoulders as she screamed her pleasure. She loved him so much tiny tears formed at the corners of her eyes.

He left her and came moments after her, his hand pumping his member until he'd shed the last drop. When he looked up, he had tears in his eyes also.

Leaning forward, he kissed her again while his hand left her hair and he fumbled to close his breeches again. He smiled.

"I love . . . your hair."

Emiline knew that. It's why she wore it down. For him.

He covered her again and got up. His knees popped. The smile died on his lips, and he turned his back.

Today seemed more tropical than most. Emiline had purposely tamed her hair this morning and carefully arranged it in a chignon so that now she could delight in every salty breath of sea breeze that tickled and cooled her neck.

Standing at the window, Emiline looked out onto the town of St. George's, capital of Grenada. When she realized her nervous fingers were playing with the brocade curtain, she quickly brought her hand down. She didn't really know exactly why she was stalling.

Emiline, I'm going to leave.

"You look lovely today, Emiline."

With a thankful nod, Emiline turned, looking straight into the keen eyes of Monsieur Améliore sitting in a huge leather chair behind his desk. He was a good-looking man even though he was old enough to be her father. His full mop of dark blond hair was only faintly dusted with gray; his braid emphasized it was graying slightly more so at his temples. He was impeccably garbed. The laces around his neck were tight, but not too tight, spilling in abundance out of a periwinkle waistcoat that high-lighted his cornflower blue coat. Emiline supposed it was diffi-cult to take Paris out of a Parisian. Fashion and good manners were inborn to the French. She of all people knew that.

Just then Améliore wrinkled his forehead. Emiline had been silent far too long. She took a step closer to the small chair in front of the desk. "Any news of your nephew?" Last year the French had joined in King George's War, and Améliore's nephew had gladly enlisted. "Is he still in—"

"Yes, Louisbourg is under siege. Just this morning I got a letter that's about four months old, dated April 29, 1745. By now I suppose the British have breached the defenses and are happily helping themselves to anything they can loot and pil-lage." Améliore spoke with a light growl through clenched teeth. An animosity toward the British was inborn to the French as well.

"I'm sorry to hear that, Monsieur Améliore."

He shrugged. "That's neither here nor there, Emiline. Would you care to discuss why you're here today?"

At first, Emiline was shocked that Améliore had so rudely cut to the heart of the matter, but on second thought . . .

Connor O'Driscoll had business with Améliore. When he arrived, the secretary assured him that even though Améliore was currently occupied, he could wait. Connor nodded and strolled to the seating arrangement by one of the open windows right next to Améliore's office.

The late-morning breeze whispered over his face and made him sigh with bliss as he settled in the cushioned rattan chair. It was cooler indoors, a pleasant, slightly moist freshness that couldn't be drawn away by the sticky hot weather. The large windows were wide open, and the white brocade curtains danced excitedly like debutantes at their first ball.

He sat back in the cushioned chair and enjoyed the solitude. It was quiet here, almost absolutely silent but for the tiny scratching of the secretary's quill and the low murmur flowing toward him from the office in the next room. The voices were that of a lady mixed with the deep, smoky timbre of Monsieur Améliore's, the best lawyer in St. George's.

The *Coraal* had arrived just this morning, and as captain of the ship, Connor had dutifully seen to it that all the cargo went for the best price possible. Then, after having been at sea for several weeks, he had spoiled himself at the local bathhouse, indulged in scented steam and a shave, and afterward floated in rose-petal water until his fingertips were white and shriveled.

Feeling cared for and contented now, Connor let his head fall against the back of the rattan chair. An unruly strand of hair escaped its braid and danced around the tip of his nose. It tickled, skipping over his face. He wrinkled his nose a few times with a dreamy smile on his lips. The effort to brush it away seemed like too much at the moment.

The breeze was quite pleasant and cooling. He was sure his friend was staying cool as well. At that thought, Connor opened his eyes and looked over the town out of the open window. His gaze was immediately drawn to the red roof of the most dubious and finest house in all of the West Indies. He knew Reinier was there. They always met there.

But business came first. Connor sighed and let his head fall back again, closing his eyes to the soft voice of the lady inside Améliore's office. By the tone of her words, she was polite and well educated, and very feminine.

His mind was lulled into a dreamlike state by the sweetness of her voice. Something in the way she talked sounded familiar to Connor. For the life of him he couldn't say how; nonetheless, he felt as if he knew her. Yet, such excellent ladies rarely associated with the likes of him or his friend. Not normally, anyway.

Not that Reinier and Connor weren't well respected. Quite the contrary, the proprietors of the Barhydt-O'Driscoll Shipping Company were very well-respected men. It was more that ladies like her didn't play the games they liked to play. Not normally, anyway.

Outwardly, such ladies thought themselves much too good, too sophisticated, and above all too decent to enjoy the degree of decadence Reinier and Connor indulged in. But he knew better. Appearances were deceiving—especially with ladies. And most pointedly with lonely ladies who needed a strong hand . . . or two or four.

Yet, it could be equally as wonderful to enjoy the talents of less-respected, highly adept women with no inhibitions. They didn't need to be convinced they'd like this or that. They already knew they'd enjoy themselves immensely.

Connor smiled and folded his arms over his chest while stretching his long legs. Oh, yes, he and Reinier had had a lot of adventures together with such ladies.

The breeze slowly died and the two voices, the soft, feminine one and the gently croaking one of Améliore, seemed so loud that Connor could overhear their conversation now. He shouldn't listen, he knew, but he couldn't help hearing them through the open windows as clearly as if they were standing right next to him.

"My dear," Améliore was saying, "I've known you since you were a child. Are you certain this is what you want?" He was coughing a little. Améliore always coughed when he felt highly agitated. Too many cigars, Connor assumed, yet out of politeness he'd still brought him a box of the finest the West Indies could offer.

"Yes, Monsieur Améliore, I am. This marriage, which exists only on paper, I might add, has brought me nothing but grief. I haven't seen my husband in over four years, and I do believe we have both moved on. He will be delighted to sign the papers, I'm sure."

Améliore murmured something into his fist; Connor could hear the muffled mumbling. He knew the lawyer used to do that when he was deep in thought.

"Your father—" the lawyer set out but was cut off by the lady again.

"My father!" she exclaimed, and judging from the sound of a chair scraping over the hardwood, followed by the rapid clicking of heels on the floor, she was up and pacing. "May his soul rest in peace, my father died four years ago and my good-for-nothing husband didn't even send a note of condolence, much less come to his funeral. I wish to be free of this marriage. At once. It's quite obvious my husband doesn't desire to have anything to do with me or Bougainvilla."

Instantly, Connor's eyes snapped open and he felt a frosty shiver down his back. He was wide awake—and careful not to breathe too deeply and miss a bit of the conversation that was to come.

Could it be? When had they last seen each other? At the wedding?

8

"Very well, then," Améliore muttered reluctantly.

Connor heard him get up from his seat as well and, so he assumed, the lawyer walked to the huge old sideboard where he kept preprinted documents. Connor leaned forward, alert.

Améliore sat down at his desk again. The slight protest of the lawyer's chair told Connor so. Then he heard the lawyer grunt, "So, do you know where we might find Captain Barhydt to make him aware of your request?"

"I'm sure I have no idea where Reinier is at the moment. Most likely, he's on the ship he built with my dowry. But I'm also sure you can hire people to track him down. Last time I saw him, he was blond. I'm afraid I cannot recall anything beyond that, having seen only his back as he ran."

Sarcasm? Connor's jaw dropped. So, the "little, too sweet-tempered and naïve wife," as Reinier had described her, was asking the family lawyer, who also happened to be the lawyer of the Barhydt-O'Driscoll Shipping Company, to draw up the divorce papers? Now that was an interesting twist to his day.

Not that he could blame her. In fact, Connor wasn't really surprised. Reinier was restless and always sought the freedom of the sea.

When Reinier had married her five years ago, Emiline du Ronde was no match for the Dutchman. She was barely 18, privileged, and judging from what little Reinier had told him, infinitely spoiled. Reinier had built his ship and ran soon afterward. She hadn't been able to hold him.

Never in Connor's wildest dreams—and they could be quite wild—would he have thought it could turn out like this.

He quickly walked over to where the young secretary sat, asked him for a paper and a quill, and wrote a short note to Améliore. But just as the salt had dried the viscous ink and he was about to fold the note, the door to Améliore's office opened.

Connor stood straight and smirked when his eyes met the

turquoise blue depths of Reinier's wife's. He saw recognition cross Emiline du Ronde-Barhydt's lovely face; then she halted and inhaled deeply. Despite her delicate café-au-lait complexion, she blanched. Her eyes widened with what must have been shock at seeing him, her husband's partner, right there by the secretary's desk.

"Monsieur O'Driscoll," she murmured civilly as she curtly bowed her head. The coolness of her tone made his name sound like that of an evil sprite one wished away.

Connor felt his smug expression broaden as he bowed to her in turn. "Mrs. Barhydt, what a pleasure to see you here."

Emiline's eyes paled to a chilly light blue at the deliberate address. She said a quick farewell to Améliore and left the office without looking at him again.

Connor watched her speedy retreat, the smile on his lips slowly vanishing. A very interesting twist, indeed.

Emiline was careful to uphold a calm, sedate exterior when she ducked into Polilla's, the tiny bookstore right around the corner. The instant she entered the bookshop, she felt better. Not only did the coolness calm her overheated body, as always, the scent of old paper and ink, vaguely moldy and bitter, had a soothing effect on her.

Emiline loved books. They were her escape from the burdens her life had become. There was no more need for decisions, no responsibility, no more hard work to do while she lost herself in her books. Poetry was her favorite; it made her feel again when everything else had dulled her.

Polilla, the owner of the shop, was a frail, old bookworm, but his eyes twinkled with delight when he saw her standing in his gloomy little store. "Ahh, Señorita du Ronde, how wonderful to see you," he greeted her warmly. Before she could answer, he promptly bent under the ancient counter to retrieve a

"Very well, then," Améliore muttered reluctantly.

Connor heard him get up from his seat as well and, so he assumed, the lawyer walked to the huge old sideboard where he kept preprinted documents. Connor leaned forward, alert.

Améliore sat down at his desk again. The slight protest of the lawyer's chair told Connor so. Then he heard the lawyer grunt, "So, do you know where we might find Captain Barhydt to make him aware of your request?"

"I'm sure I have no idea where Reinier is at the moment. Most likely, he's on the ship he built with my dowry. But I'm also sure you can hire people to track him down. Last time I saw him, he was blond. I'm afraid I cannot recall anything beyond that, having seen only his back as he ran."

Sarcasm? Connor's jaw dropped. So, the "little, too sweet-tempered and naïve wife," as Reinier had described her, was asking the family lawyer, who also happened to be the lawyer of the Barhydt-O'Driscoll Shipping Company, to draw up the divorce papers? Now that was an interesting twist to his day.

Not that he could blame her. In fact, Connor wasn't really surprised. Reinier was restless and always sought the freedom of the sea.

When Reinier had married her five years ago, Emiline du Ronde was no match for the Dutchman. She was barely 18, privileged, and judging from what little Reinier had told him, infinitely spoiled. Reinier had built his ship and ran soon afterward. She hadn't been able to hold him.

Never in Connor's wildest dreams—and they could be quite wild—would he have thought it could turn out like this.

He quickly walked over to where the young secretary sat, asked him for a paper and a quill, and wrote a short note to Améliore. But just as the salt had dried the viscous ink and he was about to fold the note, the door to Améliore's office opened.

Connor stood straight and smirked when his eyes met the

turquoise blue depths of Reinier's wife's. He saw recognition cross Emiline du Ronde-Barhydt's lovely face; then she halted and inhaled deeply. Despite her delicate café-au-lait complexion, she blanched. Her eyes widened with what must have been shock at seeing him, her husband's partner, right there by the secretary's desk.

"Monsieur O'Driscoll," she murmured civilly as she curtly bowed her head. The coolness of her tone made his name sound like that of an evil sprite one wished away.

Connor felt his smug expression broaden as he bowed to her in turn. "Mrs. Barhydt, what a pleasure to see you here."

Emiline's eyes paled to a chilly light blue at the deliberate address. She said a quick farewell to Améliore and left the office without looking at him again.

Connor watched her speedy retreat, the smile on his lips slowly vanishing. A very interesting twist, indeed.

Emiline was careful to uphold a calm, sedate exterior when she ducked into Polilla's, the tiny bookstore right around the corner. The instant she entered the bookshop, she felt better. Not only did the coolness calm her overheated body, as always, the scent of old paper and ink, vaguely moldy and bitter, had a soothing effect on her.

Emiline loved books. They were her escape from the burdens her life had become. There was no more need for decisions, no responsibility, no more hard work to do while she lost herself in her books. Poetry was her favorite; it made her feel again when everything else had dulled her.

Polilla, the owner of the shop, was a frail, old bookworm, but his eyes twinkled with delight when he saw her standing in his gloomy little store. "Ahh, Señorita du Ronde, how wonderful to see you," he greeted her warmly. Before she could answer, he promptly bent under the ancient counter to retrieve a package. "Come, have a look. I've had these ordered exclusively with you in mind."

She quickly shed her crochet gloves and let her fingers run gently over the exquisite leather bindings of the two books. She examined them, well aware of Señor Polilla closely watching her. It was too rare that somebody shared her passion for books, but Polilla did.

"Señorita, if it weren't for you, I would have had to close this shop years ago."

All he got was a tentative smile when she briefly glanced up from the poem that had captured her attention.

"Pray, forgive my speaking so openly, but there should be more in your life than printed words. I do think you need a husband."

She shut the book a little too loudly. The smile on her lips froze to a friendly grimace at the mention of a husband once again.

"Pardon. I shouldn't have . . ." Polilla bowed, averting his eyes.

"I'd like both of them. Thank you." Emiline's tone was warm and friendly to silently reassure him that she hadn't taken offense where none was meant.

Gnarled fingers wrapped brown paper around the two books, and a simple twine secured the bundle. "Shall I keep these here for you until you're ready to sail?"

"No, thank you. I'll take them now." Emiline reached for the purse in the small pocket of her gown and paid the old bookseller. Then, holding her precious package to her chest, she braced herself against the temperature outside.

Her feet carried her quickly back down the winding road to the harbor. She made her way swiftly through the dozens of sailors, traders, and marketers. St. George's was the main port in the Caribbean to purchase and advertise all manner of traded goods like sugarcane and indigo, among other things. At this time of day, the Carenage, the deep water harbor, was buzzing with traders and buyers involved in heated discussions about quality, quantity, and prices, but a good many of them were bargaining for bargaining's sake alone.

Emiline tried to blend in with the masses. She barely noticed the mixture of scents wafting through the port, from the delectable fragrance of spices to the strong, distinctive smell of coffee and tobacco all tinged by the stink of fish. She just wanted to get onboard the *Sea Gull.*

The crude wooden plank swayed under her feet as she ascended. Her maid, Justine, had returned from her errands along with the *Sea Gull*'s Captain Blanc, who had been so kind to accompany Justine. Emiline had wanted to be alone for the business she'd concluded today.

The Anglican Church proudly looked over the town and the port, its chiming bell bidding farewell to the *Sea Gull* slowly passing through the horseshoe-shaped harbor. The ship's belly was now empty of its cargo of sugarcane from Ronde, the small island just north of Grenada that was her home.

Emiline held her white crochet-covered hand over her eyes to shield them from the bright morning sun, smiling up at her entourage, a horde of quibbling sea birds with their tuneless cacophony crudely imitating a fanfare as the *Sea Gull* made her way out of the port.

On his way to the most excellent house in town, Connor didn't pay attention to whether he was walking in the shade or in the sunlight. He was too distracted. He had to be sure of his plan before he entered Madame Poivre's establishment and met with Reinier.

It was quite unfortunate that the advice he'd given his friend years ago had turned out like this. As second son, Reinier hadn't had too many options to make a fortune for himself, and since he was definitely not meant for the church, Reinier had started his career on a ship. One night Connor had told him half jokingly that Reinier needed to marry money and get his own ship. Had he known Reinier would take his advice that literally, Connor would have been more careful.

One didn't go off and marry a young, besotted girl if one wanted to marry rich. One looked for a lonely, but wealthy—and if possible, passably attractive—widow. Connor supposed Reinier had never thought that part through and had certainly not taken heed of the consequences for her.

Reinier valued freedom above anything else. Never feeling tied down was his main ambition in life, and he was determined to achieve it. Yet, Connor had known him long enough and well enough to see a new restlessness in his eyes. Something was amiss. Reinier needed to settle down, whether he was aware of it or not. He needed to find a sense of peace before too long.

Is this the right choice? Connor wondered. *Does he really have a right to meddle with his friend's life like this?*

Perhaps he wanted to do this to silence his own conscience. Reinier had taken his thoughtless words too seriously.

Nonetheless, Connor was sure he mustn't tell Reinier about the divorce. In his current state of mind, Reinier would sign the agreement only too gladly. Four years was a long time. It changed people, and by the tone Mrs. Emiline du Ronde-Barhydt had laid into her words, as well as her determination to be rid of her husband, she seemed quite the opposite of how Reinier had described her. She might not have been before, but perhaps now she was exactly what his friend needed.

By the time he was taking two steps at once to climb the stairs to Madame Poivre's, Connor had convinced himself of the best course of action. What he'd come up with may not have been the best of all lies, but it would do. Connor knew Reinier was competitive, especially when it came to what he regarded as his own.

What a shame. The world would certainly mourn the loss of a glorious rake such as Reinier.

"Bonjour, Monsieur O'Driscoll. This way." A young maid greeted him, opening the door with a curtsy even before he reached for the bell. She must have been spying from behind the curtains.

They walked in silence toward a private room at the back of the house. Quietly, she opened the double doors and motioned with a quick gesture for him to enter. Bobbing another curtsy, she closed the doors to the room, giving the men some privacy.

Three very spacious armchairs surrounded a tiny table in the elegantly furnished room. It was polished and classic, a place where a man could relax before indulging in other, very pleasurable activities.

There were no silly-looking cupids around anywhere, no lush red carpets, no strong-smelling perfume in the air covering more undesirable scents that would indicate this was an establishment of the worst kind. The tasteful and timeless elegance made Madame Poivre's an outstanding place, genteel and chic, an establishment of the best kind.

"What took you so long?"

Connor's head snapped toward the voice. He could see only Reinier's legs stretched out lazily and his hands hanging elegantly over the arms of the chair he was lounging in. Instantly, Connor felt his lips twitch into a smile again, but this time it wasn't a forced smile. No, there was genuine delight in it—and a certain amount of playfulness as well.

He went to the armchair opposite his friend and made himself comfortable. Reinier returned the smile with one of his own, only his was more. It was enigmatic. It was meaningful, it was charming and unspeakably seductive—a direct assault to one's senses.

He wore his hair loose today. There was no need to tie it back for what they had in mind. His blond hair was generally straight, but it curled slightly at the tips, and now, as he lounged in the armchair as confident as ever, his mane surrounded his head and brushed over his shoulders like a halo.

His unique eyes were translucent, crystalline jewels of lush green that became so bright they looked as golden as the sun in the center—almost like a cat's eyes. It was precisely those bright, hypnotizing eyes that were taking Connor in from head to toe and back. The perusal sent a pleasant shiver of awareness through Connor's body.

"So . . ." Reinier purred, a husky sound full of heat. "Where have you been?"

Connor relished in his friend's sensual mouth gradually changing, the corners wandering up until he smiled his typical, breathtaking smile. Reinier knew his appeal, and he took great pleasure in seeing how it affected others.

Letting Reinier's rich, velvety words trickle down his spine, Connor tried to sit more comfortably in the chair. The fly of his breeches had become dangerously confining.

Slowly licking his lips, Reinier leaned back more. The delightful physical pressure that was an immediate result of their arousing game was too sweet. Reinier loved anticipation. He adored the sensations brought on by withholding what was inevitably to follow.

At last, Connor found a position he was comfortable with. Now it was time to put his plan into action. He knew if he didn't do it now, he'd forget about it all later. But how to begin?

"Business kept me from joining you sooner," Connor finally replied. "But what I really wanted to tell you is I have heard some juicy rumors about one of the lonely wives on the islands around."

"Is that so?" Reinier let the words out in a bored sigh and

looked away. He studied a nonexistent piece of lint on the turquoise sleeve of his coat that boasted elegant patterns of gold.

He had definitely caught Reinier's attention with that. One corner of Connor's mouth flitted up. If only Reinier knew how much his taste in garments matched his wife's—matched Emiline with her turquoise eyes and the golden highlights in her chocolate brown hair.

"I hired a new sailor at Ronde when we last stopped there to load up with sugarcane. But I am a little disappointed with him. He seems to not be able to stop prattling on about how he was wrongly accused of theft and thrown out by the mistress." Connor deliberately paused for effect before he added, "And her lover."

Now, this wasn't quite the truth, but it could still be excused as a little white lie. Perhaps it wasn't that little, after all, nor was it exactly white. But Connor knew Reinier well enough to trust it wouldn't fail to rattle him.

Wrinkling his forehead, Reinier's detached façade was unwavering. He was even too disciplined to grind his teeth, although inwardly he felt anything but calm. A flashing memory of brilliant turquoise eyes skirted through his mind. Their recurring image had been haunting his dreams lately.

She'd never do that, Reinier told himself. Not to him. She wouldn't dare make a cuckold of him.

"Gossip." With a wave of his hand he brushed off the rumor.

"Yes, it is," Connor agreed, seemingly unaware of how this all affected Reinier. "But isn't it entertaining? I thought it was highly amusing myself."

Reinier snorted with contempt. Closing his eyes, he carefully hid the anger churning in him. If Connor saw his gaze darken, he'd know for sure his mood had changed, and there was no need to give him proof. Most times having such unique eyes was a blessing, but not around somebody who knew him so well, somebody who could tell what Reinier felt just by looking into his eyes.

Why did it even bother him? Everyone who married for convenience sought pleasure outside the marriage. It was almost expected.

Why did he feel that odd twinge in his chest, then? True, he'd married Emiline for practical reasons. But it wasn't quite that simple. As soon as he realized he'd fallen for her, it became quite inconvenient.

"It was only a matter of time before she felt lonely enough to do it." Connor's low voice held a slight hint of reproach.

Only a matter of time. The words echoed in his head. Damn it. If Connor only knew how badly she'd broken his heart. Leaving her had been the only way to make sure she wouldn't take his soul as well.

As soon as he felt certain he'd rid his eyes of any sign of treacherous emotion, Reinier opened them again to linger on his friend. His teeth ground now, but he made sure his eyes remained blank.

She was his, whether he liked it or not. She was his, whether she liked it or not. She had no right to act like this. She wasn't free. She wasn't independent. She belonged to him. Emiline was his wife.

Reinier rubbed his chin in thought. He had pushed that part of his life aside for far too long. She was a pretty girl when he left. Naïve, yes. And eager to please him, that too. Demanding, yet oh-so-unchallenging. At least that was what he had eventually convinced himself of.

Of course, he was completely over that immature infatuation.

Reinier took a deep breath, held it, and then let it out in a rush and along with it the memories that had come to life.

Perhaps it was time he reminded her of her place. A submissive wife needed a dominant husband. He would show her her place in the world—in his world.

Instantly, his wicked mood was completely restored with the prospect of the task ahead. "Connor," he said, his decision final, "I do think it is time I take the southern route. I appreciate you doing it for the last few years, but I feel like going to Ronde again myself." His lips twitched into a sly smile. "I'll set sail tomorrow morning, so that leaves two more days for you."

Connor bowed his head as a sign he understood. They had played this particular game before, after all; Reinier would leave and Connor would follow in a few days. If that was really necessary. Quite honestly, Reinier expected it wouldn't come to that. If she still was who she was, she'd be no match for his honed seductive skills. And speaking of which . . .

"Madame Poivre said she had someone special for us."

He didn't feel guilty about his "leisure" activities, not anymore. What he did here or elsewhere was something men in his position did, period. It was ridiculous that all of a sudden he'd think of it as something damnable.

"Someone special, you say?" Connor's eyebrows rose with curiosity, distracting Reinier's pensive mood and pointing it back in the right direction. "Where is she, anyway? I could do with a glass of port."

At that, the double doors opened and Madame Poivre came in with a tray that held two glasses of the finest wine her excellent establishment offered to only its best of clients.

With her cloying perfume, the much-too-round and much-too-small matron of the maison close of St. George's dressed a little too indecently for her age and for Reinier's taste, wore a little too much rouge on her cheeks and lips, and hid her graying hair under an absurdly large turban that bobbed like a pecking robin whenever she moved her head. But Madame Poivre had exquisite taste in deciding whom she'd let work for her. Reinier had to grant her that.

Turning his head, Reinier smiled at her. "Please have a seat, madame, and tell us about this latest and oh-so-special acquisition of yours." He accompanied his words with a graceful show of his hand, indicating she take the still-empty armchair.

"Ahh," Madame Poivre set out and nodded. "*Certainement.*" Her acquired French heritage almost hid her cockney accent completely.

She placed the now-empty tray against the side of the third armchair, then sat down and leaned back, casually folding her legs. Obviously, she enjoyed the men's attention and drew it out for her own sake. Finally, when she had arranged herself, she declared, "The young woman is completely inexperienced in this métier, messieurs."

Connor turned to her and interrupted rudely, "But she is not a virgin, is she? If so, I won't—"

"Oh, no, no!" Madame Poivre shook both her hands like the flopping wings of a butterfly, the turban on her head bouncing in tandem. "She isn't all that innocent anymore. But she still needs some guidance as to what will be expected from 'er in the future."

Reinier tilted his head in thought. "Why us, madame?"

Laughing, Madame Poivre's elbows rested on the arms of the chair while she brought her fingertips together excitedly, as if applauding herself. "You seemed the right choice to introduce 'er to the ways of 'er new profession."

Reinier raised both his eyebrows and looked at Connor, who, in turn, shrugged as a sign that he didn't understand either.

"Messieurs." Madame Poivre rolled her eyes. "I 'ave other girls 'oo 'ave already 'ad . . . shall we say . . . the pleasure of making your acquaintance? It was their ceaseless rhapsodizing that made me decide you should be the ones to educate 'er."

Reinier laughed low, an understanding, knowing purr. Connor chuckled into his fist.

"I feel obliged to tell you, though," Madame Poivre pointed out, "she is unattractively thin despite 'aving been 'ere for two weeks already. Moreover, she is unfashionably tall for a woman and 'er face is distorted with ghastly freckles."

Connor sat up and leaned forward. "Freckles, you say?"

Reinier hid his smile in his handkerchief as he watched him. He already knew the Irishman could be quickly and easily charmed by blond, flaxen, golden straw or even tawny hair as long as it came with a lovely face. Personally, he couldn't care less. Reinier failed to imagine how a woman with such a fair complexion could have ended up here, in a whorehouse in the Caribbean Sea, but he, too, did not think freckles could be classified as a "distortion." For Connor, it was probably quite the contrary.

Madame Poivre sighed. "I'm afraid so."

Perhaps it was time Reinier scattered Madame Poivre's worries about the woman's "unattractiveness." He knew she'd be appealing. Madame Poivre had a good eye for beauty, after all. Therefore, Reinier stated dryly, "I do believe freckles pose no hindrance to our performance."

"Certainly not," Connor chuckled.

Madame Poivre sighed with relief and bowed her head gratefully.

"So," Reinier concluded, "we are to be the ones to give her her first lesson in licentiousness?"

Madame Poivre bit her lower lip to swallow the mischievous grin crawling up her round face. "Do you feel up to it?"

2

Madame Poivre was swaying her broad hips more than usual.
Reinier could tell because he was right behind her when she
was showing them up the stairs. Something was on her mind,
something exciting, something besides money. He would have
liked to wonder some more, but she opened the door to the best
suite on the second floor and, stepping aside, murmured a low,
"Amusez-vous, messieurs."

Reinier stepped inside and let his coat fall over the one chair
in the room. Hearing Connor sucking in his breath, he turned.
His friend had stopped short, eyes fixated on the woman standing by the windows. Reinier pivoted to see what had Connor
so captivated.

Her exceptionally long, strawberry blond hair fell down her
sides like an exotic veil. Her hair was straight, as straight as her
back when she heard the door close, and she slowly lifted her chin
to meet their gazes. She wore a flimsy white dressing gown over
a matching corset that was cut below her breasts. The long under-
garments emphasized her slim calves and delicate ankles.

Reinier felt his eyebrows raise in surprise. She was tall and thin, but nevertheless beautiful. A rare jewel to be sure. Not as rare as turquoise . . . The thought of her had his expression turn to stone, so he reined in his wandering mind.

She was pale, which only emphasized the dark green quality of her eyes. And as Madame Poivre had pointed out, freckles were lavishly strewn over her features and décolleté. Although her lips were broad and a little too thin for Reinier's taste, they seemed created for luscious pleasures. She was beautiful, indeed. She was a very beautiful whore.

Turning back to Connor, Reinier saw that his friend seemed to have stopped breathing altogether. He looked spellbound, almost frozen in place.

As realization dawned on Reinier, his eyes briefly widened and he felt a knowing, albeit sad, smile on his lips. He'd been there. Reinier knew only too well how it felt when instant attraction hit and rattled a man like lightning.

The poor boy. Somehow Reinier had a strong feeling that this was a woman the Irishman wouldn't be able to easily walk away from.

Tilting his head in thought, Reinier licked his lips slowly. After all their adventures before and after his marriage, Reinier had not thought it could ever happen to Connor. He could only hope he would have far better luck with it than Reinier had ever had.

His gaze was locked with Connor's as the Irishman shook himself out of his trance, his eyebrows puckering in a whimsical way. Reinier ignored Connor's quizzical look and crossed the room to sit on the bed. Casually, he leaned back, bracing himself against the mattress. He was not going to start the game this time. If Connor was, indeed, feeling what Reinier thought he was, he would have to decide the next step to take.

That instant, when both men were looking at her, she cleared her throat, lowered her gaze, and self-consciously tried to cover herself. "Gentlemen," she began tentatively and quietly, "I have been instructed on what you expect. So, what would you have me do?"

A fleeting glance at Connor told Reinier that he was too hypnotized by her smoky voice to react, so Reinier drawled, "Patience. We have all afternoon and half of the night for this." Reinier paused before he added, "At least I do. I believe my friend can stay even longer."

If it was possible, she blanched even more at those words, swallowed, and looked down. Finally, Connor found his way out of his stupor, threw his coat carelessly on top of Reinier's, and stalked toward her. Moving around her, he eyed her from all sides. His sapphire eyes glittered with appreciative sparkles. Subtly leaning forward as if he was trying to catch the scent of her hair, Connor closed his eyes. "Tell us your name." His words were barely more than a whisper.

Instead of answering, instead of maybe even giving them a false name, she only shook her head. Just as well.

Then Reinier saw her shudder and he couldn't help feeling a little bit for her. She was frightened to death. But there was no need to be. He knew that if Connor still wanted this, they would both skillfully seduce her. It was an art they had perfected a long time ago.

Connor walked around until he stood right in front of her. "Are you cold?"

He captured her hands in his. Reinier noticed she wanted to pull away but apparently thought better of it.

"Come. Sit down," Connor offered, guiding her to the bed until she had no choice but to perch on the edge beside Reinier. The Irishman sat down on the other side of her, gently massaging her hands in his. "I am Connor. And this is Reinier."

So, it was to be the both of them? Inwardly, Reinier was surprised at Connor's choice. But maybe it was better this way.

She refused to look at either of them. Instead, her eyes were fixated on a spot on the floor.

"Tell us something about you," Reinier encouraged, hiding the low, purring note in his voice. "Where are you from?"

She raised her head slowly at that and stared at him, full of suspicion. But when she looked into his eyes, her face relaxed and her cautiousness eased. She was fascinated.

Reinier's singular eyes were indeed a blessing most of the time. One would think he would grow tired of others' reaction to them, but all too often the advantage served his purpose.

The woman before him vigorously shook herself out of her enthrallment and looked down again upon replying, "*Éire*. I was born and raised in Ireland."

Connor stopped caressing her hands and his eyebrows drew up in obvious surprise.

Reinier's and the Irishman's eyes briefly met over her shoulder. They had both noticed the sophisticated way she expressed herself.

"Born and raised?" Reinier repeated her words as a question to nudge her to tell them more. Meanwhile, Connor tenderly rubbed her upper arms. She let it happen; in fact, she didn't seem to notice at all.

She nodded to emphasize her story. "I am a maid's daughter. My father is unknown."

Perhaps if she'd looked him straight in the eyes, Reinier could have believed it. As it was, it was clear that she had diligently made it up.

Reinier tried his best to hide a grin. "You look like you loved to ride through the vast green fields bareback."

Eyes wide with astonishment, her mouth opened and closed. Her eyes began to sparkle unexpectedly, as if with fond memories. "Indeed, I did! Much to my cousins' dismay, though." She laughed. "But was it my fault that their horses weren't as fast as mine?"

Mirth made Reinier purse his lips as he, again briefly, locked gazes with Connor. He, too, was smiling mischievously. They had caught her unawares with that.

Now Connor leaned forward and breathed into her ear, "You had a horse?"

Her laughter died as abruptly as it had erupted. She blushed and her eyes widened, realizing she had been caught red-handed. Reinier felt smug. He enjoyed playing with her as much as Connor did.

Quickly regaining her composure, she came up with another facet to her story. "Of course not. I only helped the groom so often that he let me secretly ride a horse when the masters weren't home."

At the indignant glare Connor received along with her words, his eyes dilated. Reinier was sure that never in Connor's life had reproach been that arousing for him.

"You were grooming horses when you didn't work in your masters' household?" Reinier took one of her elegant, slim hands into his. His eyes flicked to Connor's. Receiving Connor's minuscule nod, Reinier brought her hand up to his mouth.

Connor's caress on her upper arms changed, slowing and softening to a light touch up and down her arms.

Reinier kissed her palm, a palm that was not flawed by calluses and old scars from blisters as a maid's would have been. He decided to let it go. She must have her reasons for this. Besides, they had said quite enough.

Feeling the slight tremble of her hand under his lips, Reinier looked up at her. He slowly guided her hand in his to his abdomen and placed it there, letting her feel his body through his garments.

Connor's fingers brushed her hair from one ear. She shivered when he brought his lips close. Leaning forward, Reinier mirrored Connor's caress at the other side of her neck. Their lips whispered over her skin, raining featherlight kisses, lavishing gentle nibbles.

Her fingers on Reinier's abdomen twitched, betraying her arousal. Not only that, her skin was already so sensitized, it rippled beneath his lips. Her head fell back a little and she gradually began to subtly move against them.

She was a highly sensual creature. Despite her obvious shyness, this was very promising.

A particularly precious aroma filled Reinier's lungs and made his head light—the faint nuance of delicate white roses surrounded by a deeper note of sweet sandalwood, Connor's natural fragrance. Reinier knew it so well by now, and still it did not fail to pique his arousal. The spice in the air mingled with his own darker scent and was accentuated by her feminine musk, growing and wrapping itself around them all.

As if that had been their cue, both he and Connor parted their lips. Their tongues wet the silken skin of her long, elegant neck. Again, she shivered. Then she sighed.

Never ceasing his attentions on her neck, Reinier knew Connor's hands wandered down her sides to play with the little ribbon that held her gown together. The gown slipped down her shoulders as Connor nudged it off her arms and parted it to reveal her upper body to them. Obeying the slight pull, her arms fell to her sides and the fabric came off.

Reinier drew back just long enough to see her sensitive peaks harden, pleading for attention. He cupped her chin to gently urge her head back a little more now that Connor's nibbling and caressing lips wandered down her shoulder. Subtly moving closer, Reinier spread his fingers over her delicate neck; then they wandered lightly down to the top part of her breasts.

Cupping one of them, he gently squeezed it. Connor's hand came up to cup her other breast. His thumb toyed with the hard peak in his hand; Reinier could feel it, because the back of Connor's hand brushed against his chest at the same time.

When Reinier's lips found the frantically beating pulse at the base of her neck, he opened his mouth a little more and waited for another blissful gasp from her. As soon as it came, he gently bit into the satiny, frail skin.

She jumped at the erotic assault and bowed to allow them both better access to her body. Her body's subtle movements against them became more urgent. She was restless. Her other hand grabbed the bedcover, but before she could ball it into a fist, Reinier snatched it and guided it to the buttons of his shirt.

"Undress me," he whispered against her skin and helped her with the first button, noticing that Connor was busying himself opening the laces of her corset at her back. It slipped away just as Reinier's shirt fell open far enough that he could shed it.

The garment hadn't even touched the floor when Reinier's lips found her skin again and his hand found hers. He guided her to him just like before, making her touch him. She complied, but when her fingertips brushed his breeches' seam, she stiffened. At the sudden change in her, Connor's head snapped up.

To be honest, Reinier was gradually growing a bit weary of her highly improper decency. He rolled his eyes with mild impatience at Connor, who bit his lower lip as if struggling to ban his obvious mirth from erupting in an audible chuckle.

Reinier resigned with an inward sigh. If this was going too fast for her, they'd do it another way. Capturing her earlobe between his lips, Connor's hands came round her waist again and wandered up her front until he reached her breasts. He squeezed them just enough so that they stood up, begging Reinier for a lick, a taste . . .

Mouth closing fully over one puckered flower, Reinier suckled her until the erect pebble was right between his teeth and he could gently nip at it. His effort was not in vain. His reward was her honeysweet gasp full of want. Another shiver shook her, this time more intense than before. She threw her head back against Connor and Reinier took advantage of her distraction, quickly opening the lace that held her undergarment. He locked his fingers into its seam, and while Connor lifted her up a little, Reinier rid her of the last piece of cloth shielding the rest of her body from their seduction.

She blanched briefly at being fully exposed to them now, but Reinier paid that no mind. She'd blush with hunger in a moment, sigh and moan and beg for more. He knew it.

Connor laid her back onto the end of the bed but left them, crawling farther up and, leaning against the headboard, watched their performance. Looming over her, Reinier let his lips draw a path of wet kisses and mild nibbles down her body. Bracing himself against the bed with one arm, his other found her thighs and nudged them apart for his exploration. At his touch a ragged sigh escaped her throat. Instantly, her hips were rolling in a slow rhythm as old as time.

Connor's eyes were sweeping over them both, lingering here and there. Reinier could feel it. The heat in the Irishman's gaze provoked ripples of gooseflesh running over Reinier's skin and his nostrils flared. He could smell her syrupy musk, intense but not quite ready for the taking. Lust exploded in his mind. Anticipation sizzled through his veins.

Just as he was about to let his tongue flick over the hollow where her neck met her shoulders, he saw her balling her hands into the bedcover. Reinier's eyes narrowed. This would not do.

His hand wandered over her thigh and up to her lower belly just above her mons. He heard Connor's low, appreciative rumble. He was watching as Reinier let his index and middle fingers draw a luscious path down to her warm, welcoming heat.

At first, she moaned low as Reinier let his fingers play over her, caressing her, spreading her. Then her body heaved off the bed as his fingers found her erect nub. He circled it, then concentrated on it. When he rubbed it gently, she keened, her hips arching wildly to his touch as she climbed toward release. She was ready, primed to climax.

But Reinier stopped his caress altogether and she groaned in her abandonment, breaths coming shallow and fast. His hand remained completely still while he delighted in her frustrated moan. At that, Connor chuckled, a low, sultry sound, like velvet rubbing against Reinier's back.

Looking up, Reinier watched Connor touch himself, his broad hands brushing over his belly and lower still. When he reached the fly of his breeches, Connor rubbed the impressive bulge in the garment. Reinier's lids lowered, and hissing through clenched teeth, he felt his own hardness twitch and strain against his breeches.

Another surge of her slickness bathed his fingers resting in her dewy folds and drew his attention back to her. Parting his fingers suddenly, Reinier spread her core and bent down, buried his face against her, and let his tongue delve and play over her with the exhilarating finesse of an expert, continuing what his fingers had started.

Once more her body heaved off the bed. Once more she moaned and Reinier burrowed deeper, tasting her, and swirled and toyed with the exact spot that made her writhe and shudder under his touch.

But just like before, he halted. And just like before, release did not find her.

Reinier moved off the bed to crouch between her spread legs. His eyes traveled slowly over her glistening core and the moment he saw, he understood. So, this was her secret. It all made sense now, her shyness, her lack of experience. But the bed was moving; Connor was getting up and stalking toward him.

Quickly, Reinier covered her moistness with the flat of his hand, disguising the protective gesture with a rolling movement against her. Her breaths came in sighs. Her lids fluttered close. She wanted it. Every fiber of her body screamed for it. So, Reinier kept silent. He stored her secret for later, though.

The gentle, exquisite pressure against all of her center had her hips meet his hand with a steady rhythm. Connor crouched down behind him. He pressed close, fondling the soft tissue of the scar on Reinier's back. Longing streaked through his body. When he turned his head, their eyes met. Leaning forward, Connor's arm came around Reinier.

"Let me have a taste. She smells so sweet," Reinier heard Connor whisper. Parting his fingers, Reinier exposed only her sensitized bud for Connor's kiss.

His body pressed fully against Reinier's as his tongue flicked over her for a quick sample. Then the Irishman's dark head bent and his mouth closed entirely over her most ticklish spot. Connor licked and swirled his tongue over her, light and fast, until she squirmed on the bed and moaned helplessly. His tongue was pleasuring her, taking her higher and higher. Suddenly, her arms snaked up and her hands fisted in Connor's hair.

"Please," she sobbed, begged.

Reinier smiled when he heard Connor's muffled chuckle. One last flick of his tongue and Reinier saw the coil that had been nourished spring free. Her body was shaken with tremors, tiny, violent quakes of ecstasy. Connor continued his sweet, gentle caresses, lapping at her with the flat of his tongue until her body stopped trembling with the force of her climax.

Connor drew back and left Reinier also to crawl up the bed to her side. Elbow braced against the mattress, the Irishman's gaze settled on her passion-flushed face while he cupped her breast and squeezed it gently, pressing a fleeting kiss to her earlobe. Reinier came to lie on her other side just as Connor's arm came around her limp body and her eyes fluttered open.

Reinier saw the light of understanding in her eyes. She had been told to give, but now she comprehended that she was supposed to take pleasure in return.

Tentatively, she brought her hands up and placed them on Connor's sculpted upper body. Gooseflesh rose where her hands explored, and the Irishman closed his eyes lazily. Seemingly emboldened by his reaction to her touch, her fingers, although hesitant, ran over the prominent bulge in Connor's breeches.

Reinier let his head rest over hers to watch her progress. He pressed his front into her back, and instinctually her body started moving against him. Reaching down, Reinier entwined her fingers with his to help her unbutton Connor's fly, and as soon as it was open far enough, he guided her in.

Connor hissed when Reinier wrapped her small hand around his hardness. His own hand grasped her wrist and he showed her how to stroke him. Down he guided her, then up.

His tongue flicked over the sensitive skin beneath her earlobe, his breath cooling the wet trail just a little. "Slowly," Reinier breathed into her ear. "But hard, lass. Squeeze the tip just a little before you let your hand slide back down again." Hearing Connor's deep, throaty purr sent a yearning quiver through Reinier. He moved against her more, his own hardness riding the cleft of her cheeks.

She answered them both with a soft moan. While her hand on Connor became bolder, her body moved, rubbing against them like a lazy cat at first, but soon her motions became more urgent, faster.

Receiving their attention only for the moment, Connor wrapped his arm around both their heads and Reinier grabbed her free hand. He entwined her fingers with Connor's and sat up, guiding them to her mouth. She needed a little encouragement, though, so he pressed their fingers against her lower lip until she parted her lips to welcome them.

"Yes, sweet. Take his fingers into your mouth. Let them go a little, then suck at them again."

She did as he had instructed her; quickly, Reinier laid her on her back and nudged her thighs apart while she continued to suckle Connor's digits. Braced on his arms, he settled between her legs, pushing his cock, still painfully confined in his breeches, against her creamy core. Then he leaned down, his tongue flicking over her earlobe. "Now let your tongue run around his fingertips every time they almost slip from your lips."

He saw she obeyed; her throat jumped as she rolled her tongue, and her cheeks hollowed as she sucked Connor's fingers deeper into her mouth.

Reinier's breathing was coming hard. Her honey soaked his breeches, cooling his hot flesh for just a tiny moment. "Very good," he encouraged her, well aware that his voice was hoarse with hunger.

He wanted more. Now. It was high time they got to the heart of the matter. Rolling off her, Reinier shed his breeches, then crawled a little farther up the bed to lie on his side.

He cupped the back of her head. "Wrap your hand around me and stroke me."

She let go of Connor and turned to her side to face Reinier. She was studying him closely now, and Reinier had to press his lips together not to chortle at the mixture of fascination and bewilderment on her face. Tentatively, her hand wrapped around him. Immediate, sizzling lust shook his body at her touch.

Reinier noticed the bed move under him. Connor must be getting rid of his breeches also, he thought, and when he looked down, he saw Connor's arm come around her waist, his dark head bent over hers.

"Use your mouth on him," Reinier heard Connor instruct her.

Another surge of quivering sparks, both hot and cold, washed over him as he heard the Irishman's sensual command. Lifting her chin, she met Reinier's gaze and hesitated. Her eyes flicked from his cock to his face and back. Timidly, she bent and opened her mouth. Reinier's blood was pumping harder, every inch of his skin alive and burning for more. Her tongue snaked out to lick over his tip. At that, a shiver ran through him.

Her lips explored him, the taste, the feel of him. Reinier's hips bucked on their own accord, his flesh straining to be engulfed by her, feeling that hot, wet mouth surround him, taking him in . . .

Finally, she wrapped her lips around him, wiggling them a little to accommodate his width. With a pleased sigh, Reinier closed his eyes and bent his head back. The world ceased to exist. He breathed joy. He tasted lust. He felt longing. He saw flickers of desire dance merrily before his eyes.

Then he felt her hand on his rod too. Connor must have guided her there. As if from far away he heard him rumble, "Let your lips follow your hand."

After a few tries she found the right rhythm.

"Open your throat. Don't swallow. You can take him even deeper then." Reinier had to suppress a moan. When she did as Connor had instructed her, the sensation became scalding. The suction was harder as well. Just the way he liked it.

Soon she was teasing him and Reinier's body was shocked with electrifying sizzles from head to toes. She was sucking him hard just before her mouth would slide loosely over him. Reinier arched to her caress with a gasp of pleasure.

"Methinks we have just discovered her major talent, my friend."

"I expected as much," Connor chuckled hoarsely, the amusement in his voice clearly drenched with lust. "Her skill must be outstanding, having been blessed with lips as gorgeous as hers."

Reinier felt light-headed, as if he were floating. His laugh became darker and ended in a blissful sigh. Bringing his head forward, he watched Connor spreading her legs again. He tested her readiness, and when she moaned against Reinier, the vibration echoed in his body and made him close his eyes briefly at the pleasant shudder running through him yet again.

They shifted. Connor was kneeling, arranging her shoulder-down and bottom-up while she continued her ministrations on Reinier, who lay down farther onto his back, all the while observing Connor position himself behind her. He'd never tire of watching the Irishman at that.

Connor's hands clamped around her waist. Then his hips rolled forward with what seemed like agonizing slowness. He stuffed her inch by inch. He must have been halfway in when she released Reinier and threw her head back with a gasp that soon turned into a moan.

Reinier urged her head back down onto him, his gaze settling back on Connor, who was smiling dreamily with his lids lowered. Connor always savored that moment. His eyes slid closed completely and the expression on his face soon relaxed entirely. He parted his lips slightly at the soft shiver shaking his body. Reinier knew then that Connor was seated deep in her, almost up to the hilt.

Her pace on Reinier changed, settling into the rhythm Connor dictated. His thrusts were slow at first. Connor pulled out again almost completely, only to push back into her, but still he was taking his time with it. Momentarily, his thrusts deepened, and so did her eager mouth on Reinier.

Their dance was faster now, more urgent. The primal rhythm was taking over. She trembled and whimpered each time Connor thrust into her, shuddered and sighed when he moved his hips back.

Her moans scorched through Reinier's veins. Fiery, voluptuous embers showered him. Feeling her mouth around him echoing Connor's slide in and out of her was almost too much. His whole body stiffened with his impending climax.

Stop. Reinier needed her to stop. Now. Let them finish, he thought; he'd have his turn later.

His hands clamped around her head to keep her from moving. The desire lashing through him protested, but eventually his iron will won over. Reinier hissed with both relief and anguish when her lips freed him.

Reinier kept his eyes closed, reveling in the soft glow of passion not quite gratified. The bed was gently rocking beneath him. With those movements he could feel Connor easing his thick shaft out of her hot moistness and gliding back in. She moaned every time he filled her, sighed each time he pulled out. The rocking quickened. Connor's strokes must have become more intense.

Connor was close.

The thought swirled in Reinier's mind, a vague idea at first, rolling, rocking like the bed under him.

Just in time, Reinier opened his eyes to see Connor's body trembling with his climax. He cupped his flesh and spilled his seed over the small of her back, his hips moving slightly still while he squeezed himself until he was spent. His eyes remained closed the whole time, his lips slightly parted. When he opened them again, they were dark, dilated, contented, as was the smile he gave Reinier just before he fell to the side with a sigh.

Now it was his turn, or at least Reinier thought it would be. Their union could have freed Connor of that recent possessiveness, or it could have enforced it. But there was only one way to find out.

Reinier came to kneel behind her, the satiny skin of her legs tickling against the tiny hairs on his hard thighs. He rubbed Connor's quickly drying seed into the skin of her back and down her thighs, while his other hand was bathing in her juices. Reinier was drawing her moistness up her cleft to make sure he wouldn't hurt her when his exploring finger entered her where she would surely least expect it. If his suspicions about Connor were correct, he—unfortunately—wouldn't get anything beyond his hand near her tight bud.

"What—" She jumped and gasped at the intrusion at first, but as soon as Reinier started his arousing game there, moving very slowly in and out, she relaxed immediately with a deep, breathy moan.

At that Connor's eyes snapped open and he sat up quickly, placing his hand on Reinier's stomach to bar him from moving any more.

"No." Connor's growl was impressive. Poor Irish bastard, the siren's call had him now.

Reinier lifted his eyebrows in mock surprise. "Why shouldn't I?"

Connor didn't reply. He only shook his head. Reinier had to avert his gaze to hide the telltale glitter of understanding in his eyes.

How sweet. Connor felt territorial. But it was a shame, really. The world would certainly mourn the loss of a glorious rake such as Connor.

"I see," Reinier gasped a little exaggerated and somewhat disappointed, but he wasn't bothering to hide the triumphant, meaningful smile he felt. "Seeing that she is out of the question, I might have to find someone else for it, though," he whispered, leaning closer, so close to Connor that their lips almost met.

Reinier had expected anything but Connor's surprising response, a sly curling of his lips into much the same enigmatic smile he himself had felt on his own face mere moments ago.

"You are charmingly incorrigible." Connor smirked. "Go ahead and tease me now. But you'll see. You'll soon see, my friend."

Now it was Reinier's turn to look—and feel—quite perplexed.

3

"Mistress!"

Emiline was stopped by Justine's breathless, distressed squeal as soon as she entered the house. Hands in her apron, the lady's maid who had been on Bougainvilla since Emiline's childhood seemed quite agitated. Her eyes were unnaturally wide, as was her mouth.

With a sad smile, Emiline remembered when she had last seen Justine like this. It was when one of the downstairs maids had broken several saucers of her mother's most precious china.

Emiline cut the maid off with a simple, weary shake of her head and continued toward the stairs up to her room. "Justine, whatever has you flustered like this, whether it's another piece of the china or something similarly dramatic, please stop. I'm too tired and I long for a bath."

Justine clapped her mouth shut. Then her forehead wrinkled. "But . . ."

Once more Emiline shook her head and handed the maid her old hat and worn leather gloves. Justine could wait. It had been another exhausting day in the fields. A long, hot bath would ease the ache in her back a little and the stiffness in her muscles too. Besides, it was part of her daily routine. After a day in the fields, she'd relax in steaming water; then she'd have tea in the parlor and read a little or brood over the ledgers in the study until it was time for dinner.

When she entered her chamber, Emiline leaned against the door, closing her eyes with a sigh. She felt so tired. The people of Ronde all worked hard for her and she worked with them. There was no day off for the Mistress of Bougainvilla.

When her father had died, Emiline had to learn to take a man's role, to take on all the responsibilities the trade required without complaint—and she had. She'd made Bougainvilla the most profitable sugarcane estate in the West Indies.

She pushed off the door and began to open the laces of her plain linen dress that was mended in too many places and now dirty from the fields. Emiline made her way to the bathtub in the adjoining room and let herself sink into the hot water.

Having scrubbed herself clean until the water was white from the soap, Emiline allowed herself to linger a little longer. She leaned back, feeling the soreness in her muscles ease.

The scent of bougainvilleas wafted to her through the open windows. That's where the name of the estate came from. They'd been her mother's favorite flowers, and the villa was surrounded by them.

The estate and the tiny island were Emiline's whole world, and she ruled it. She had to. There was no one else to do it for her.

Sometimes she felt very alone. But that was ridiculous really. She had a busy life. There was nothing she lacked, and she was a very successful businesswoman. There was no need, she told herself, for a family.

Once she'd thought herself in love. Once was enough to teach her. That love had been so fierce and all-encompassing, it burnt her. Oh, it had definitely been enough.

The ever-present, soft breeze from the sea through the windows reminded her that the water had turned cool already, so she stepped out of the bathtub and grabbed a towel.

While rubbing herself dry, she was thinking about the parlor. She'd have tea there, as usual. Sometimes, when she was sitting in the parlor, she caught herself still looking out the window there. It had a wonderful view of the little harbor of Ronde.

Some days there'd be ships there. Ships waiting to purchase a load of the finest sugarcane or rum the Caribbean had to offer.

For a long time she'd searched the harbor for the one ship that would bring her beloved home. After a while, her tears had tasted bitter and stung her cheeks as she watched for the ship that might carry her husband back to her. He'd never returned, and eventually there were no more tears left. That fountain dried and her heart shriveled with it.

He didn't want her and she wasn't looking for him any longer. And that was just as well.

Still, the annoying habit of looking out of the window in the parlor when she was having tea remained. And still she chided herself for it.

But Emiline would be in control of even that eventually. She controlled every other aspect of her life now. She'd master this too. Only one little obstacle remained in the way of her absolute independence. But that was well in hand and would be taken care of. His whereabouts would be known soon, and the papers would be delivered to him.

Elated by that thought, Emiline went to her wardrobe and chose a simple beige linen afternoon dress to wear for tea. She mustn't forget to take one of her new books with her, she thought and snatched it from her bedside table before she closed the door behind her. Blessed solitude and tea were waiting in the parlor for her.

Reinier was annoyed. Simply being here irked him immensely. It was bad enough that he'd had to interrupt his very pleasurable life to come here and bring his wife to heel, but waiting this long for her to finally grace him with her presence was enormously irritating.

He felt the muscle in his jaw twitch furiously. He should have known, though. She was probably up in her room making herself look pretty. She shouldn't flatter herself. He was over that animalistic affection he'd felt years ago. Besides, he hadn't come here to stay, and he surely hadn't come here to take care of her loneliness. He was not going to be intimate with her, so there was no need for her to try and impress him.

Reinier had only come to tell Emiline what he expected of her, and he assumed that she'd meekly accept it. Once he'd saved his reputation, he would leave again as quickly as he'd come. Maybe even with the evening tide. He had a shipping business to run and quite a few other pleasurable things to get back to, after all.

The tiny island only felt confining. Especially this parlor he was in now while waiting for his spoiled wife to arrive. Even though he was standing by the window and looking out at the sea, he felt as if his hands and feet were shackled and he was chained to a wall. He longed to be out there, experiencing the salty breeze of freedom on his face.

He remembered that stifling feeling only too well—his past. Sometimes he thought it might still suffocate him, throttle him, and immobilize him. Like he'd felt when . . .

The nervous clatter of teacups on delicate saucers interrupted his somber memories, and out of the corner of his eye,

Reinier could see a maid setting the table for tea. She was struggling not to look directly at him.

His lips twitched. Yes, he was here again, but he'd soon be gone—with the evening tide for sure.

Reinier heard the maid leave as unobtrusively as she had entered. By her quick footsteps, she seemed eager to exit the room. Why? Was it because his wife would soon be here? He really hoped so, because the evening tide waited for no one.

He heard footsteps again, slower this time. The doorknob turned and the door squeaked. Then suddenly there was complete silence, as if time stood still for that very moment.

But the enchantment fled as unexpectedly as it had come when something fell to the floor and there was a sharp intake of breath. Reinier turned around and met the aquamarine blue depths of Emiline's stunning eyes.

By God.

He'd forgotten how stunningly beautiful she was. His gaze traveled over her appearance. No, she was not simply stunning, she took his breath away. Still.

Gone were the round, youthful cheeks she'd had five years ago, gone to be replaced by sharp features, a little hollow now, but amazingly it emphasized her strong cheekbones. Her arms weren't as soft looking as they used to be either. They were leaner, muscled.

But, he thought and his face lit up, her ample curves were still all there. He'd always adored her soft curves. They fit to his body perfectly.

And her skin, how could he forget that fascinating bronze color that came from the perfect mix of her father's dark Afro-Indian coloring and her mother's pale French complexion.

Seemingly frozen in place as she stood in the door, Emiline's full rose petal lips were slightly ajar. Goodness, he still remembered what it was like to kiss them, how gentle they were, supple, trembling under his shortly before she'd melt in his arms and arch her body into his. And they tasted like sweet strawberries, seductive, yet innocent.

Perfect.

It's what he'd thought when he'd first seen her as well. She was perfect. Flawless perfection come to life.

Reinier had forgotten how much he'd wanted her. How much he still wanted her now that he saw her again after such a long time. It all felt so new, yet it wasn't. Still, it was exciting. Still, she was enticing. Simply seeing her again had his heart pumping heavily in his chest. And something else farther down as well.

He'd always felt physically attracted to her—almost to the point of madness. Yes, he'd always thought he'd go insane if he couldn't have her.

Time and distance hadn't lessened her appeal like he'd hoped it would.

She wore a simple linen dress, but nothing looked just plain on her. Whatever she wore, she looked like an angel, especially now that she had her hair down, her still-wet, wild curls fell down her back. He knew they smelt like strawberries as well. Small wood strawberries, like the ones he'd gathered when he was a boy back home.

Reinier also remembered how silken her hair felt on his skin. He'd drape it over him in the night, and lose himself in her utter femininity and mild, soothing fragrance.

The evening tide was almost gone. Almost.

So, while he was here, he might as well renew his memories; he might as well enjoy her soft, pliant body against his. It would be only natural. He was her husband and . . .

Suddenly remembering why he was here, a cool jolt of reality drew him out of his pleasant musings.

He was not just her husband. She'd made him a cuckold as well. He'd had a purpose coming here, after all.

* * *

Upon entering the parlor, Emiline thought she saw a ghost, an evil ghost from her past that had come to unmercifully haunt her. But Reinier was real and standing there in her parlor by the window with his back to her. When he turned around, she thought her heart had stopped beating altogether.

Now he was moving, gracefully, with a certain swing to his every movement, like the predator she thought him to be. Reinier was coming up to her and she knew she should run, should do something, anything but just foolishly stand there, paralyzed by his presence, mesmerized by how he looked at her.

He bowed to her and Emiline blinked. What was he doing? Was he formally . . . ? Emiline gasped as she saw him lifting the book she hadn't noticed had slipped from her fingers. Absent-mindedly, she took it from him and clutched it to her chest, held on to it as if she needed something that felt solid, real.

Nonsense, she chided herself. She needed a shield.

What was he suddenly doing here? Why was he back in her life now?

"Emiline."

She had to repress the warm, gentle shiver that snaked through her when she heard Reinier's voice again after such a long time. It was deep and there was still that certain kind of husky mystery in it. Oh, how she'd missed it, how she'd missed hearing him speak, hearing him say her name. He always laid special emphasis on the last syllable, gave it a particular sensual quality that made her skin crawl with delectable memories of how he used to caress her cheek after he'd made love to her and he'd say her name in almost a whisper. . . .

Good Lord.

Emiline had expected anything but this. She'd never again take Justine's distress lightly. If only she'd listened.

Now not only did she see his eyes wandering up and down

her body, she also felt them as they whispered over her. She almost trembled with the sensation that he knew exactly what was underneath her dress.

Her treacherous body instantly started to heat up. When she saw the left corner of his ever-smiling lips move upward, she was so stunned that all she could think was how could she have forgotten how breathtakingly handsome Reinier was.

Yes, his lips were so full that he always seemed to smile, and they made him look soft and sweet. She knew what he was thinking by the way his eyes, his still amazing bright citrus eyes, began to glitter.

She still felt like a rabbit staring at a cougar that had suddenly pounced out of the bushes, just like she had all those years ago when she'd first seen his intense gaze taking her in. All she could do was blink once and swallow hard.

Once more she was mesmerized by his fair beauty. He wasn't just the most handsome man she'd ever met in her life. Now she remembered why she'd fallen so easily back then. He had a way of making one willingly do almost anything just to hear him say their name, experience his lips against their own, his hands on their body, his body against theirs, his hair tickling their neck and other places the mere thought of which made her blush.

Damn him.

His smile was triumphant even now, because he knew how she felt when he merely looked at her like that.

And curse him. His skin was a sun-baked tan, and Emiline even caught herself wondering for a moment how far his tan would go. His hair, neatly tamed at the back of his head, had faded to a lighter shade in the sun. Now he had small wrinkles around his eyes. Barely there, but they made his alluring, seductive gaze even wilder than ever. He wore a jacket that was exactly the same shade as the green part of his swirling eyes, and his elegant, golden breeches did little to hide the muscular columns underneath.

The years had added to his good looks. She'd thought him handsome then? Well, he was as beautiful as an angel now. So beautiful she'd weep if she could. But she couldn't do anything at all. She was too stunned.

She bowed her head and gave him the friendliest smile she could manage. "Reinier."

When he presented his arm, she took it and let him guide her to the table where their tea was set.

Aloof politeness was the right course, Emiline decided while she was sorting through the chaos in her mind. Maybe he'd be gone by the evening tide. If it wasn't too late for it already?

Emiline busied herself by filling their cups with tea. She could deal with him. She was a strong woman. She was in charge.

Emiline almost believed herself if it hadn't been for the tiny voice in her head that snickered evilly that she controlled every aspect of her life—save him. But she had a plan to remedy that as well, didn't she?

The awkward silence in the room now felt oppressing. Emiline brought her cup up to her mouth and sipped elegantly while trying to find a way to start a pleasant conversation with Reinier. But what could she possibly say?

Reinier leaned back and watched her craning her head a little, blinking at him like she always did. She wasn't showing him any kind of emotion at all. But she had to feel something. Elation or, more likely, anger. Anything that showed him she felt—for him. But she didn't. Had she ever?

He noticed her hands were trembling. When she put the cup down on the saucer she was holding with her left hand, it clattered. Emiline cleared her throat at the embarrassing noise.

Reinier laughed softly.

"What amuses you?" She was only smiling at him, her stunningly bright eyes searching his face, and as always she didn't have the slightest idea what he was thinking.

"I see that nothing has changed."

"Oh . . ." Emiline set out, but he rose to leave and she didn't continue.

Reinier had had enough for the moment. If he'd missed the evening tide, then they had plenty of time to talk before morning. "Since I feel fatigued after the journey, I will retire until supper. I expect you to honor me with your presence, Emiline."

Her mouth opened and closed a few times, but in the end, she nodded, "Of course."

Reinier hid his disappointment behind a detached but self-assured smirk, an expression he'd practiced well over the years. He'd have preferred her sneering at him, or screaming she'd rather starve or eat maggots than dine with him. But no, he wouldn't get any emotional reaction from her.

Emiline. Always polite. Ever the perfect wife.

He'd forced himself to forget, but he remembered now why he needed to stay away from her. She filled his sweetest dreams and haunted his nightmares. Yes, he had loved her. But he hated her for not loving him back—and that was why he could not forgive her.

4

Emiline had lingered in her preparations for dinner hoping to annoy Reinier by making him wait, but now she decided that was a much too petty and cowardly tact for the Mistress of Bougainvilla.

Her foot was tapping with apprehension as she sat at her dressing table. She pictured him down in her parlor, with his typically triumphant smirk, the smile that she hated and loved at the same time.

She mustn't let him get to her. Not again. Not ever. He wasn't worth it. Each emotion Emiline let him pull from her was like another stabbing pinprick, and she wanted them to stop. She ruled here, and now she was overly anxious to get downstairs and show him just that.

Justine was humming softly to try and calm her. "Be still, child, or I'll never be done."

"Sorry." It wasn't a complicated style, just a simple pile of curls to go with her simple tan silk dress and ordinary sea-green cap-sleeved jacket. Still, Emiline found it hard to remain still enough for Justine to finish her hair.

"I don't blame you, though. That man would try the patience of St. Rita of Cascia popping up here out of the blue like that."

"What possessed him to come here, Justine? Why didn't I throw him out of my house as soon as I saw him?" Was it really just a coincidence that he'd returned right when she'd asked someone to find him? Emiline pricked her thumb with the pin she'd been playing with and threw it carelessly on the vanity table.

"Worse of all, my brain was so addled before I could think of any kind of witty reply, he just left—left me alone in the parlor with my tea and a million questions."

"No use fretting about it now. If I know my girl, you'll be thinking much more clearly at dinner. Don't you worry."

Emiline took a deep, calming breath. "Thank you, Justine. Yes, I do believe I am thinking much more clearly now. It's of no special consequence that Reinier came here past that of convenience." She refused to say he'd come home. "I hadn't thought it was important to meet in person, just that we could handle the matter like any other business transaction. But it might be fortuitous he's here. This way I can get the things over more quickly."

"The quicker the better, I'd say." Justine added the last pin to Emiline's hair. "You sure you don't want me to do anything else? Maybe add a string of pearls or pull a few curls down?"

Emiline looked at the plain style in the mirror. "No, this will do fine. Thank you." She didn't need to make any kind of impression. There was no need to take any special care whatsoever with her appearance for a man, not husband, but just a man she barely knew and certainly didn't want meddling in her life anymore.

"If you wish, but I say the more armor, the better to face the devil." Justine took one more quick look over her handiwork.

"He's not the devil, Justine, just a shrewd businessman. You know, even if I hadn't realized it in the beginning, our marriage wasn't anything but a business transaction. Why shouldn't the end of it be the same?" She'd make it through dinner with just a little small talk and then casually remind him of how well they've both done apart from each other.

Justine's snort was derogatory. "If you say so, but, darling, I was there when the honeymoon was over and you suddenly found yourself alone. If only you'd listened to your father's warnings before it was too late."

"I know." Emiline sighed, thinking back on how she'd told her father time and again that Reinier wasn't like the others. Eventually, her father gave up trying with a sympathetic, sad smile. You know there's nothing I can deny you, he'd said, kissing her forehead.

Emiline knew now she'd been overconfident in her youth. She thought she was oh-so-special and her love was enough to hold Reinier. She'd been completely happy to give herself up to being the perfect wife—had, in fact, believed it would be enough for him.

But bitter realization had woken her from her dream. Reinier Barhydt had never wanted her love, hadn't wanted the burden of responsibilities that came with being master of Bougainvilla and being her husband. He had only wanted her money. And just as her father had predicted, she couldn't keep him with her on Ronde.

Emiline walked to the full-length silver mirror and took one last look. "We're both businesspeople now. I'll make him see the logic and tremendous profit in him signing the papers. If all goes according to plan and he agrees, then maybe he'll even be gone from *l'Île de Ronde* and our lives by the morning tide."

Justine knit her brows, her frown deepening. Paying that no

mind, Emiline opened the door. The stage was set; now all she had to do was play her part. It was easy, really.

"From your mouth to God's ears, child." Emiline heard Justine's murmur just as she stepped out of her room.

Reinier paced in front of the open French doors of the dining room. The fresh evening breeze and scent of bougainvilleas, sugarcane, and sea did nothing to lighten his mood.

He stopped to look out at the cliffs above the caves, wondering again what the hell had really made him come. One thing was for sure, as Captain of the *Sirene,* he had a reputation to uphold. If word got out that his wife was cuckolding him and doing as she pleased, his ability keep his own house in order might be called into question, and thereby his ability to keep his business dealings in order as well.

Not that he actually wanted any real part in having to keep his own house in order. It was rather annoying to have to take time out of the life he so enjoyed to be forced back here to bring his wife in line. Hopefully it wouldn't take too long to charm her into agreement; then, after a very pleasurable night of husbandly duties, he could be on his way. Maybe even on the morning tide.

He checked the clock on the mantel above the fireplace again and his frustration grew. Obviously, his spoiled little island beauty hadn't changed at all. Still playing childish games by keeping him waiting.

But when he turned at the sound of delicate yet determined footsteps coming through the door behind him, all his previous thoughts were forgotten and lost in the vision of someone he didn't recognize standing before him.

This moment Reinier knew she wasn't the same. This faultless beauty standing just inside the doorway to the dining room was not the girl he'd married.

Already a very appealing and exquisite, comely girl, Emiline had become a stunningly gorgeous woman. As his intense gaze examined her appearance, taking her in slowly from head to toe, he noticed her chin inched higher with indignation. But Reinier paid that no mind. He looked his fill. If anybody had a right to do it, it was him—whether she welcomed it or not. On the contrary, her reluctance to enjoy his sensual perusal made the task even more luscious than it already was.

He was glad she didn't favor the busier fashions of the day with all their ribbons and lace and bows. She didn't need them. Her eyes were jewels, her skin was warm silk, and her hair was entwined with its own strands of gold. They were all the accessories she needed. And he hoped to see her with nothing else very, very soon.

Also, Reinier noticed that she was, it seemed, a woman as impatient as he'd just been by the look in those magnificent blue-green eyes.

He moved toward her to lead her to the table set near the open French doors to catch the breeze. The table by the doors had been set without its leaves, creating an intimate and casual feel as if this was how the master and mistress had their dinner every night.

His gaze, he knew, was predatory; perhaps much more revealing than he had at first intended. But it was only natural. She had achieved the impossible by becoming more beautiful than ever, and Reinier couldn't seem to help the attraction he was beginning to feel for the improved looks of his wife.

The servants, arms laden with food trays, were moving into the room from a side door. Emiline gave Reinier a small nod, lightly placed her hand on top of his, and without a word let him guide her to her chair.

They ate much of their meal of prawns, citrus-glazed chicken, roasted yams, and fresh fruits in little more than an awkward silence.

"You had fair weather sailing in?"

"Yes, it was quite nice. The prawns were excellent. Were they caught this morning?"

"I believe so; there should have been mussels as well."

"Wonderful."

It wasn't that they didn't have a lot to say to each other. He assumed she, too, was carefully testing, trying to find a way to lead the conversation in the direction she wanted. They both had their agendas, he was sure, only it seemed that no occasion would arise to allow either one to finally start the topic they intended to talk about.

Finally, Reinier had enough. He broke another long stretch of silence right before she could seize the chance to make her excuses and take her leave for the night. "I must tell you, madam, Bougainvilla seems to be doing quite well. Of course, I haven't had time to see too much of it as of yet, but it seems to be thriving. Who's your man, by the way?"

Her fork clattered on her plate; the tips of her ears pinkened. Reinier's lips twitched into a mean smile.

"My man? Sir, whatever do you mean?" She blinked innocently and her gasp was exaggerated. "I was under the assumption that you were under the assumption that it was you."

Her eyes sparkled with the cold, calculating certainty of her quick mind. Reinier was taken aback with that bit of sarcastic wit. It tasted just a tiny bit of hostility. It would seem that more than just her outer carriage had changed.

"Touché, madam." He winked quickly.

If she wanted to challenge him, he was more than up for the task—in more than one sense of the word to be sure. If irritating her made her react to him in more than the usual slightly bored and superficial way, then more's the better. After all, it meant she felt something for him and wasn't just trying to keep up appearances and be the perfect wife. Just that thought alone made his chest tighten and his breath come quicker.

Reinier took his napkin from his lap and placed it on his plate. "I was speaking of business, not personal matters—for the moment at least. Who have you got running things for you here? He should be commended."

Her eyes grew unnaturally big. "I don't wish to seem obtuse, but I'm afraid that I am the man you speak of. I run Bougainvilla on my own. I am the sole mistress here."

On her own, did she? Reinier didn't quite believe that. On the other hand, her father had been very smart when it came to business matters. If he'd taught her enough before his unfortunate death, it was indeed possible that she had run the estate ever since, with her lover's help, of course.

"My apologies, madam. Then you are to be commended for taking on such heavy burdens and succeeding." For a very small moment her mouth became slack and was in danger of dropping.

"Yes, well, I wasn't left with much choice." Her tone was quite sharp and she looked down her nose at Reinier. "And as you can see, I do quite well here—alone. There really was no need for you to bother coming by."

At that, Reinier snickered. She didn't know the half of it. Yes, she was rather agitated, maybe it was because he was here and she had to hide her lover or just because he'd annoyed her. Whatever the reason, it was a small victory on the path to triumph. He'd only just begun to play with her.

She staked a piece of mango on her plate and tried to ignore the offending, low chuckle from Reinier. Did he suppose a woman couldn't possibly be as successful as she was on her own? How insufferably arrogant could he be?

It wasn't like her to be easily provoked, but her initial irritation turned into white fury now. Why was he now interested in the estate? To get a share of its profits instead of the payoff money she planned to offer to be rid of him? Oh, that was just like him. The estate was none of his business! He was underestimating her if he thought her naïve.

She refused to look at him until her emotions were under control again. When she spoke, her tone was aloof but polite. "Whatever the reason, whatever the circumstances, sir, it is very fortunate that you've come here. There is a very small matter I'd like to discuss with you." She set her napkin on the table and began to rise from her seat.

Reinier rose when she did. In one stride he was in front her, barring her escape from the room. When he inhaled, his nostrils flared. His eyes closed lazily as he tilted his head to the side.

"How do you feel now that I'm back?" Reinier leaned subtly closer.

Emiline halted and stared up at him unblinking, her indignation blazing through her.

"You must feel something." He walked around her slowly. "Are you angry with me?" He whispered against her lips, looming even closer.

She turned her head away. "No, I'm not angry with you." She'd given up feeling anything for him a long time ago. Stepping around him, she continued toward the door to get the papers from the study. He could sign them now and be gone. Out of sight, out of mind.

She grasped the doorknob with both hands, but Reinier had caught up with her again and held the door closed with his arms braced against it. A shiver ran through Emiline when she felt the heat of his body, although he was careful not to touch her.

"Or could it be that you're glad I'm back, Emiline?" His words were low, sensual. Her name on his lips sounded like a promise, whispering over her treacherous skin that rippled with desire as her knees became dangerously weak. Closing her eyes, Emiline remembered what it was like—what he was like when he was on his most charming behavior, when he told her all the sweet things she needed to hear. She could feel his words tickling against the shell of her ear . . .

Emiline willed herself to come to her senses. She'd be damned if she didn't go through with the plans she'd made.

Rudely, she thrust her shoulders and upper body back so that Reinier had to give her more room. His arms fell to his sides just as she turned to face him. She wasn't the naïve girl he'd left behind anymore. She was a woman now—a strong businesswoman at that. He wanted to make this a tough business negotiation? Little did he know that she'd just begun.

"It is of no special consequence to me that you are here." Her look was cold and callous. "Once again, I do not have any choice in the matter."

Reinier captured her smaller hand in his and brought it up between them. "Oh, but there is always a choice, wife." His voice was seductive and dangerously low.

Emiline felt the blood drain from her face as he held her hand. No man had ever dared touch her like that, not since . . . well, not since their honeymoon. She felt herself quiver inside.

"I wonder . . . Do you ever wish to be free?"

Did she ever . . . Oh! Emiline understood now. He wanted a divorce as well! What a very fortunate twist of fate for her. "Of you?" she blurted out, speaking faster than she could hear herself think. "Yes, of course! In fact—"

"No," Reinier cut her off with a patronizing snort. "No, not of me, I'm afraid." He used her hand, held close to his heart, to guide her back to the table again. Her fresh hope shattered, Emiline was now more confused than ever. She blinked up at him as he released her and backed up slightly from the table.

Reinier spread his strong arms wide. "Free of all this."

What was he talking about? The mental image of what he asked was outright ridiculous.

The way her expression changed, the way the light in her eyes died to be replaced by cool determination and prudent intent was simply amazing for Reinier. He found himself eager to taste her confusion in the air. The scent of strawberries filled his mind and let sweet memories tickle up and down his body. He wanted to catch a bit more of her spice, even more alluring now that she was angry with him.

He leaned down and set his hands on the arms of her chair. "All you command. What I mean to say is . . . Have you ever wished for someone else to be in control? To turn over the burdens of rule, to let go of all the responsibility and control, and just be free to follow?"

Reinier could read it in her eyes. The mere thought that her mind had instantly gone in the right direction was so very arousing. She'd wished it already. But did she have any idea how far this would go, how far he'd take her if only she let him guide her?

He pulled away from her and gave her the space she needed.

Emiline rose from the table without Reinier stopping her this time, and she moved across the room toward the small fireplace in the center of the east-facing wall. She turned to the empty hearth, placing one hand on the mantel. Eventually, she pressed out between clenched teeth, "You do not know me."

Reinier moved to the fireplace and stood directly behind her. He touched her dark, smooth shoulder lightly with the back of his knuckles and let his breath caress her perfect neck, marveling again at what true beauty he'd sailed away from.

"Oh, but I want to know you, wife," he whispered.

At that, Emiline spun quickly, too quickly for Reinier to catch her small hand before it connected with his cheek with more force than he'd ever imagined she could have. The smacking sound reverberated throughout the room, the candles on the mantel flickered, and even the natural music of the West Indian night outside seemed to stop in time.

His last words had definitely struck a chord—his tingling cheek was proof of it.

They stood as they were for what seemed like hours but could have been only seconds. In those moments the morning tide was completely forgotten. Reinier couldn't think of anywhere else he wanted to be tomorrow. He had no intention of rushing things, he decided as he rubbed his cheek tenderly. He was always in the mood for a good challenge—thrived on it, in fact. Right then he was quite determined to spend a few days learning all about this new side of Emiline, the angry, passionate, and quite alluring facets of his wife he'd never seen.

Well, learning and then teaching, of course.

Emiline's eyes were wide. She seemed horrified by her loss of control. The memory of how she shivered to his touch earlier was still echoing in his mind, but now hatred must be tickling her palm as well. Was she just as furious at herself as she was at him?

In a slow movement, meant to give her enough time to react while the dark light in his eyes dared her not to, his hands lightly gripped her forearms. When he spoke, he hoped the rich sweetness of sensuality in his voice was adding insult to injury for her.

"You've changed, Emiline. I have definitely seen—and felt—that now." He laughed lightly. "But the facts are as they are: You are my wife. And this is my home when I choose it."

His fingers started to move over her skin on their own accord. There was a brief moment when he asked himself how he could have forgotten how magical her skin felt. His hands followed his fingers, slowly moving up and down her arms.

Telltale goose bumps rose on her flesh, but he could see she was determined not to show any reaction either to his words or his touch. Reinier might not have known in the beginning, but he had been waiting for this moment since he'd first stepped foot back on the island. He leaned down until his lips were a hairsbreadth from hers.

"I have rights here—like it or not." His breath tickled her soft lips. "I think there's been enough discussion for our first night. Now, come to bed, wife, and we can continue this tomorrow."

Emiline stood frozen as she watched his pale, freshly shaven cheek turn an angry crimson and quickly start to fade again. In some small way it should have been a satisfying feeling, but it wasn't. Nothing about her wayward husband was as it should have been. Looking farther up, she saw those cool, pale citrus-colored eyes twinkle.

Her spine tingled at the thought of what his kiss might feel like. For only a split second she let herself remember what his lips tasted like, how gently they could draw her in. But then she pulled away from Reinier's arms with all her might.

He had no rights here after sailing out of her life on the ship her money had built. Oh, she would make sure those papers were signed and he was off her island sooner rather than later.

"As I told you, Monsieur Barhydt"—Emiline thrust her chin up indignantly to make her point clear—"I rule Bougainvilla, and I surely do not take your commands. But you are right about one thing, sir. We will continue this discussion tomorrow. Good night."

Turning away and marching toward the door to the main hallway, the breath flew from her lungs as Reinier quickly came up behind her. His muscular arm gripped her small waist when he crushed her tightly against his body. Through the silk of her dress, she felt him aroused and straining against his breeches.

Once again, a deep blush moved from her cheeks to the tightening tips of her breasts.

His breath was hot and demanding against her throat. "You may very well rule Bougainvilla, madam," he purred into her ear, passion and promise all rolled into one. "But before I leave here again, I will rule you. And rest assured, wife, you will beg me to do it."

Emiline's whole body stiffened in resistance. As suddenly as he'd captured her, he let her go.

She wasn't sure if it was his words or the definite twinge of excitement she felt that scared her most, but she knew she hated him for it. For that and the fact that this man she now considered barely more than a stranger somehow saw into the farthest part of her mind—a part that she only admitted to herself in the darkest of dark and lonely nights.

Not looking back, Emiline moved out of the room as quickly as she could without breaking into a dignity-killing run.

5

In her hurry, Emiline barely made it into her room without stumbling and almost ran into Justine, who had been waiting to help her undress and had jumped to her feet as soon as Emiline had opened the door.

"By that look and your haste, I take it things didn't go as well as you'd hoped?"

That was quite an understatement. "Just a minor setback." Emiline moved to the dressing table and began to remove the pins from her hair. "Nothing I can't handle, truly."

Justine walked up behind her. "Well, you can tell me all about it while I help you get ready for bed."

"There's no need. I can put myself to bed. You go on to yours and we'll talk about it tomorrow." Emiline caught Justine's eye in the mirror. "I'll be fine, really. I love you, but I'm not a child anymore. Now shoo."

Justine sniffed at Emiline's dismissal. "It's not that. But if you say so, good night." The maid curtsied and left.

Sighing with relief, Emiline rushed to the door and quickly

bolted it from inside, then ran to the adjacent door that connected Reinier's and her dressing rooms and bolted that door as well. That would show Reinier just how much she despised his being here.

He thought he had rights to everything here including her? Well, she'd be damned if she let him have any of them.

Her hand grasped the soft silk of her dress right above her wildly beating heart. Breathing hard, she told herself her hasty retreat was not an act of cowardice, but sensible and prudent. She'd been much too much of an easy prey for him the first time, but she knew his tactics now.

Emiline bit her lower lip and pushed away from the door. Stomping her foot, she couldn't believe he was playing his games with her. Again.

She'd believed she'd learned from her mistakes. She'd succeeded in convincing herself that the spell between them was broken. Yet when he touched her, she knew she'd only deluded herself. She was still attracted to him.

But how could she be when he was nothing but a supercilious fop, the worst libertine she had ever met! Did he really think she didn't know? Didn't know that he had run off to sow his wild oats, never thinking about how he left her wounded and brokenhearted, left her to live with the certainty that she'd failed as a wife?

Reinier was too sure of himself. But he'd always been like that. It was part of what had attracted her in the first place. She had chosen him because he was the best, the one with more appeal and more drive than all the rest. Suitors had come en masse and left just as quickly after her rude refusals. Her father had only sighed and called them crazed tomcats. She'd laugh with him and say she knew they weren't love-crazed over her personally, rather lusting after her dowry.

But then she'd fallen for the roaring cougar among the yowling tomcats. As soon as she'd first set eyes on him, Emiline had forgotten to be guarded. Her father had known, though. He'd warned her that cougars were solitary creatures. They weren't meant to be tied down, and no one would ever be able to hold one. At least not for long.

She'd set out to prove to everyone she could be the perfect wife to the one no one else could tame. But as it turned out, her efforts had been in vain. She'd fallen in love and he hadn't returned those feelings.

Emiline had been another person then. Now she knew that her life before him was ill spent. She'd lived through every day like the spoiled brat she'd been, too consumed with herself, too sure of the power she'd had with her father's tremendous wealth. Looking back, she despised who she'd been then. There was nothing left of the girl he'd once married.

And now she was feeling miserable at her own confusing reaction to him. She sank to the floor and let her head rest against the solid wood of the door while her hands balled into fists.

Why did she feel so torn inside? Why did he have to be so charming? Why did he have to be the most irresponsible man on earth?

Emiline quickly turned her ear to the door. She could hear his footsteps and laughter in the other room. Why did that make her tremble?

Closing her eyes, she winced ever so slightly at the creak of the wooden floor in his room.

She really had forgotten how breathtaking he was. She'd made herself forget how sensual and incredibly reckless he was. How could she, after all those nights she'd spent in desolate loneliness, still want him? Her weakness was disgusting.

His words echoed in her head. He had been speaking of giving up her precious and hard-won control to him. Of course, her first reaction was that she'd been there, had tried that, only it hadn't been enough.

Her eyes were getting weary, and slowly Emiline got up from the floor. She fumbled with the last few pins in her hair until it was freed and fell loosely over her shoulders again. How she hated when she had to capture her hair in such a tight imprisonment.

Come to think of it, she'd started to wear it down when Reinier asked her to all those years ago. It was just to spite him that she had wanted to wear it up on her head again and hide its wild fullness from him.

Emiline slipped out of her shoes and unceremoniously kicked them into a corner. Her dress followed in much the same fashion. Once she'd put on her flimsy dress for the night and her nightgown, she felt calmer. She inhaled deeply as she sat down by the vanity table again and began to brush her hair.

She remembered only too well how proud she was to tell her friends she was engaged. They'd giggled in a silly manner, clapped their hands and congratulated her, and had shared more or less valuable insight on what to expect. That she should hold back and meekly accept his attentions, for men did not appreciate their wives being happy to welcome them. Also, they told her that what happened between husband and wife in private was something one could endure at best, or that men always sought their entertainment elsewhere; there was nothing you could do against it.

She scoffed at those pearls of wisdom she'd been given by her friends back then and threw the brush down with a frustrated huff. It occurred to her that none of her friends' advice had done her any good. No matter how hard she'd tried, she knew he had never really loved her, just her money. He'd wanted a warm bed while he built his precious ship and that was that.

Recalling when she'd first sensed he was pulling away, she bowed her head in despair as the feelings revived once more. The more he'd kept to himself, the more she'd given. There were a few times when she hadn't held back despite her friends' advice and had come to him, wanting to, needing to feel him, craving to touch him as he touched her, giving him everything just to get his love in return. But it was useless.

The yearning to hold him to her grew as she caught him looking out to the sea with such a deep longing in his eyes. Soon he began to spend the evenings alone at the shore, watching the sun going down as night ascended, and only then, when every star finally flickered, had he come into the house. Emiline had felt it. She was losing him.

With a heartfelt sigh, she rose from the chair and walked to the French doors of her room. Opening them, she welcomed the fresh night breeze as it whispered over her. Her skin tightened with the sensations of the wind drifting under the gown and nightdress. The light material seemed unbearable all of a sudden, so she let the gown fall to the floor.

Without realizing it, she cupped her breasts with her hands. Their weight was heavy. They felt swollen, and just touching them made her gasp. She quivered inside as the tingling sensation of lust rushed through her like a bolt of lightning and pooled right between her legs.

She made it to her bed, lay down, and brought her knees up. Her nightdress slipped up to her waist. The breeze was now the only thing that kissed her aching, exposed core as her legs fell open.

Her folds were warm and moist, her sensitive nub hard and aching. She let her fingers play over it, bathed them in her sweet dew, and slowly circled around the most eager spot. She knew how to draw her own pleasure and give herself what she needed.

Her other hand found her breasts and cupped them, one

after the other, squeezed the hard peaks just enough until her whole body started to quiver with the sensations she brought herself.

Her sides tingled and tickled with anticipation. Only then did her fingers find the hard pebble and rub over it in small circles.

Oh no, she thought just then and rubbed herself faster, she surely didn't need him, not for this, not for anything. In all these years she hadn't needed him, she hadn't fantasized about him as she did this.

Soon that familiar edgy pressure built in her that demanded an urgent relief. But she wanted to draw it out, and she had enough discipline to prolong her pleasure.

She didn't want to yearn for his touch. She didn't. No. She hadn't needed him, not once in all these years, years of distant longing to run her hands over his powerful body again, years of hungering for his kiss, years of feeling his member in her, move in her, thrust into her again, and again, soft, slow . . . or hard, yes, so hard he'd force the air out of her lungs with each rolling, pumping motion of his hips.

A fresh gush of moistness bathed her fingers and she almost slipped.

No, it didn't turn her on even more to think about him while rubbing harder and faster.

Her other hand came down, too, and she thrust a finger into her, then two, mimicking pumping movements.

No. Thinking about him didn't peak her desire. Not at all. Imagining him, how he looked covering her, how his hair tickled her face and breasts, how he threw his head up when she scratched his back and he smiled, rumbling his deep, masculine approval that he'd made her forget herself. . . .

Don't hold back. Never hold back with me, Emiline.

The pressure at the end of her spine built. Her body heaved

off the bed. She threw her head back and closed her eyes as she felt the pleasant shower of memories wash over her.

Her hand was moving harder now, on the place where he loved to kiss her most, he'd said, because she tasted like strawberries all over.

Her body remembered his touch only too well, his teeth, scraping the inside of her thighs, raking each and every inch of her body in those almost bites that made her squirm. His satin lips nipping and pinching her nether lips . . . kissing her until her body caught fire . . . how his tongue swirled and danced and then flicked over her sweetest spot . . .

Emiline didn't want to remember how he could make her body sing to his tune alone, how he could make her ache for him in simmering pleasure or greedy lust. She refused to recall his breathtaking tricks with his clever tongue, his wicked hands, his glorious member. . . .

Damn him, she was her own mistress now. Emiline had learned all about her body's yearnings and responses in all those years alone, not remembering, not fantasizing about . . . No, she didn't need him anymore.

Come, Emiline. Come for me. Now.

Her body coiled with the growing tension, her blood catching fire. Falling through a pitch-black hole, she resurfaced on the other side in a shower of blissful sparks that licked at and then scorched her skin.

Twisting on the sheet, her eyes snapped open. Emiline gasped, then wheezed in a deep breath and held it, trying not to make a sound. Her body shook hard in tiny, luscious spasms that seemed endless, intense, so much so that in the end she couldn't hold back the low moan she'd been fighting.

Exhausted, her head and limbs fell limply to the side. Trying to catch her breath, heart thundering in her ears, she licked her lips.

Wickedly wanton. Amazing. Like never before.

That wasn't quite accurate, though.

Sadly, she knew the truth. She'd just come harder than ever before by fantasizing about him.

Reinier was back again and he'd asked for what was rightfully his. In spite of how hard she was trying to fight the attraction, her body demanded the opposite.

Did he have any idea how tempted Emiline felt by his presence, by his words?

Probably.

No! She was too strong to give in. First thing tomorrow she'd have it over with. She'd get Reinier to sign the papers, then send him packing and back to his ship still hard and wanting what she wouldn't let him have. That would show him.

Having turned down the offer of a servant for the night, Reinier crossed to the dressing room and began to remove his boots and coat himself. At the sound of the bolt sliding into place on the door that connected their dressing rooms, Reinier couldn't help but laugh out loud.

She'd made herself crystalline clear. As bad as his reputation deservedly was, he'd never force himself on anyone—that didn't want him to at least—and he wasn't about to start with his own wife. He might not be the most moral of gentlemen, but he was one nonetheless.

Stalking from the locked door to her dressing room into his, he wondered why she'd stayed in the smaller mistress's suite and not moved in here. She'd said herself she ruled Bougainvilla.

He wasn't sure if he felt comforted or disconcerted by the fact that at least in this tiny respect he still had a place here. At first he'd thought maybe the lover Connor had spoken of had been using it, but when he'd first arrived there hadn't been any evidence of a lover currently in residence. Reinier had turned his suite all but upside down—twice—and either her staff was beyond remarkable or no one else had recently occupied it.

Reinier ran his hand across the soft-washed navy silk of the dressing bench at the end of the bed, remembering a time when she'd come to him wearing only emeralds and citrines begging him to let her make love to him right here on this bench, in fact.

That had been close to the end. Probably she'd already begun to feel him pulling away. It had been one of the very few times she'd approached him instead of meekly awaiting his attentions. It had finally been a much welcome change from the smitten, immature girl that hung on his every word and was more than happy to lay back and let him have his way with her, body and money alike.

But it had been too little too late. His heart and mind were already at sea with his new ship and his newly formed partnership.

Reinier slipped into his dressing robe and went to see if the cabinet beside the large armchair had been stocked with any of the island's famous rum. Indeed, it was, and he poured himself a tall glass and sat in the overstuffed chair.

The silky dark liquid was still as warm and soothing as the first time he'd tasted it. It had been the night he'd met Connor. He and the impertinent Irishman with his raven hair and midnight blue eyes had become fast friends soon after.

Another sip of the burning, smooth liquid had Reinier pacing the soft oriental carpet, harking back to the first time he'd come to Bougainvilla.

He'd been desperate for freedom then, anxious to be free of the *Galatea* and her monster of a captain. Not willing to settle for just another position on just another ship, he'd decided to follow Connor's advice. Reinier easily charmed his way into an invitation to the carnival ball on Ronde, hoping one way or another to find backing for his own shipping venture.

He'd been willing to do whatever it took to find some freedom and enough money to control his own destiny, but he surely hadn't meant to set his sights on the Master of Bougainvilla's daughter. In fact, he wasn't sure if at the time he'd even remembered that the master had a daughter until he saw her. But when he did, he knew that was the prize he'd sought all along.

She was the most exotic and unique beauty he had ever seen. The added forbidden allure in the contrasts to himself made her impossible to resist at the time. All soft feminine curves, she had skin like creamed coffee, so much darker than his own, and those dark, wild curls strewn with hints of gold made his fingers itch to dive in. But the final straw had been those eyes. Those perfect, clear aquamarine flames behind luscious charcoal lashes drew him like a moth until all he could think of was finding out if bringing her to climax would make them darken or lighten even more.

But having her in his bed wasn't an easy prospect. She was young, educated, highly respectable—and looking for a husband, not a lover.

Finally, he'd decided that the sacrifice of marriage would be worth it to have such a rare jewel in his bed—and her father's money for his shipping company.

Looking back, it had been easy really. Her inexperience had been no match for his well-heeled seductive skills; plus, her father was fortunately the doting kind who could never say no to his daughter's wishes.

What started out as a marriage of convenience for him soon turned into his worst nightmare, though. Not that she did anything wrong, quite the contrary. Emiline did everything in her power to make their marriage work. And she charmed her way into his heart.

Yes, there was a point in his life . . . He remembered when he woke up one morning and she wasn't by his side that he knew he'd fallen in love with her, helplessly fallen in love with her. He thought he'd go mad without her being near him. Nothing else mattered for him anymore, not the shipping venture or anything else. She was all he needed to breathe, to live. He craved her presence, yearned for her touch, longed to lose himself in her arms. He'd have given up everything for her. It was love so consuming it had him despair and hope at the same time.

That helped to make the hardest decision of his life. It wasn't easy, but in the end he was convinced it was the only thing he could do to save his soul, because he knew she didn't return his feelings. Not one bit. For her, he was just another thing she'd conquered, and their marriage was just another thing she'd master. He'd heard her say so to her friends. She had shown him off like a prize stallion to them, vowing to be the perfect wife to the one no one else could tame, happily unaware that he was standing right outside the room where she'd made that little speech.

Her words had broken his heart.

Yes, Reinier had had to get away to save himself.

The weight of the chains of being a full-time husband and one day master of the estate, which he knew absolutely nothing about, were too much for his wounded heart. The call of freedom his new ship would bring grew too seductive. So he'd left and never looked back. Until now.

Refusing to delve any further into the past, he threw back his head and finished the rum in his glass.

The time apart had served its purpose. Reinier could be near her now without the oppressing weight of his feelings. He could face her with just as much indifference as she faced him with.

Suddenly, there was a sound that caught his attention. He cocked his head and stopped breathing. It was a sound Reinier remembered only too well. It caused a lazy smile to spread over his lips. Oh yes, he'd heard many over the years, but hers was special—no, it wasn't just special, Reinier corrected himself, it was . . . singular.

Instantly, his insides burned with rage, yet he felt himself harden as the sound of the soft, low moan in the other room reverberated in his head.

So she'd rather take matters into her own hand? More's the pity, she would have appreciated his . . . help. He could have made her come so many times, could have made her weep in pleasure.

Good Lord, had he lost his mind completely? The only thing weeping right now was his rigid cock. It surged even higher thinking about burying himself in her tight, hot, wet sheath.

Reinier growled in frustration, setting the now-empty glass still in his hand down hard for fear of breaking it in his hand.

Feeling more than restless now, he left the room to make his way downstairs to her study. He'd roam the house until he was calmer.

In the study, he lit the lamp by the door. Reading always helped. That is to say, it usually did.

Reinier was highly impressed once he made his way to the bookshelves. This was an extraordinary collection. And it was a legitimate collection. So many libraries these days were filled with books bought by the boxloads just to fill the shelves. Their spines hadn't been cracked in years, if ever, and certainly wouldn't be again, but here he could tell each book was chosen with care and well read as they should be.

Carefully, he set the lamp in his hand down and let his fingers glide softly over the spines of books on the shelf.

There were the classics: Homer, Chaucer, Malory, Sir Thomas Moore, and Shakespeare. What struck him the most, though, was her collection of more recent poetry: Alexander Pope, Jonathan Swift, James Hammond, who he himself had only recently read, a collection by Thomas Cooke that he hadn't been able to procure as of yet, Andrew Marvell, Thomas Traherne, Henry Vaughan, George Herbert . . . Amazing indeed!

Some of the older works could have been her father's, but these were too recent. These had to have been her choices.

For Reinier, it was hard to reconcile a woman with this kind of love and taste in books with the girl he'd left. This contradiction, combined with how much spirit and resolve she'd shown since he'd arrived, had his mind racing with questions and possibilities about this intriguing new side of Emiline, a side he'd never imagined she'd have.

His eyes were glued to the books, taking in the names and works repeatedly, flicking over one after the other, just like the soft light of the lamp was flickering and illuminating them. How very fascinating that Emiline shared his fondness for and taste in poetry. Perhaps they could talk about it—as soon as Emiline got over her unreasonable irritation, that is.

Reinier took a step back, away from the shelf. He let his gaze take in the study once more. A rather strange but at the same time cold and hot pricking made the small hairs at the back of his neck stand up. Everything seemed the same as when he left, yet . . .

How much had she really changed? Had he been wrong about her? What was it she'd been so eager to talk to him about after dinner? If only he'd listened more carefully, read between the lines . . .

And perhaps more importantly, what was it going to take to make good on his threat to seduce her?

Reinier had to find as many clues as he could. When his eyes fell on the large mahogany secretary, he decided to start his search right there. He stalked to the desk, determined to find information from among her private papers. The writing surface wasn't locked, so he lowered it quietly. Reinier brought the lamp over and picked up an ivory-handled letter opener to work the locks on the two tambour slides.

He began to pore over the ledgers in the dim light. To his astonishment, he lost any sense of how long he'd been there. With each moment that passed, his admiration grew exponentially. He prided himself on Barhydt-O'Driscoll being one of the most savvy, tightly run, fair, and highly profitable companies in the Caribbean, but it would seem that they had nothing on his wife and her estate. Her father had always done very well, but Emiline had raised the margin of profits by twenty percent at the least. Oh, and was she ever clever about it. Some of the things she'd tried were unprecedented, especially with her workers. Some ideas hadn't worked out, but enough had that she was able to do what no one else had seemed to do, treat her people kindly and fairly, and still turn more profit than anyone. It was incredible, really.

An aching strain in his neck from studying the ledgers so long made him stop reluctantly. Reinier leaned back in his chair and took a deep breath in a weak attempt to calm his wildly pumping heart.

The glow of pride tightened in his chest. In that moment, he was surprised at his reaction, but—goodness gracious!—the smartest sugarcane producer in the islands was his wife. Who'd have thought?

He couldn't wait until tomorrow when they could talk about it all. Although Connor was a wonderful captain and had a good head for business himself, he never seemed to find the enjoyment in discussing business that Reinier always did.

Who'd have guessed he and Emiline had that in common—the love and fondness for business? The certainty of that, given the evidence right in front of him, had him smiling dreamily.

Charming his wife with talk of something that interested

him keenly also was infinitely appealing. It actually promised a very pleasant day at Bougainvilla—

An almost pleasant day, Reinier corrected himself.

It might not be so bad to have to play the husband for a day or two, after all. What a beautiful, clever, and savvy business-woman his wife was. They may not be soul mates, but Reinier felt some kind of bond now, after all.

When he placed her ledgers back exactly as he had found them, though, another document caught his eye. He recognized im-mediately that it had been drawn by the family's lawyer and couldn't resist a peek at its contents.

Despite the warm night, his spine went cold.

They were divorce papers.

Reinier read over them five times before he let himself stop to think.

He should feel good. He should be happy that she'd thought of it first; after all, he had made himself believe—no, he'd thought their marriage was a burden for the last years.

Nevertheless, he'd appreciate it if she just did as he said and kept her admittedly appealing mouth shut.

No, it didn't make sense. His thoughts raced through his mind, one contradicting the other.

How could she! How dare she try and cast him off!

Well, by the terms laid out, she must have assumed it would take a large sum of enticement—that was clear. Emiline had been rather gracious, actually, if one looked at it objectively. It was very well thought-out and precise. It would make good sense to do it.

But Reinier found himself feeling anything but rational or objective. Right now he felt like the bull in front of which one had waved the red cloth once too often. His nostrils flared, and hot, crimson anger crept up his neck and stuck stubbornly to his cheeks. He felt the urge to ball his hands into fists, papers in them or not, he didn't mind. He wanted to throw the papers through the room and roar with outrage.

Breathing deeply, he forced the muscles in his arms and neck to relax. He wouldn't sink that low and allow himself this kind of emotional outburst, even though the tightening in his chest he'd felt for the last few hours had turned into a stinging lump of pain now.

He'd let her do it again; he knew he mustn't allow himself to feel for her for his own sake. In the end, it hurt too much.

Reinier fought his way back to his senses. None of this mattered. He had his charms, he knew, and he'd use each and every one of them.

He didn't feel wounded by her irresponsible show of defiance anymore, not even in a small way. No, he actually took this predicament as just another challenge, a game to play and win before he moved on to the next thing. He felt as if he was back in his element where he was comfortable and in control.

Pinching his lower lip and thinking of how he would play this game, he suddenly remembered the small box of "treasures," as he called them. He always had them with him, and right in that moment he knew that the fortune he'd spent on them was more than worth it.

Reinier decided exactly how he would go about it. First, he'd appeal to the savvy businesswoman in her. Then he'd spin his net. If she wanted his signature on a set of divorce papers, then she'd have to bargain for it. He knew what he wanted—and she would realize it only when it was too late for her.

The games had begun, and he had just enough time to set a few playing pieces where he needed them and get a little sleep before his next move. Emiline might not be aware of it, but her action hours before gave him the clue to just how he'd start out.

As quickly and as quietly as possible, he put everything away and locked the secretary. When he rose from the desk chair,

Reinier rubbed the front of his dressing gown, finding himself rock hard and aching once more.

As much as he hated to have to take care of things himself, Reinier was afraid if he didn't give himself some relief, sleep would never find him. And he'd need some rest. He'd have to have all his wits about him for what he had planned for his beautiful, smart, and defiant little wife.

6

Despite how angry and confused Emiline felt last night, she had a good night's rest. So good, in fact, that she started the next day with a hum on her lips. Today she'd show Reinier just how much in control of Bougainvilla she was; not just the estate, but the whole bloody island. She'd make her place—and his—perfectly clear.

She could almost taste victory in the air when she was bouncing down the stairs. Justine had been instructed to tell the staff they should set a big breakfast table. Emiline and Reinier would sit at the opposite ends, with both leaves put back in. That would make her attitude toward him quite clear. This was going to be a landmark win for her in their battle for control.

Wonderful, Emiline thought as she approached the breakfast room. Reinier was already up and about. She could hear him in the room saying thank you to someone.

As Emiline entered, the young maid bowed and, with a quick, uncertain flick of her eyes toward her mistress, hurried out of the room. Emiline wondered what that was all about, but soon enough she halted, robbed of breath.

The table was set with the leaves in, just as she'd wished it, but the china and silver were set right next to each other. Reinier, insufferable lout that he was, stood right next to his chair, his arm leaning against the back of it with a sparkle in his eyes she didn't care for at all.

How dare he contradict her orders? Emiline remembered to breathe again just in time so that Reinier couldn't mistake the outraged, flustered blush on her cheeks for anger or, God forbid, shyness.

"Emiline." Reinier bowed, the twinkle in his eyes becoming more intense for a moment. "Good morning to you. I trust you slept well? How nice of you to join me for breakfast."

She glanced from the plates set so intimately next to each other to him and back. Then, putting all the disdain she felt at him into her glare, she held her back rigid and with an almost regal stance stared at Reinier coolly. "It seems I do not have a choice. Once again. I must say I find this all rather tiresome."

Reinier's lips twitched before he took a step forward and presented his arm to guide her to the table.

"Truly? I'd have thought you'd be happy to have me back at least for the moment to oversee things so you could concentrate on embroidery or—"

"There is little use or time for embroidery," Emiline interrupted, taking her seat without bothering to look up at him.

"Or," Reinier drew the word out, ignoring her objection. "You could concentrate on other things that might interest an accomplished woman. Do you still play?"

He sat down then, leaning toward her with a despicably amiable smile on his face. "Has your skill with the harpsichord finally improved? I must say—and we both agree on that, I believe—you never took your play seriously, although it should be tremendously important for a modern woman."

Emiline felt her molars grind, but she was determined to ignore him. Taking the napkin, she flicked it open and placed it on her lap.

"Or what is it that strikes young women's fancies these days? Fashion! Yes. Ohh, you'll tremendously enjoy having time for all that now that I'm back."

Emiline never knew he loved to hear his own voice so much. He most probably expected applause to commend him on his ridiculous monologue.

Instead, Emiline balled her hands into fists. The nails biting her palms reminded her that it was essential she stayed calm. But how could she stay calm with him blabbering such nonsense?

"Furthermore, sir, there is no use for fashion or any other fancies on Bougainvilla. So you see, I do not require or desire your help."

Reinier sighed. "A pity! You always had such a good eye for fashion. You never looked less than stunning as I recall."

Emiline took a deep, fortifying breath and narrowed her eyes at him. The unbearable smile on his face was not wavering; if anything, that peculiar gleam in his eyes flashed even brighter.

"My compliments, sir. You have the memory of an elephant or so it seems," she pressed out, her words barely void of the unladylike growl she felt.

Reinier tried to hide his amusement behind his hand, elbow braced on the table. Either he'd been in the sun on deck of his precious ship for too long and was suffering from the consequences of serious sunstroke, or he had become a little daft through the years. Why wasn't it getting through to him that she didn't want him here?

"By the way, I have asked Captain Blanc to see you off at the docks whenever you're ready to depart."

Rolling his lips under, Reinier only busied himself with his own napkin. A strange, unpleasantly cool sensation skittered down her nape.

Just as Emiline was about to demand he disclosed his thoughts, the servants entered and set breakfast. There was no need for them to witness a scene, because if she spoke now, she knew she wouldn't be able to control her temper, and she and Reinier would end up having a nasty argument. She never raised her voice in front of the servants, and she wouldn't let him make her do so now. He wasn't worth it.

As soon as they'd left, however, Emiline let all the contempt for him fill her glare, but his cold, calculating stare stole her thunder.

"I have to say your wish to be rid of me again so quickly has me concerned." Reinier's face was void of any expression, his voice callous. The contrast to his amiability before was chilling to the bone. "Emiline, could it be there's something you're trying to hide?"

Heart hammering in her throat, she swallowed hard. She needed to remain calm.

"Hiding?" Emiline cocked her head. "What on earth would I have to hide? And from whom? You—someone who hasn't stepped foot on Ronde for four years?" She shook her head with a derisive bark of laughter. "Why would I bother?"

Leaning his head back a little, his eyes narrowed.

Emiline drummed on the wood of the table with her forefinger. "But more to the point: Why have you bothered coming here?"

Reinier averted his eyes and licked his lips. He gave a bored shrug and stirred his coffee.

Yes, she had him now. Her heart was pumping so hard with

the certainty that he was going to admit it was a mistake, perhaps even ask her forgiveness . . .

He met her eyes straight on. "Frankly, I was a little bored. And Connor was otherwise occupied, so I thought why not come here for a bit of fun, she is my wife, after all."

Reinier saw it snap, the last straw that held her calm, dignified carriage together. Throwing her napkin on the table with a little too much force, the smile she gave him was brittle.

"Well, then, Monsieur Barhydt, I think I might have just the excitement a savvy businessman like yourself would be interested in."

Very promising. Indeed, something in the way she'd called him "Monsieur" struck him in a very interesting way. There were possibilities in that.

Reinier marveled at her spirit, truly admired her strength. What a worthy opponent she was in their joust. But he knew he'd win this tournament of words.

He uncrossed and recrossed his legs, leaning back in his chair, feeling comfortable and infinitely smug. "Do tell, madam."

She inhaled deeply through her nose. "Since I've been running Bougainvilla on my own these past years, rather successfully I might add, and you've shown no interest, I thought it only practical and fair that we make our separate lives official. That way I can legally have full control of what I'm already managing, and you can carry on just as you've been doing—with ample compensation to you, of course."

Reinier waited to see if she remembered to breathe. "Spell it out, Emiline. What precisely do you want?"

She wrinkled her nose as if she were disgusted talking to him. "Fine. I want to be free of you. I want you to give up all rights to the property and to me. In short, I want a divorce."

"Give up all my rights to my property? To all of my property? Including you?"

Emiline nodded once.

"That is highly unlikely."

Lips grim, she narrowed her eyes at him. "Perhaps you failed to hear me correctly. I am willing to pay very handsomely to finally be rid of you."

Reinier shrugged again. "No."

"What?"

"No, I'm not interested in your proposal."

She blanched. "Why not? You obviously don't want me—"

Reinier clicked his tongue at that. She had no idea how much he wanted her, but she'd see soon enough. "Besides," Emiline went on, her tone slightly sullen. "You haven't even heard exactly how much I'm offering."

"It doesn't matter. I don't want or need your money."

"What, then?" she snapped. "What do I have to do for this to finally be over?"

He inhaled slowly, his nostrils flaring. Then he brushed his sleeve, gently, like he'd caress her skin. "Everything." Uncrossing his legs, he leaned forward. "Anything and everything I could possibly ask you in every way."

There was this certain light in her eyes, distrustful and cautious. Her eyebrows drew together. "What exactly does that mean? Explain yourself."

"Three days, Emiline. Three days under my command and at my beck and call in exchange for the rest of your life. It's hardly even a fair bargain for me."

Looking down, she bit her lower lip. Reinier could see the wheels turning.

"Three days and I will sign the papers, Emiline." The time span, Reinier was sure, would win her over.

Her eyes flicked up at him, filled with annoyance. "You know."

"Yes, I know about the divorce papers."

Emiline turned her head away from him. "Three days and you'll be gone for good?" Her voice was barely more than a whisper.

"Cross my heart."

Slowly, she nodded to herself, then looked him straight in the eyes. "We have a bargain, Captain Barhydt."

At that, Reinier's expression turned sour. "No, please. From now on you will call me 'Monsieur' and only 'Monsieur.' And I shall call you . . . my 'Lily.' Very fitting, wouldn't you agree?" His face glowed with anticipation.

Emiline pursed her lips and wrinkled her nose at her new nickname. She obviously didn't care too much for it.

"You see," Reinier explained, "a lily is a flower so delicate and precious, she needs someone else to care for her." Clearly, she set out to contradict him, but Reinier waved her argument off. "No, no. You are my Lily from now on. And remember, you will do as I say. No exceptions to the rule. These are the conditions, and you've agreed to them." His words were a cold warning.

Emiline pressed her lips together. There was a flicker of willfulness in her eyes. "Aye, captain."

She'd defied his first order. Reinier suppressed the smile he felt. Instead, he leaned into her more. "I do not care much for your bold show of recalcitrance." His whisper didn't hide the tone of command. "Perhaps I need to teach you a lesson."

At that, her eyes grew wide with confusion.

"Give yourself pleasure, Lily. Now."

Deep crimson colored her cheeks and she avoided his gaze. Her lips moved, although nothing but a whimper could be heard.

"What? Are you shocked? But why? It's not that you haven't done it before. I know. I heard you last night. So, show me. I want to see how you did it."

Emiline shook her head. "It's broad daylight. We're too exposed here. I can't—I won't do it. What if one of the servants came in?"

Reinier felt the muscles in his jaw twitch. He'd been looking forward to this, perhaps more than was prudent. Reluctantly, he had to admit that she was right. He got up, went to close the door to the main hallway, then the servants' entrance. Very careful that she didn't notice, he turned the key so that it was locked.

"Now, then. Nobody will dare intrude upon our privacy." Walking back, Reinier sat down before her. "Well? What are you waiting for?"

She turned to look to the side, embarrassment shining brightly on her face.

"Three days. You agreed to the bargain. So, Lily, expose yourself."

Her inner battle showed clearly on her face. Her hands on her thighs were balled into tight fists, but gradually, they opened.

She looked up at him. Her eyes were marvelously big, their aquamarine quality slightly paler than usual. She was frightened; this leap of faith was a very big one for her. Was she afraid he'd laugh at her?

He wouldn't. Reinier let his steady gaze convey just that. He didn't move. He simply waited for her to comply, giving her strength by locking his eyes with hers. She needed his support, and that was all that mattered to him for now.

He could see her shoulders moving. She was lifting her dress inch by inch. Reinier remained still and encouraging in his demeanor. When her skirts were finally up, bunching at her hips, her courage left her and she looked away.

"Lily." It must have been the way he said this one word, a name, her name, because she looked back at him. He rewarded her with a tender smile. Something akin to gratefulness showed in her eyes.

"Open for me."

Perhaps she was slowly grasping the idea of the game. Perhaps she was slowly understanding that this wouldn't end in humiliation, that, in fact, this was not about humiliation, far from it. For whatever the reason, she seemed no longer hesitant but did as he'd told her and opened for him to see her.

She began to move. Reinier watched her hands as they wandered over her thighs. Her fingers, delicate and oh-so-elegant, caressed the silken, golden skin on the inside, drew up, then down, and up a little farther until Reinier could see her core was gradually covered with a fine glistening sheen, the color deeper, her nether lips opening.

He suppressed the urge to lick his lips. In fact, he was careful not to show any outward sign that might betray how elated and aroused he felt.

Her fingers found the sensitized nub but didn't touch it yet. Her middle finger was rubbing to the side of it, first left, then right. Her other hand grasped the inside of her thigh. She finally found the spot that would give her release, stroked it, and at the same time squeezed her thigh. It made her gasp and she let her eyes close, her head falling back.

So she loved the sensations brought on by the sweetest of pleasure-pain, not quite pain, not just pleasure anymore. Good to know, Reinier thought as he kept observing her every move, every shift, watchful not to miss a thing.

Her hand left her thigh and cupped one of her breasts, squeezing it as well. He could see she had increased her speed, her fingers flying expertly over her shining, wet core.

Her fragrance found him. The heady mix of musk and strawberries raged through his body and mind. Her scent tingled under his skin, tickling his scalp, wrapping him into its sweetness, drawing him in. She'd always been an aphrodisiac, a drug he couldn't get enough of. Biting his lower lip, Reinier swallowed the masculine grunt he felt churning in his chest.

After a time her breathing quickened, and soon little sighs could be heard every time she exhaled. His own breathing became deep and heavy in response.

He asked in barely more than a hoarse whisper, "Are you close?"

Gasping, she thrashed her head from side to side, arching her body to her own touch, opening her legs wider. "Yes, close. So close."

Reinier slipped off his chair and fell to his knees before her. His hands found her knees and pressed them apart even more while he brought his lips closer to her core. Saliva gathered in his mouth. He couldn't wait. He needed to taste her now, needed to feel her honey trickle down his throat.

Breathing through his nose, he saw the tiny stir cooled her heated flesh for only a brief moment as gooseflesh rippled her skin. When he inhaled her sweetness, his eyes slid closed. He nudged her hand away and instantly replaced it with his mouth, letting the flat of his tongue travel over her first.

Her breath pitched. With a low, sultry moan, her hands found his head. Reinier reveled in the sharp twist of his hair when she grabbed him tighter to hold him to her, and he burrowed his face deeper against her creamy flesh.

He closed his lips over her, his hands traveling up her upper thighs until his thumbs brushed her core also. His mouth left her and he brought his thumbs together, teasing her nub while he raised his eyes to see her writhe with pleasure, her eyes half open and blazing with dark aquamarine fire.

Bringing his lips back down, they closed over her bud and his tongue flicked over her fast. Her body convulsed and she came hard, with a noise erupting from her throat that was half moan and half shriek. Reinier continued to lap at her through her orgasm, slow, gentle strokes, tender enough to prolong her pleasure, soft enough to keep her arousal on a high level.

Eventually, her body relaxed. He left her to look up just as she brought her head forward. A mixture of emotions were in her eyes. Reinier could see delight tainted by confusion, then awe.

"That was beautiful, Lily. You were magnificent." Reinier rolled back on his heels, got up, and retreated to the corner where he'd hidden his little box of treasures the night before. Pivoting, he felt her eyes on him.

He was more than content with her performance. But now it was time for the next step. He saw her eyes were studying the small box in his hand, trying to figure out what it contained.

Reinier kneeled down before her again, the box hidden away between his knees for now. Tilting his head, he let one hand play with her again, bathing in her honeysweet moistness. His other hand found her nape, wrapped around the base of her skull, and brought her forward just far enough that their lips were a whisper from each other still.

He let one finger slide into her slick cunny and tasted her gasp on his lips. She was tight, but her muscles grabbed him and sucked him in. He complied, giving her what her body demanded. He added a second finger and her muscles accommodated eagerly.

Her head was moving, her lips sought his, but Reinier moved back just a little every time she tried to steal a kiss.

She gave a whimper of protest when he left her and brought his wet fingers up to her lips, tracing their perfect outline. He kissed her, savored her hungry lips on his, drank her keening moan as he sucked at her tongue.

His fingers grasped the box between his knees, found the clasp, opened it, and retrieved its content. He rubbed what moistness of hers was left on his hand over the two jade balls attached to each other by a delicate gold string. Quickly, he brought them up to her core and slid them in. Her sheath opened and swallowed them until only the chain could be seen.

Their kiss deepened, became more intense. She melted into him, welcoming his exploring tongue and following it back. Her hands found his shoulders and she pressed him to her, her nails pricking his skin through the shirt he was wearing.

When Reinier ended their kiss, she was breathless, her eyes dilated, her body screaming for more.

This was where her first lesson ended—and her second began. After rearranging her dress so that it properly covered her once more, he righted his hair as well as his attire, then sat down in the chair opposite of her.

"For the rest of the morning, how about you show me the estate? I must say I'm very curious what you did to it and how it's become so prosperous."

Emiline blinked at him. Eventually, she stood. A visible shiver ran through her, and with a gasp, she grabbed the table-cloth to steady herself. Reinier was instantly there, giving his support and helping her stand.

"What is this?" Emiline's words were seductively breathless.

"Just a little toy I once purchased. I thought I'd put it to good use with you."

Emiline turned her head, eyebrows furrowed. She was more puzzled and wary than ever.

"Come now, Lily, let us walk." Hoping that every use of her new nickname would be a subtle reminder of the bargain they'd made and what she'd agreed to, he reached for her.

Eventually, she accepted his proffered hand despite her obvious unwillingness to do so. At first her steps were finicky, but soon her pace quickened.

Just as they reached the door, Reinier leaned close and whispered in her ear, "Before I forget. You are not supposed to climax unless I allow it."

Reinier saw her lips move; they opened as if to contradict, but she shut them quickly. She was so charming being baffled, overwhelmed, and willful all at the same time.

This was going to be a wonderful day, indeed.

7

The tour of the island so far had been a mixture of heaven and hell. Emiline was tortured by the erotic sensations she felt at every step and cursed him silently with every new shiver that racked her, all the while being forced to appear outwardly calm. How she had made it through chatting with the workers and answering his blasted mundane questions Emiline couldn't say.

She didn't know how much longer her legs were going to support her. She felt like a jellyfish and they were just making their way to the well house used for cool food storage. Thank goodness they had already visited the windmill, the boiling area, the crystallization house, and the rum stills.

The jade balls Reinier had placed inside her felt like . . . like nothing she'd ever experienced before. At first, their tinkling sounds caused crimson heat to blaze over her cleavage, up to her ears. But the muffled noises weren't Emiline's major concern any longer. They bumped against each other and against places inside her that sent fissions of electricity through her whole body. They tickled and clicked, and jolt after jolt kept her on the edge of bliss with every step.

Once again, she had to stop moving or else she would have climaxed. Reinier took her elbow to steady her and to her chagrin, watched her every movement, how she took deep, calming breaths, how she rubbed her face to feel something else, anything else. He grinned devilishly. The bastard enjoyed each moment of her torment.

"Are you all right, Lily?"

She answered only when she finally managed to get her annoyance under control and could speak calmly. "Yes, of course."

Reinier let her elbow go and they continued on with the tour.

They now stepped down the five feet into the well house with its thick stonewalls sunken deep into the earth. Emiline was so focused on the cool air finally giving her some blessed relief from the fire raging though her that she never heard his question, neither the first or the second time he asked it.

"LILY!" The volume and sternness of his voice brought her back to the present and she jolted, turning to face him. His infuriatingly beautiful eyes were glittering with reproach, and his terribly striking lips were pressed into a tight, pale line. "That's twice now I've addressed you without a response. I expect you to address me promptly when spoken to."

Emiline thought she heard a low growl swinging with his words also.

Three days. Just three days.

Biting the inside of her cheek, she remembered what he expected and eventually responded, "*Oui,* monsieur. Pardon, monsieur."

The smile he gave her then was one of pure unadulterated male satisfaction.

Before she could tame her wild emotions, her heart skipped a beat at the powerful angelic presence he created. She couldn't even begin to examine all the far-reaching, treacherous emotions creeping in from every direction.

His "treasures" kept her on edge, and she was almost thankful they held those thoughts at bay for the moment. But Emiline wondered if he knew that, and if perhaps that was part of his plan.

Reinier placed his hands around her upper arms. Goose bumps covered every inch of her flesh, both from the stimulation and the temperature. His crystalline green gaze fixed on hers, eyes heavy lidded. His grip loosened and his warm hands ran up and down her arms. "I was asking how it remains so cool here," he repeated with a low, sultry purr, and Emiline could see his pupils dilate.

Emiline tried her best to focus on the question and not his touch. "The well that feeds the troughs is very deep and the water is very cold. The depth of floor underground and the thickness of the stone walls above keep the coolness in." Hating how her voice came out as a husky whisper, she pressed her lips together.

"I see." His gaze flicked from the corner where bacon was hung from a pole in the ceiling to the opposite corner where thick earthen jars were filled with goat's milk.

Before Emiline knew what happened, his grip tightened and he pulled her against him. Gasping with surprise as one of his hands moved to the small of her back to press her into his body, she tried to escape his commanding embrace. Her hands braced against his upper arms, but his strength held her in place.

The long, strong fingers of his right hand wrapped lightly around her neck as his erection pressed into her lower belly. Emiline closed her eyes and swallowed a groan. Next thing she knew, his thumb was caressing her lower lip.

"Open for me, Lily."

Without thought, she parted her lips slightly and his thumb

traced their outline, sending bouncing tickles from her mouth straight to her lower belly. She shivered yet again from the sensation.

His thumb slipped in and Emiline's eyes widened as she stared up at him. Reinier raised one eyebrow nonchalantly. She knew what he wanted. Her lips closed around the digit and she lightly sucked at it while circling it with her tongue.

Her eyes flicked up to see his lips curling into a lazy smile, his lids lowering even more. His hand on her back began to move, circling her backside. At first it seemed to relieve some of the pressure, but then his touch pushed her back against him again, and the intimate closeness had scorching tremors running through her.

Her mind was screaming in outrage. She should be affronted, she thought, but she wasn't. She told herself it was only because she was playing along for the sake of their bargain.

But a small voice whispered at the back of her mind that maybe she had missed his touch, that maybe she wanted this regardless.

Both rebellion and prudence were shushed when his ravenous mouth replaced his thumb. Emiline heard herself moan as she felt him grind his erection against her lower belly.

Her core fluttered once more, and in response Emiline kissed him back with equal hunger, using her tongue to joust with his, tasting him as deeply as she could. Reinier plundered even deeper with his mouth, his movements against her increased, and her arousal began to climb again quickly. She whimpered into his mouth. She was seconds from release when he suddenly pushed her away.

Emiline stumbled not knowing whether she was angry or elated that they'd stopped. She labored to catch her breath, and when she looked up she saw Reinier was taking a few shallow, shaky breaths himself. Her lips curled down in frustration.

Sympathy lit Reinier's gaze for only a moment to be replaced by something darker that had disquieting shudders run down her spine.

"Try to kneel down." He placed his hands lightly on her shoulders and brought his lips to her ear. "It should ease the sensation."

She pushed back and gave him a questioning look, but at the slight pressure of his hands, her own hands fisted in her skirt to lift the hem and her knees bent to kneel. Bowing her head, she opened her fingers and began to smooth the fabric over her thighs, thankful that she did feel much calmer now. Just when she was about to tell him so, the fingers of Reinier's left hand went to her chin to lift her gaze even more.

"Now that you're feeling better and since you're already down there . . ." he drawled, his right hand working the buttons of his fly, freeing himself. He was grinning from ear to ear, as if he'd just won at cards.

Her anger flared, but suddenly all her disdain fell silent when his musk crept up her nostrils. A balmy, velvety tickle whispered through her. Her body instinctively recognized his, coming alive even more and humming keenly. Her breath came faster. She had to lick her suddenly dry lips. Her eyes were riveted on his engorged flesh. He stroked himself, twisting his fist as it moved from root to tip several times. Then he brought his erection to her lips, almost touching them but not quite. Desire lashed through her.

Reinier didn't move to force himself into her mouth. He stayed where he was, still stroking himself.

"Show me you still remember what I taught you, Lily." His words were a sensual, deep whisper.

She was mesmerized by the sight of his member so close to her and found herself recalling all too well what he'd taught her in that blissful year. As much as she'd have loved to, she'd never been able banish him or his body from her mind. The sight, feel, taste, and scent of him were etched into her soul, and she'd never been able to wash them away.

He'd made her burn then; he'd made her burn today, all day. She not only remembered the techniques he'd shown her, she also remembered how he reacted. A smile flitted across her lips.

Her hands reached for him. They traveled over the linen of his breeches, feeling the hard muscle underneath. Emiline couldn't suppress the shiver that came with that touch. He'd always felt . . . glorious to her, and after so many years, he still did. She knew she should feel abashed, but she was too far gone for that. Her core was throbbing and aching, and her lips were hungry to taste him again.

Her fingers wandered up over his hips. She leaned slightly forward to get closer to him. His natural perfume lashed out at her senses, and closing her eyes, she inhaled deep to take more of its sweetness into her lungs, her body, her mind.

One hand curled around the base of him, displacing Reinier's, just before she brought her cheek close and caressed his soft flesh. He was pulsating and hot beneath her skin, the contrast in feel almost as striking as the contrast in their skin tones. Her lips explored lazily where her cheek had touched before, fingers trailing with a tantalizingly slow pace over him.

Emiline lavished his member with tiny kisses as if she needed to refresh her memory of him. His response was a jerky twitch.

At last she came to the tip of his big rod and her tongue darted out to tickle the small opening; then quickly it found the nub on the underside right below his glans, stimulating his most sensitive spot carefully. When she heard Reinier suck in his breath, she lifted her chin to meet his gaze.

His usually bright eyes were hooded, and what little she could see of his lime-green irises was almost swallowed up by his dilated pupils. The look on his face was utterly erotic, full of heat and anticipation. Emiline felt her heartbeat pitch as her stomach fluttered and her core trembled.

Her tongue rotated around him quickly, and his hips moved forward and back rhythmically. She repeated her sensuous game of licking and tickling him, taking her time with it, making him wait deliberately.

When Emiline saw hunger darken his features, she felt powerful. There was no other word for it. She did to him what he was doing to her; she made him wait, made him long for and anticipate her next move. His cock twitched against her lips.

She wrapped her lips around him in a sudden assault. A keening moan ripped from Reinier's throat and she saw his eyes were closed, his head falling back an inch. And she'd only engulfed the tip of him for now.

Her tongue never ceased rotating around him, not even when she took him a little deeper into her mouth. She felt his hand on her head, the tips of his fingers digging deep. She also felt him harden in her hand and between her lips, signaling her to take him deep into her throat.

At another moan, she felt her eyes close as well when she tasted the first drop of salty ecstasy at the back of her palate. Only when she heard Reinier hiss did she realize that it hadn't been his moan, but her own. How she had missed this.

His hand fisted in her hair and his hips started to move as if to urge her on. The certainty that she could give him such pleasure was potent, made her head light. If she could make him smolder, she could make him burn even brighter.

Her lips chased her fingers wrapped tightly around him until they reached the root; then her fingers would follow her lips in an increasing rhythm. She was in charge regardless of how his hips moved into her or how his hand fisted in her hair to urge her on.

She sucked him hard a few times, only to let her lips relax

and glide loosely over him until she opened her lips completely and only her tongue explored him, his shape, his texture. Next time she began her tantalizing game of alternating between lavishing intense attention and playful teasing; his hips' movements grew more urgent, more frantic in response.

Emiline stopped, her eyes flicking up, her gaze locking with his. She opened her throat as if to swallow and took him deeper, and deeper still. The muscles in her throat were working at him now, constricting and loosening, convulsing, then slackening.

Reinier threw his head back and groaned. Unintelligible whispers trickled from his lips, beginning with sighs and ending in soft moans.

That was when Emiline realized part of the thrill was the knowledge that she could make him forget himself, all his sternness, all his austerity. To know she'd just turned the tables and she could bring him to his knees with her touch, with her kiss alone, was almost overwhelming. She began to like the little game they were playing even more now. No matter what he claimed, in this moment, she was in charge.

Working him some more, faster and harder, just like he wanted it, Emiline ignored the pricking in her scalp as his grip in her hair tightened.

The first of a series of trembles ran through his flesh. Emiline felt it in her fingers and lips and tongue. Just a little more, she thought, and continued her ministrations. Once more, once more . . .

Then she stopped, freed him from her grasp, and leaned back. He was so hot, he was almost steaming in the cool air of the well house.

Reinier sucked in a sharp breath. His eyes snapped open and his jaw dropped. Emiline's heart was pumping so hard she felt it in her throat and mercilessly lashing in her core. His eyes found their focus and she gave him an innocent stare.

"Is that anywhere near what you'd had in mind, monsieur? I'm not sure. My memory seems rather vague, you see."

With every little breath that left her lips when she spoke, she saw him twitch from out of the corner of her eye. It didn't matter that her words were hoarse; she was sure the same honey-sweet layer of lust she felt also covered his throat.

"Vixen," he pressed out, half hiss, half chuckle, his hand in her hair fisting even tighter pulling her back to him. "Finish what you started."

She knew her grin was wicked, saw its mirrored image in his eyes. She was still smiling when she opened her mouth again to start her sensual game of kissing, lapping, and sucking from the beginning.

Reinier closed his eyes and a moan tore from his lips. Again, he threw his head back, his hips meeting her every time she took him deeper.

That was Emiline's cue. She slowed down, her grip on him tightened, and she brought him deep one last time as he convulsed in her mouth, his hot seed splashing against the back of her tongue, flowing down her throat. She moaned and drank what he offered greedily. The air left his lungs in a ragged, blissful sigh, and her lips curled around him as her hand milked every last drop of him.

She finally released him and watched him smile at her fully contented. Pride pulsated and fluttered deep in her.

The feeling spread and changed. All too soon she became aware of her body's demands. Tasting him had aroused her to the verge of misery. Her thighs were drenched with her own desperate longing. Forcing herself to take even, deep breaths to suppress her own hunger, she accepted the hand he offered and stood as gracefully as possible under the circumstances.

It was exhilarating that she'd just succeeded in making him forget himself, making him completely lose himself in her caress. Still reveling in her feminine prowess, she let her body lean into his while looking up at him.

His hands once again rested on her forearms, and his eyes still showed a flicker of that fire she had stoked. Would he kiss her now? Would he claim her like he almost had after their episode at breakfast? Had she driven him that far? She hoped she had.

With a triumphant smile on her lips, she lifted her chin an inch to show that she knew the hunger she'd stirred. She wouldn't deny him; her own desire had passed the boundary of reason.

But instead of pulling her even closer, he forced more distance between them.

"Don't look so smug, darling, we've barely just started."

Before Emiline could even register his words, he had the fly of his breeches closed again and turned to leave, but not without offering his arm. "Now, Lily, I'd like to see the small stables we passed before. Do you still have that haughty little dappled filly?"

Placing her shaking hand on his arm, she barely suppressed a growl. "*Oui*, monsieur, of course, monsieur," she murmured, wondering if he'd ever let his mask of indifference fall again.

8

Reinier could see the aggravation clearly in her beautiful, sea-colored eyes when she stepped beside him and accepted his arm. As they made their way out of the well house, he had to admit at least to himself that she'd had every right to feel smug. He couldn't remember when, if ever, a woman's mouth on his cock had felt quite like that. The deliciously cool air, his hand fisted in her ebony and gold hair, the perfect feel of her mouth . . . It was all part of a memory he was sure he'd think of quite often after he'd left.

But it also made him wonder again about her lover. Had his wife been perfecting her skill on him? Because perfect it was, perfect she had been. Reinier shook his head a little as they walked along as if it would help to scatter his thoughts, but it seemed nothing helped. He wondered if she and her lover had strolled the estate like the two of them did today?

Did she happily share with him the things she was so reluctant to impart to him, her husband? That thought was extremely vexing.

It was of no consequence now, Reinier decided. He was here now; she was his to command at the moment, and that was all that mattered. He turned his head to measure her. She held her head high, her shoulders straight as they walked along.

He thought he saw a shadow, and instinctually he flicked his gaze down the front of her dress—and his eyes widened. He wanted to laugh out loud while at the same time his heart missed a beat. She hadn't noticed, of course, but there were two very prominent dirt smudges on the front of her yellow-washed silk dress. It would be obvious to anyone that she'd been on her knees for one reason or another in one of her best morning dresses. And given the fact that he was struggling not to grin like a simpleton at the mind-blowing orgasm she'd just given him, it would be very hard for an onlooker not to jump to the right conclusion.

Oh, she'd be mortified when she saw it. Emiline was master of this place. The people here loved and respected her, and he was sure it had taken her years to achieve that. As captain of his own ship, he understood what it took to gain that much affection and respect. He'd never let that be jeopardized. If there were any chance that her people might lose some of that admiration now if they thought she'd been on her knees for the man who had married her and left her soon after . . .

The consequences would be a disaster. For one, she would never forgive him. For another, her reputation would suffer beyond repair. He knew that.

Reinier was relieved that they hadn't encountered any of the workers on their way to the stables. Finally there, they stepped out of the bright sunlight and into the building.

It was smaller than most with only four stalls. However, it reflected her father's wealth in the materials, her mother's taste in the French style, and like everything else he'd seen so far, it was immaculately maintained by Emiline.

Reinier inhaled deeply. The warm, soothing scent of horses and the soft, dry fragrance of hay welcomed him. Beneath all that, the faint nuance of leather wafted toward him and made him feel completely at ease. Well, at least there was one place on this whole bloody island that welcomed him and made him feel at home.

He felt her hand slip from his arm and turned, thinking she might be unsteady again from the stimulation of the jade balls. But she'd stopped dead and was now staring with pained expression at the stains on her dress.

"Reinier! Why didn't you tell . . . What must people . . . I mean . . . Just look at my dress!" Her words were little more than a hiss. Even though she'd struggled not to raise her voice but to keep it low, the tremor of anxiety was all too clear. Her eyes flicked from the stains right above her knees to him, to settle there with a healthy amount of disdain tinged with enough helplessness that he understood how humiliated and embarrassed she felt.

At almost the same moment and before Reinier could say anything, the clip-clop of hooves could be heard coming into the barn from the other end. Giving her a wink, he scooped her into his arms then, quickly silencing her small shriek of surprise with a kiss. "Never fear, my lady."

Seeing them, the young groom stopped, then rushed forward with the dappled filly in tow. "Mistress, are you hurt?"

Reinier allayed the groom's concern. "She's fine, just had a little fall. Her beautiful dress and her pride took the worst of it. Why don't you leave the horse to me and we'll give your mistress some privacy to recover?"

Instead of trotting off right away at Reinier's dismissal, the groom looked straight to Emiline for her approval. "Are you sure, miss?"

"Yes, John, I'll been fine."

Emiline patted Reinier's shoulder to signal him he could let her down, then balled her dress in one small fist to hide the stains. She leaned into him, and when he stood her back on her feet, she added, "Go on home. I'm sure your mother can use your help with something around the house."

The groom's affection and loyalty for Emiline was apparent. With a smile and a nod, the boy handed the reins to Reinier's now free hand and almost skipped as he headed home.

The horse wasn't saddled, so Reinier guided her into her stall and, rolling up his sleeves, found a comb and then brushed the horse a few times before leaving her in the stall. After washing his hands in a barrel of fresh water, he found Emiline exactly where he'd left her, looking lost and deep in thought. She glanced up when the tip of his boot lightly touched the tip of hers.

"Thank you." The quiver in her whisper spoke of her inner turmoil.

"You're welcome. Part of our bargain is that you are in my care, Lily. Never forget that. What kind of care would that be if I let your reputation be tarnished? You've earned their love, and I know how hard that is. I wouldn't dream of doing anything to hurt that."

She nodded but still looked pensive. He couldn't blame her. There was a lot to their dynamic he didn't quite understand either, but deep in thought was not where he wanted her to be right now. Looking around, his eyes soon fell on the door to the small room at the back. Reinier felt his lips curl up. There it was what he was looking for.

He took her hand and led her into the well-appointed tack room, the seductive scent of freshly oiled leather delighting his senses as he surveyed the room. He noticed the neat arrangement of crops, bits, and leads among other promising things along one wall, a freshly polished saddle on its stand, and a sim-

ple but well-made couch in the corner. He couldn't help but
muse to himself that Madame Poivre had almost an identical
room in her fine establishment. Yes, this would do very nicely.

"Let's have a seat, shall we?" Turning to her, Reinier guided
her to the settee that was normally used to take one's riding
boots on and off.

She nodded her agreement and they settled into the small
couch. Wrapping his arms around the small of her back, Reinier
pressed her closer to him. Their eyes met and he saw her lower
lip quiver; then the pink tip of her tongue snaked out to wet it.

He lowered his head and brushed his lips against hers, breathing in the whispered moan she couldn't stop. Reinier laughed
low against her lips. What a tremendously sensual creature she
was, it was almost a pity that he'd have to deny her relief for a
little longer.

He began to rain kisses and light flicks of his tongue along
her neck and down to her décolletage. Her warm tan skin tasted
of salt and sunshine, but also of musky strawberries, the scent
of her arousal, a thick, syrupy spice on his tongue that made
him want more. His hands moved up to loosen her dress and to
his delight, her breast sprang free with one good tug downward.

Delighting in her small gasp when he cupped one golden
breast, he kissed her, a hard, open, wet claiming of her mouth.
His tongue thrust deep while his hand found her soft, round
breast with its impeccable fit that molded into his hand as if it
belonged there. Her skin was like precious auburn satin, and he
drank her muffled, breathless whimpers like a man who had
been adrift at sea for far too long.

Her nipple puckered and she bowed in his arms. While
kneading her tender flesh, he felt her small hands burrow into
his hair. She wanted more and Reinier was in the mood to give
her a little more just now. Ending their passionate kiss and lowering his head, his tongue laved her dark nipple.

His other hand worked its way under her dress and found the insides of her thighs slick with her arousal. But his hand didn't stop there. Momentarily, his fingers found her moist folds and parted them to his touch.

Her quick breaths were enchanting, and her fingers kneading his scalp sent pinpricks of lust through him. Every nerve end of his body was sizzling with the need to take her, even more so given he knew it would have to wait a little longer.

She had turned out to be so much more than he'd ever expected, and he couldn't even begin to fathom all the possibilities before him. Never ceasing to squeeze and suckle her supple breast, his fingers entered her until they touched the jade balls deep inside. He leaned forward, his erotic assault intensifying, his fingers pumping in and out of her. She followed his lead, her hips meeting him hungrily with every little thrust, and she leaned back until she lay with her head against the rounded arm, giving him easy access to everything he wanted.

She arched her back as he worked the jewel treasures. His teeth began to gently graze the tight bud of her nipple. He felt her core spasm around his fingers and small, musical moans escape her with every breath. She was getting too close. It was time to pull back. She hadn't quite earned her prize just yet.

But just as he began a slow withdrawal of his fingers from inside her, she quickly released his hair and gripped his wrist tightly with both her hands. Her strength surprised him as she held his hand against her most sensitive nub. Pumping fiercely, she found her release in seconds.

Her sigh as her orgasm claimed her thundered through him, making his skin crawl with pleasure. Reinier narrowed his eyes, not that she'd notice. Her grip loosened and he pulled his hand away as if she'd burned him.

Sitting up, he turned away from her, his elbows on his knees and his hands in his hair where hers had been just moments before. When he turned back, he saw his Lily lying, eyes closed, in a dreamy, satisfied sprawl, looking once again every bit of the triumphant Venus.

If it hadn't made him so mad, it would be highly amusing . . . or infinitely arousing . . . or both. Something had to be done about that.

Cheeky girl, she just wasn't getting it. Unfortunately, she was turning out to be a much more difficult student than he'd ever thought. Something definitely needed to be done about it.

"Lily." His tone was sharper than he'd intended, but he told himself he was only annoyed with her repeated failing to obey him, not bothered that he'd overly enjoyed seeing her climax.

"Hmm?"

"You are going to have to pay for that, my dear. What did I specifically tell you before we left?"

Eyes still closed, a wonderful shine on her content face, she rolled her head. "My mind happens to be in a slight fog at the moment. What on earth are you talking about?"

Surprise and anger both raged through him at the same time. How dare she? That was it. His playing nice and bringing her along slowly was at an end. "Lily, stand up. Now."

She opened her eyes but stayed in place, looking up at him obviously confused at the harsh tone in his voice.

Reinier stood and took her hands, dragging her to her feet. She looked so sweet in her total bewilderment that he calmed instantly. The sigh he let out then was that of someone trying to show great patience with a wayward child.

"My dear, have you not played enough games to know that there are always penalties when you break the rules? You failed to address me correctly earlier, and I specifically told you that you were not to climax without permission. You chose to disobey both, and there are always consequences to every choice." Reinier left her and turned, pointing at the saddle on its stand before him now. "Lift your dress and bend over the saddle to accept yours."

From out of the corner of his eye he saw her sputter, trying to form a protest, but she didn't move otherwise. She fell completely silent and only stared at him with a cautious look, trying to understand it all.

Once again, he turned to her, grasped her hands that hung limply to her sides, and brought them up to his lips. He began to pepper her knuckles with soft kisses.

"You made a promise," he reminded her, and saw the spark of wariness light up in her eyes. That look was promising. Hopefully she was battling her instinct to fight with the desire to give in that he knew was there. His fingers cupped her chin and lifted her face to make her look him in the eyes. "Do you trust me, Lily?"

Could she truly let herself admit that she wanted him, wanted this? That after all these years of control and sacrifice, of taking on all those responsibilities, was he right? Did she truly have a desire to see what it would be like to let go? Did she have enough courage to trust Reinier with her care?

Emiline couldn't understand all the things she'd felt since he'd returned and their bargain began. She had given her word. And it was such a short time. Truly, it would be a shame not to see what would happen. Knowledge was power and she needed to understand these new feelings.

But did she trust him to show her?

She thanked some old Norse god at that moment that he had seen fit to gift Reinier with those haunting, expressive, pale citrus-colored eyes of his. There was little they hid, and she saw sincerity in them now.

Did she trust him? Could she?

Did she want to?

She was no coward. She wouldn't back out now.

"Oui." The word was barely over a whisper, but to her it sounded like thunder. In response, he squeezed her hands once before giving them one last kiss and letting her go.

Turning without another word, Emiline walked to the warm leather saddle on its stand. She began to gather her skirts with slow deliberation and quiet grace until they bunched at her waist. Still not quite believing what she was about to do, she leaned delicately over the saddle, focusing on its soft warmth rather than the cool air on her backside.

She could hear his boots moving to the wall of tack, then heard the click of something being lifted from its hook. She waited. Her body tensed with each echo of his steps coming closer, but at the same time she noticed her desire was surprisingly ever present.

Instead of stopping behind her, he came around to squat in front of her. She shuddered at the sight of the crop he held. Then he lifted her chin with his other hand for her to meet his eyes. He kissed her once before he rose and moved behind her.

She jumped when she felt him pulling at the string as the jade spheres were removed from her core. She felt so empty all of a sudden. But she had no time to muse over that. She heard Reinier step back.

"You will try and remain as still and quiet as possible. If you cry out or move away, it will only add to your punishment. Is that clear?"

The tone he'd laid in his words made it crystal clear that he didn't welcome defiance at this point. Its superior callousness made her cringe, and she felt herself nod reluctantly.

Good Lord, what had she agreed to?

"A nod isn't good enough. Say you understand and accept, Lily. Say it and mean it."

Emiline sucked in a ragged breath of air and held it as blind obedience battled with irate reason. Biting her lower lip, she let the air out of her lungs in one long, slow breath. She had promised. A bargain was a bargain.

"*Oui,* monsieur. I understand."

"Now get a good grip on the edge of the saddle."

She felt the soft touch of the crop that stung just a little. "That stroke had a strength of three. Two is less, four is more. The spanks can go up to ten. I expect you to call out a number that will indicate the strength of the next stroke. So, what strength shall it be, Lily?"

She hesitated. A quiver ran through her. It was part dread, part curiosity, and part anticipation. Emiline plucked up her courage and uttered a palsied, "Five."

Holding her breath, she perceived the sibilant noise of the crop cutting through the air just before she felt the sting on her cheeks. It was much more prominent this time, but it tingled in its wake so it was still manageable. Maybe she should pick a higher number next?

"Seven." She again held her breath, but this time she had difficulties not to cry out. It stung too much, never mind that the tingle that followed was quite delicious.

"Six," she breathed, then jumped as the next stroke hit.

No. She shook her head, swallowing a low groan. "Five." That was definitely her favorite.

"Five, you say? Very well, then. Spread your legs a little wider and try to relax. I think twenty-five should do."

Was he joking? How could she relax? Widening her stance would only expose her more fully.

But something in his tone had changed and was now drenched with that ever-present deep, masculine purr that was infinitely arousing. Emiline felt herself comply. Her knuckles whitened on the leather and she waited. Her anticipation was unnerving.

Then it came. The crop sang in the air and landed on her soft skin with a cracking flick. That wasn't the strength of five, she thought, and jumped when the sharp pain made her skin ripple. She closed her lips tightly, but a small sound still escaped at the sting of the crop across one cheek. It hurt. She bit her lower lip hard not to let out a whimper. She felt her skin pucker where the crop had landed.

But then . . . before she could process the feeling completely, the next came and the next, each one in a slightly different location than the one before, each one stinging, then leaving in its wake a strange, pulsating warmth like after a bee's sting. Then the hurt mellowed even more and the resulting sensation . . . wasn't unwelcome.

The air around them seemed to still and all sounds stopped but for the snap of the leather crop as it connected with her soft flesh again and again. Her senses sharpened. She could hear his breathing come harder, could taste his desire in the very air licking at her skin. She could see lonely straws littering the floor and would have even been able to count them, but the crop sang its dreadfully amazing song again.

When the leather came down on her skin her surroundings blurred, yet became clearer, the colors more intense with the sting on her backside turning into the sweetest tingling. The vague notion that he was speaking finally filtered through and she realized he was counting.

"Seventeen . . . eighteen . . . nineteen . . ."

The strokes came closer and closer to her core. Her grip tightened. Her breathing became more labored. She continued to toil to not move or cry out at each new sharp pain that rocked her body.

Little by little, Emiline began to realize that it wasn't shock or discomfort, but it was her climbing desire that she struggled against. The pain had somehow become pleasurable, dissolving into smooth warmth that made her core weep with joy.

She couldn't stop herself from moving against the saddle,

anticipating each stroke now in desire, not dread—wanting it, afraid of it, and not understanding it all at the same time.

She tried to focus, to find her way out of the haze, but her head was light and her heartbeat was frantic as each new sting took her pleasure higher and higher. She could feel the wetness of her core bathing the leather of the saddle. Her head fell against the cantle and she could hear herself moan.

"Twenty-two . . . twenty-three . . ."

Suddenly, he paused. She couldn't move, was too boneless to do anything. Her whole body was tingling. She didn't know how much longer she could bear this. Nothing made sense, yet it all was so clear. She wanted him to stop. No, she wanted him to go on. What was happening to her?

His breath tickled the shell of her ear. "Come for me, Lily." His low whisper wrested a groan from deep in her chest. "Come for me. Now."

The crop sang through the air. Its melody was higher now, the slap on her skin earsplitting, but there was no pain. A tremor ran through her body; her secret muscles clenched. He'd given her an order.

Again, the crop whistled. She felt the air move against her skin under the swing. Emiline threw her head back. Leather touched her.

Slap.

She was lost, bucking against the saddle and crying out from deep in her throat, unable to stop herself. Her mind slipped free as she lost her grip. Her body convulsed; savage contractions rocked her pelvis and singed her secret muscles. She exploded into nothingness, floating in the sensations clouding her mind.

As if from far away, she heard herself sob in bliss as wave after blinding wave of her climax washed over and through her. The contractions turned erratic and her senses dulled.

She felt overwhelmed. How could she . . . ? Why did she . . . ?

It didn't make sense. She was weeping, both confused and desperate now that her body was coming down from its divine flight.

The next thing she was aware of was her dress back in place and she was cradled on her side on Reinier's lap on the settee. She blinked to stop the tears that continued to well in her eyes. She gripped his neck and buried her face in his chest. His heart was racing under the soft fabric of his shirt. It beat against her cheek. She noticed he was fighting to calm his breathing.

"Don't you see now, my beautiful Lily?" His words were a throaty, hoarse croak. "Relinquishing control doesn't mean you've failed. Letting go at the right time is an act of true grace. It's beautiful and powerful." His arm, wrapped around her, tightened its grip and he was raining soft kisses on the top of her head.

Gradually his words sank in. Was it truly? Could she ever think that way? In that moment she didn't know what to think, but she was honestly starting to believe it.

As Reinier held her, all he could think of was how she was perfect for this, made for this. It had never been this way before. He'd never felt quite so awed, powerful, mad with desire, touched, and he wasn't sure what else. For just a moment, he let himself believe this was heaven, this was perfection—this was home. If she continued to open up to the possibilities, continued to take his instruction with such elegance and passion, then she'd see how wonderfully mated they were.

But then cold reality made sure he remembered where that kind of thinking could take him. He'd witnessed it firsthand. He knew it only led to weakness or madness or both, and he wouldn't let her take him there. He was stronger than that.

Besides, the point was moot given the fact that she didn't really want him. This was only a means to an end for her.

No, his first thoughts had been rash and unrealistic. This

117

wasn't anything special, just an amusing interlude. Just like the others, like so many others.

So, given that and the fact that his time was sadly limited, he resolved he'd best make the most of it, all of it. Now.

"I want you, Lily."

She only mumbled something against his chest and held him tighter. His heart constricted for a second until his determination overshadowed it. "I have been waiting since the moment you stepped into the parlor yesterday to take what is mine and plunge myself into your sweetness. That wait is over. When I lift you up, I want you to stand on your knees on the cushion, facing the wall and gripping the back of the couch."

She lifted her head and looked at him then. The wonder still held in the depths of her blue-green eyes made it obvious she was still too caught up in what had just happened to deny him.

If only . . . yes, if only she would look at him like that always.

But she wouldn't.

No, he mustn't do that to himself. He wouldn't allow her to draw him in. She was nothing special. Not anymore. He knew her tricks and he wouldn't fall for her.

That singular light in her eyes died when he lifted her, but she complied. Just as well. It helped him to find his focus; it helped him remember what this was all about. Indeed, he could have easily remedied that expression of hers by explaining the prudence of it. After all, the position he'd placed her in was for her benefit, because her admittedly very lovely backside would still be a little too sore to lay or sit on it at the moment. But he wouldn't tell her.

He lifted her dress, resting the folds in the elegant dip at the small of her back. Besides, he thought while holding back a moan of pure adulation as he gently smoothed his hands over the marks he'd given her, there was nothing like admiring one's own handiwork while one took their pleasure.

At his touch, goose bumps rose all over her creamed coffee skin. He continued to caress each and every fading line with one hand, trying to remember if he'd thought to bring some of that ointment he'd also purchased from the Chinese man who'd sold him the jade balls. He could look in his trunks later; he impatiently brushed the thought off and let his other hand work the buttons of his trousers. A low moan of relief escaped him when his cock sprang free from the confines of his clothing.

Reinier eased her legs farther apart and settled himself between them. One hand was braced against the wall trapping her while he positioned himself. Just gazing at her entrance for now, he saw and felt her whole body shudder when he barely touched her.

A wave of her liquid heat trickled over the head of his erection. He had done that to her. What a gorgeous sight this was.

It had all led to this. This was his alone and she wanted him to take it. He'd make sure she'd never ever think of wanting another man between those delicious legs again. Leaning forward, he kissed her temple. "Do try to remember this time, Lily, pleasure is not yours to take, but mine to give."

Her quiet, lilting "yes" was lost in a loud moan that seemed to come from deep in her throat when he drove home in one quick motion.

The feel of her throbbing so tightly around his aching shaft took his breath away. It was everything he'd remembered and more. Placing his other hand on the wall as well, Reinier held still for the next moment, struggling to find his composure. This was his game to play.

He took a deep, fortifying breath and slid halfway out. Rolling his hips, he began moving slowly, easing in and out of her slick depths with controlled deliberation to draw out both their pleasure. He felt her heat, as it fluttered around him to adjust to his thickness stretching her. Stroking her to sensuous delight while the friction had burning, prickling waves of pleasure spread through his body and mind made him arch his hips a little faster, not much, just enough so that he slid into her even deeper than before.

Lily began to move then, too, thrusting against his withdrawal. She wanted more, was silently demanding her needs be met. How he loved that part. His mastery. His control. It was all in his hands alone. Reinier stopped, moving one hand to her soft, flat belly to hold her still against him.

Careful not to touch her heated backside too much when he leaned forward once again, he dragged the flat of his tongue across the shell of her ear. His breath teased the wet trail on her sensitive skin.

"Be a good girl, Lily, and don't move." Reinier put special emphasis on each word now. "I will give you what I think you need, as much as I think you need, at the pace I choose to give it." Reinier simultaneously rolled his hips forward once, driving his shaft hard into her moist warmth to emphasize his point. "Is that clear?"

Stifling a moan, she froze in place and nodded quickly with a pleading whimper. This was true ecstasy, he thought, the purest and untainted of all power, where he would give and get everything in return.

His hand on her midriff moved to her smooth hip. Reinier rocked gently against her, heightening her enjoyment while each relentless thrust sent sparkly ripples of desire through him. His head spun. She felt so good, so hot and tight, and she was so wet, so wet for him. He became boneless, weightless; all that mattered was riding her, more, longer, harder.

Pleasure prickled through all of him and he began to move

in earnest now. His thrusts roughened and deepened. Firm, long strokes went deep inside of her and sent friction battering through both of them.

She caught her breath and let her head fall forward, arching her body to his, thrusting her backside with its pink marks up to him. Reinier hummed male satisfaction in her ear when she moaned her own pleasure.

His hands clamped around her waist, holding her captive. He fought hard against his rising need for completion now, wanting what he had waited so long to have to never end. Whether having stayed away so long made him the wisest or most foolish of men he had no idea. The erotic surge of desire rushed through him, pooling, then building to become fiercer than anything he'd ever experienced before, a riptide of ecstasy coursing through him and numbing his mind.

Reinier's thrusts intensified, got wild and abandoned, until he was pumping savagely, undulating his hips against her backside as they both cried out with each stroke.

Through the thick haze of lust covering his mind, he heard her pleading, "Please . . . please . . . I must . . . I can't . . ."

"Oh, but you will," he ground out, his voice thick with pleasure. "Not yet, Lily. Not yet."

"Monsieur, monsieur, monsieur," she repeated, breathless. Her litany sounded like a prayer, like a promise of surrender, and he couldn't stop the wave from cresting. His consciousness began to fall apart under the fire they both nourished. "Yes, Lily, come for me now."

Her scalding core spasmed around him and his own intense excitement grew like a torrent. He pumped inside her, pushing away sanity, pushing aside his control. Quickly, he pulled away to spray his seed against her perfectly rounded globes. He exploded, violent and intense, with a hoarse cry.

When he found his way out of the haze of his climax, he realized he'd leaned forward and wrapped his arms around her, kissing the back of her neck. Her breathing was little more than shallow, rapid gasps; his was no more than hard and heavy gulps of air.

Their union had been perfect. She was perfect, so much so that he felt his eyes flood with tears he quickly blinked away.

God help him.

How arrogant he'd been to believe himself immune.

She was a siren and he was a complete fool. Still.

9

Just after sunset Emiline sat on the rose silk-padded stool by her dressing table. Her fingers played with the edge of her silk robe that matched the stool's color while she watched her mother's hammered brass and claw-footed tub being filled. Absently, she replayed their day in her head again and again.

When she and Reinier had returned to the house, he was as distant as ever. But before she could say anything, he suggested she take dinner up in her rooms and rest. At least he'd made it a suggestion and not an order.

At first she'd been relieved. Now she wasn't so sure anymore.

All she'd been able to do ever since entering her rooms was think. Emiline was slowly coming to the realization that they would have ended up exactly where they had, no matter what either of them might have tried to do differently.

Well, maybe not in the tack room of the stables but together in some passionate way nonetheless.

There was something that seemed beyond their control;

something that, for Emiline at least, drew her to him despite herself.

It had always been like that with the two of them, though. There had always been this fascination, this allure between them. At least she had always felt that way. Reinier had shown her a side of passion she'd have never believed existed outside her deepest, darkest dreams.

He had bewitched her once again, but this time it was only her body, not her mind. It was only a bargain and one she fully intended to go through with. If Reinier Barhydt had shown her anything by his example in the past four years, it was that one's body and heart could operate completely independently.

"Almost ready, miss." Justine's familiar voice sent her thoughts fleeing like the chambermaids now scurrying to leave the room.

Emiline stood automatically so Justine could help her remove her robe.

"Lord!"

At Justine's sharp gasp, Emiline turned to look over her shoulder, catching her own reflection in the full-length, filigreed dressing mirror. She was transfixed by the sight. Her skin seemed to glow, especially where faint and fading pink marks still decorated her skin from the backs of the thighs up to the small of her back. When her gaze travelled up even farther, she caught a look in her own eyes she couldn't quite recognize. Her reflected expression seemed . . . proud.

Emiline was horrified by her own reaction. What had she become to feel proud of something that should be shameful?

"What has he done! Child, how could you!"

Justine's words broke the mirror's spell, and Emiline rushed to hide the marks by lowering herself into the steaming, welcoming water.

Averting her eyes, Emiline felt very much like a little girl

124

again. Even a slight blush of shame crept up her neck. "Please don't scold. I've chided myself quite enough already."

A sad, almost weary sigh came from Justine. "I'll go and get some aloe and marigold for your bath. I had heard rumors about him, but I never thought . . ."

"Heard? Heard what, Justine?"

She rushed out before Emiline could say anything else, but as soon as she returned, Emiline coaxed, "Justine, you must tell me."

The maid kept silent, adding herbs and oils to the bath. Shaking her head while biting her wrinkled lower lip, she turned and busied herself, and by the clatter of the china soap dish, Emiline knew she still wasn't happy with her.

Emiline gripped the maid's hand. "Justine?"

The lady's maid pulled her hand away and stepped back, folding her arms over her ample chest. "And why should I? Not that it will matter. It's too late now that you've let that man back in this house and let him do God knows what to you."

Pressing her lips together, Emiline looked down. Of course, Justine wouldn't know about the bargain, nor did she need to, and she didn't need to know about the details. The outcome was the only thing that counted.

With a determined upward glance, Emiline spoke low, her voice insistent and unwavering, "Justine, you have known me all my life. Long enough to know I am not a green, gullible girl any longer. I have my reasons. If there is anything you know and think I need to know, tell me now." Just in time, she added another, relatively unnecessary but nevertheless polite, "Please."

Justine's expression softened and, unfolding her arms, she reached for a bucket of warm water to dampen Emiline's hair. "It's just that I have this cousin," she began quietly while kneeling down by the bathtub. "She lives quite scandalously. She has a fancy house in St. George's, paid for by a 'benefactor,' you see."

Emiline could see her roll her eyes and in response snorted dutifully, but secretly; the thought that Reinier might be that benefactor—or anyone else's benefactor—made her stomach roll to her throat. Swallowing hard, she remained silent and only leaned her head back, waiting for Justine to continue. Emiline knew if she interrupted her now, it would be even harder to get every bit of information out of the maid.

"And . . . well, she writes to me about the most outrageous things. They make me blush something horrible. Oh, the kinds of things she writes!"

Justine giggled and Emiline tried to show patience, but it was difficult. If she would kindly tell her all that might have to do with something she'd heard about Reinier now, Emiline would be grateful, indeed.

"Oh, where was I?" Justine gasped for air and got up to get some more warm water, all the while fanning her glowing cheeks with one hand.

"You were about to tell me what all this has to do with Reinier, I believe."

Justine gave her a mocking curtsy as an apology and began to wash Emiline's hair. "I had thought they were only rumors, and you know with rumors you never know . . ."

Emiline loved Justine, but she was always prone to digressing and losing the thread of what she'd meant to say in the first place. That trait of hers could be a bit tiresome.

Justine's hands stopped unexpectedly in midmotion and after having taken another deep breath, she blurted out, "Did— did he hurt you?"

"No!" Emiline burst out, but instantly regretted her initial reaction. "I don't know," she sighed, crossing her arms over her chest. "Don't ask me about it again. Just tell me what you know."

Justine clucked at that; the noise coming from her mouth had a peculiar, pitying ring to it. Or maybe Emiline had just imagined it. Sometimes Justine's impertinence and the fact that she continued to try and mother Emiline now that she was fully grown—and in charge even—could be rather trying at times.

"Well," the maid continued and leaned closer so that she could impart with what she knew by only whispering in Emiline's ear. "Once she wrote of how . . . of how . . . well, the captains of the Barhydt-O'Driscoll Shipping Company were known for liking to entertain ladies . . . together . . . in certain . . . particular . . . well, disciplined sorta ways, so the girls say." She tugged at Emiline's hair a bit too roughly and Emiline winced a little.

"Oh, but not that they minded," Justine added with an indignant snort, making quick work of rinsing the soap from Emiline's hair. "In fact, this friend of my cousin's, the one who had confided in her, was lamenting greatly that neither one ever seemed to entertain anyone more than once, even though everyone always wanted them to." Pausing there, she leaned forward and her head came into Emiline's view again. Justine pinned her down with her glare and repeated with meaningful emphasis, "Always."

Emiline grimaced. Now that the secret was out, the maid sighed with relief. Obviously, a burden had been lifted off her shoulders. Emiline, on the other hand, wasn't sure at all what in the world she was supposed to make of it.

Had Justine meant to imply that Emiline was like all the others for Reinier? Had she just hinted at the possibility that after Reinier used her he'd leave and wouldn't be back again?

That was the sole purpose of the whole bargain, wasn't it? Three days of dancing to his tune for the rest of her life in independence. Knowing what she did now, that was wonderful news, wasn't it?

"Thank you for telling me, Justine. Go on and get your rest for the night." Her maid gave her a hesitant look but with a quick nod left the room.

After the door closed and Emiline was alone, she sank deeper into the water, trying to concentrate on how relaxing and soothing to her body it was. But the turmoil in her mind kept intruding.

So there were others. Many others from what Justine had said. Of course, Emiline had known that. She'd heard enough bits and pieces of rumors over the years to know that. She was sort of cut off from the world here on her island, but surely not deaf, dumb, and blind to what was going on around her.

Something scorched her chest from the inside out, something slightly bitter that also dulled her at the same time. Emiline decided what she felt burning through her wasn't jealousy. She was sure that it couldn't be.

She didn't care that their bargain was similar to what he'd done with others. Of course not. On the contrary, the fact that this was similar, and as Justine had said, it was never the same woman twice gave her confidence that in a relatively short amount of time she'd have what she wanted to begin with.

Yet . . . something inside her couldn't help wanting it to be different.

But it was. This was different. She was sure of it. She wasn't meekly letting him do as he wished with her like, she assumed, the others had. She was a much worthier opponent. She was holding up her end of the bargain, and truth be told, despite Justine's disapproval, she was beginning to enjoy her part.

Emiline sank all the way in, up to her chin, watching the ripples her breath made on the surface of the water.

The captains of the Barhydt-O'Driscoll Shipping Company, Justine had said. Together they had a certain way, and neither one saw the same lady again. Emiline guessed not much had changed in that regard then.

But that meant she was right and this was different than with the others. Reinier had come alone.

Connor O'Driscoll. A good deal of her initial pain and anger after Reinier had left went toward the Irishman. She had been jealous then. Not of other women, but of Connor. She'd always wondered about them. Wondered in those lonely nights when she still let herself cry what Connor had that she didn't. While her husband increasingly pulled away from her influence, Connor still held his ear. At the same time he refused to come home, he still met the Irishman in port whenever he got a chance. At first she'd been sure if not for Connor, Reinier would have stayed. She'd been confident that it had been all the Irishman's fault.

But now she understood that Reinier was very much his own man. If there were other women, if he spent his free time with Connor, it was his own doing.

Still, Emiline couldn't help the spare traces of resentment that lingered.

Taking a deep breath, she plunged under the now cooling water, then quickly emerged until she was sitting high enough in the tub to rest her arms along the edge.

So what was she to do about all of it? If she was perfectly honest with herself, she'd say she wanted to continue what they'd started regardless of Justine's revelations and everything else.

Emiline shook her head at herself while picking up the sea sponge and French-milled soap from the stool beside the tub.

How good she'd become at rationalizing almost anything. The real truth was she'd enjoyed it. She wanted to continue simply because she wanted it—wanted Reinier.

She just couldn't let that interfere with the fact that she still wanted to divorce him.

* * *

He was a blithering idiot. For the second night in a row Reinier found himself pacing the study—her study—with restless energy.

Or rather almost like a lunatic. He surely felt that way.

Oh, he was angry. He was so angry with her for . . . well, for being her. Beautiful, strong, alluring, addictive, and someone who did what she did not because she loved him but because she didn't want him.

She was nothing but a contradiction. Everything here was nothing but a contradiction. It all seemed nice and easy, gentle and sweet, when, in fact, nothing was.

More pacing brought him close to the secretary. That blasted secretary that seemed so unobtrusive, but on looking closer, one would find those damned papers.

Reiner resumed his pacing. Ruddy hell, even the night was a contradiction. Outside the window the crickets sang soft songs that floated on the gentle breeze coming in from the sea while inside the house the mantel clock in the dining room ticked away its mocking countdown of his time here. The pitiless flying by of the moments he was still supposed to stay here.

What in God's name had made him come here?

Reinier was angry. He was angry at her, true, but he was even angrier at himself. He was weak. A pitiful weakling to having reacted as he had, so emotional like that—like Emiline was something so new and so sweet and . . .

He should leave. Now.

Why didn't he leave? What was making him stay?

It couldn't be pride; with his barely suppressed tears in the tack room, he had none. Or almost none.

He knew he should have talked with her about what had happened. Not what had happened at the end, but before that.

He shouldn't have left her to struggle through it alone. In fact, he'd planned to talk to her, but he'd only had a tiny shred of pride left and he hadn't wanted to lose it completely, especially not in front of her.

Capital! He was trapped. Again.

As noble, or rather questionable, as his motives had been in the beginning, the reasons for any of this had evaporated into thin air. He couldn't go through with it. He couldn't hold up his end of the bargain. Not if it . . . well, the price was too high.

He wasn't like her. She was ruthless and unfeeling. He'd known that, and yet he'd come back.

Frustrated with pacing, Reinier sat down behind the secretary, deftly picked the lock, and pulled out the divorce papers again. He stared at them for a long time, hardly seeing them. He didn't blink. It was only when his eyes started to burn that he came out of his gloomy thoughts.

Yes, he'd sign them now. Sign them and get it over with.

Fumbling in the low light of one taper, he looked for an inkwell. When he found it, his resolve had strengthened. Now all he needed was a quill. Where had she hidden those bloody quills?

Yes, yes, he'd sign the papers and be gone before she even woke up. He didn't need her.

He shouldn't have come back.

Reinier opened another drawer only to find it, too, contained no quill, so he shoved it closed with a little more force than was necessary.

A frustrated sigh wrenched itself from deep in his chest. He gave up searching and set his elbows on the desk, running his hands through his hair. The secretary shook and groaned with the force of his frustrated gesture.

A small casket slid from somewhere in front of him, shattered on the surface of the desk, and opened. Its contents spilled.

There was the quill he'd been searching for all along.

He could sign the papers now.

Although . . . that would be just what she wanted, wouldn't it?

Well, it was more than he could say of himself. At least she knew what she wanted; at this point, he honestly didn't have a clue what he wanted.

No, that wasn't quite true. He knew what he wanted. He wanted her.

Now, didn't that sound familiar?

How much did he want her and at what price? Was her body worth his soul? Would it come to that—again?

He wouldn't let it happen. He'd just have to try harder. He'd have to try harder to be more like her. He'd have to follow her example and be the epitome of perfection for perfection's sake alone.

But that was easier said than done. Maybe he just needed a small break to figure it all out. He should take some time and work off his confusion and anger with something to tax his body and that would eventually clear his head.

If that was the case, he thought as he folded the divorce papers again and put them back in their place, he'd better try and get some sleep.

Who was he trying to fool? He knew he'd never get any sleep.

Maybe he could seduce one of the pretty little maids or one of the villagers.

Wonderful. They were basically at his mercy. Since when had he sunk that low to even think about something as repugnant and damnable?

Or he could get raving drunk—he'd surely find sleep after that. Only then trying to clear his mind with work in the morning was out of the question. What kind of impression would it make on the workers if the master vomited from a little exertion?

He was a blithering lunatic. Oh, he was angry with them both. At her . . . at himself . . .

Good Lord, this bloody island was driving him insane!

10

"That's how I used to ride the chestnut filly," Jaidyn whispered, licking Connor's ear with a teasing tongue. His hands clamped down on her lean thighs and he could feel the muscles bunch under his fingers when she circled her hips, rose off him, and sat down again, circle, up, and down again, and again . . .

Finally, she'd revealed her name. A good, solid Irish name. She was his green-eyed, Irish goddess. Her red gold hair was tickling his face, his shoulders, and his sides. Connor pressed his head into the pillow, his eyes rolling up under his closed lids.

He shouldn't have said what he had; he shouldn't have asked her to once more show him how she used to ride her horse. He almost felt sorry for himself. Almost, because her strength and stamina were killing him. God, she was good at that. Untamed and enthusiastic, and Connor wanted it to never stop.

She was riding him hard, so hard he thought he was going to burst any moment now, and she didn't seem to tire one bit. She was wonderful, absolutely lovely. At least that's what he remembered from right before her rolling and grinding her hips against his cock made him close his eyes. She was perfect, riding him just the way he liked it. No, the way he loved it; the way he'd never been ridden before.

His hands wandered up her thighs and captured her waist that was so small the tips of his fingers touched at the small of her back. Her skin was sticky, deliciously moist from the exercise.

The palms of his hands then cupped her buttocks—firm, nice cheeks. His fingers wandered along the cleft; she was even wetter there. Lower down, where she ground against him, where her slick softness met his hardness . . . He let his fingers stay there to feel her bouncing up and down on him, taking him in, then releasing his rod only to capture him again completely.

Her breaths were coming hard, and each time he met her thrusts, she'd moan, a soft, high sound, so completely different from when he rode her. Then her moans were low and rough. But whatever position they were in, however he took her, the sounds she made came from deep in her throat and washed over him, inciting him, exciting him even more.

Jaidyn paused. She sat up completely, and her long hair tickled his hands and the inside of his thighs. Connor was grateful for the chance to take one last breath, because he was certain he was going to perish.

He'd have never thought he'd meet a woman who'd respond to him so completely, who matched his need as perfectly as Jaidyn did. One touch from her and he was up and ready in no time. One touch from him and she was hot, willing, and eager at once.

They'd taken a lazy bath, fed each other grapes and oranges and cheese and bread and roast beef from a silver tray. They'd also slept just a little in between, arms around each other. That was new too. He'd never enjoyed a woman beside him for longer than it took to make her crest enough times that he was satisfied. With Jaidyn it was different. He couldn't get enough of her. They fit perfectly.

Wasn't there something he needed to do? He couldn't really remember now. There was no yesterday for him, no tomorrow. Only the present, this moment, and each moment that he was with Jaidyn. It was the only thing that counted, the only thing that was important. The only thing that was . . .

He opened his eyes to see her. He'd never forget how she looked, because saying she looked . . . beautiful didn't quite fit. She wasn't just beautiful, she was stunning. More than that. There was no word for it—at least Connor didn't know one. Certainly not at that moment.

Her skin, her perfect, smooth skin, as white as porcelain, as soft as silk and dotted with all the places he'd kissed and had yet to kiss, glistened with transpiration, shone as the pale light of the early dawn illuminated her. It made her look ethereal. Like a fairy.

Catching her hips in his hands, he helped her with her sumptuous ride, bucking his hips up against her, and she let out those incredibly arousing, soft and high moans again. She was circling her hips against him, grinding her core on him, and he watched himself slide in and out of her, glistening with her juices. Gooseflesh rippled her skin and his as well.

Connor sat up, wrapping his arms all the way around her at the same time. This was where he wanted to be. His mouth found the puckered, delicious pebble of one breast and engulfed it, eagerly sucking it until he felt her arms around his head, pressing him closer to her. He left his teeth open a little so that her nipple rubbed against them but was then caressed by his lips. She must love the gentle abrasion. Her breathy moans were lower, coming faster as her ride became harder.

Quickly, he flipped them around, never leaving her warm embrace. When she landed on her back sprawled under him, he braced himself against the mattress and pumped into her hard, rolling his hips with long strokes that sent fire pulsing through his veins. He was going to burn alive, but it didn't matter. It was all right; he'd die a happy man in her arms.

He was close and her sheath was fluttering around him. They'd come together. No, he had to hold back, he wanted to see her sigh and moan and whimper, her body rocking with another climax beneath him while he plunged into her tender flesh.

Closing her eyes, she bit her lower lip and froze, her whole body stiff with the calm before the storm. The blink of an eye later, she gasped and exploded, her nails raking his shoulders, eyes wide, body heaving off the bed in waves. Connor slowed, heightening her enjoyment, drawing it out not just for her sake but for his own. He'd never seen a more striking or mesmerizing sight than Jaidyn peaking so completely. The intensity of her orgasm shook him, raged through his body. He couldn't hold back much longer, but he had to. He wanted to.

The waves of her orgasm ebbed by degrees and her body became softer, pliant under his. She swallowed hard; then he saw the haze crawl away, and when her emerald gaze focused on him, the contented smile on her lips sent a sizzling bolt through his body. He was lost. The last conscious thought he had was that he needed to pull out before it was too late.

His climax exploded through his body and burst from his mouth in a hoarse bellow.

He pumped into the hot tunnel he suddenly found himself in, not knowing how he'd gotten there. He thought he'd pulled out. Bending his head, Connor saw that it was Jaidyn's hand that milked every last drop out of him, his semen dripping over her fingers and onto her lower belly. When he was completely spent, her hand retreated and she met his stare in which his utter amazement must have shown.

She smiled. And Connor didn't just feel satisfied. He felt

without question completely and truly happy. He wanted her to look at him that way always. He wanted her to . . .

Having wiped her hand on the bedsheet, her arms snaked up around his back and he let himself fall into her embrace. His heart was pumping in an erratic rhythm, his breaths coming hard. Bringing his hands up, he brushed a few wayward strands of her strawberry blond hair from her face.

Her body fit his like it was made for it. It was the perfect port, the only port that he'd ever want or need.

Connor mirrored her smile and brought his lips closer to hers, just an inch away. He could taste her breath on his lips, her warm, soft, luscious lips that quivered right now before he . . .

Sudden shock at what he was about to do surged through him. An ice-cold iron bar had replaced his spine and his eyes widened as realization hit him with the force of a cannonball.

What on earth was he doing? What in bloody hell had happened to him?

Cursing under his breath, Connor immediately left her arms, rolled off the bed, and stalked to the washstand. He filled the china bowl with cool water and splashed his face a few times, dragging his wet fingers through his hair. Bracing his arms against the stand, he watched, head bent, the bead that formed on the tip of his nose drop back into the bowl, rippling the surface with flawless circles. The water barely helped to cool his mind.

The sleepy early morning sun glimpsed at him through the open window. He gripped the rim of the washstand so hard that his knuckles turned white.

What had he been thinking?

He'd wanted to kiss her? A whore? Kissing didn't work without feelings. He certainly didn't have tender feelings for her, and surely she didn't have any romantic feelings about him. What devil had possessed him?

"Connor?"

He could hear her move on the bed behind him, but he wouldn't look at her and didn't answer her. He was too embarrassed. No, he was too angry.

What had she done to him?

Whatever spell he was under, he had to get away from her. Lips grim, he grabbed one small washcloth on the stand beside the bowl, immersed it, then wrung it out. He didn't even look back when he tossed the wet cloth in her direction, growling a distant "Clean up," while he did the same.

"Connor, what's wrong?"

He still didn't talk to her. Instead, he went to the chair where his clothes were and donned them hastily. He didn't even bother tying his hair back. Just before he reached the door, he looked back at her. He had to; he didn't know why.

His grandmother always used to call freckles like hers "fairy kisses."

Clearly he was under some kind of spell.

They were staring at each other. Her eyes were wide. She bit her lower lip, averted her eyes, and reached blindly for the blanket. Lips quivering, she covered herself but didn't look at him again. She turned her back, away from the door, away from him.

Connor felt the muscles in his cheeks jump. He turned and ground his molars so hard he could hear them make tiny little noises in his head, creaking and crunching like the planks of a ship at sea in the middle of a calm night.

Hand wrapped around the doorknob, he narrowed his eyes at the door's panel in front of him. His heart was beating heavily up to his throat. Something akin to dread was squeezing his neck with cold talons.

Whatever she'd done to him and that had him so . . . confused . . . it didn't agree with him. Not at all.

He turned the knob and left the room without another backward glance.

The door fell shut behind him when he was almost down the stairs. With each step he took, something in his chest constricted, more and more, until Connor had to pause to catch his breath.

He was cursed; that must be it. There was no other logical explanation for it.

"Monsieur O'Driscole!" Madame Poivre's lilt tore him out of his dark thoughts and his head snapped up to see her standing right in front of him at the foot of the stairs, barring his hasty retreat from her establishment.

"Why, you're a little pale. What 'as 'appened?"

For the first time since he'd known her, he couldn't manage his typical smirk. His eyes were glued to her and instantly he avoided her searching gaze, looking to the side, then down.

"I think you need a glass of something stronger than port right now. Come with me." She slung her arm around his, hooking in his elbow, and much to his chagrin guided him to another room at the back, even farther away from the exit. But Connor complied. The house was asleep; besides, he had too much respect for the madam to just brush her off.

Next thing he knew, instead of halfway to the harbor, he was seated in a comfy armchair in a room he'd never been in before. Madame Poivre thrust a slightly chipped lead crystal glass in his hand that was filled with golden-brown liquid. Its fragrance was familiar and it soothed his agitated mind right away. Irish whiskey. Single malt. He guided the glass to his lips in a slow and deliberate way, savoring it like it was ambrosia. Indeed, to him it was. Taking a sip, he let the liquid splash against the roof of his mouth, then linger on his tongue. Swallowing it, he felt its almost nonexistent burn down his throat, tasted the gentle, tickling whisper of its unique flavor on his palate. Connor closed his eyes as the liquid brought balmy calmness and tingling strength back to his body at once.

"You're leaving us already, O'Driscoll?"

Connor's head snapped up at her having said his name without the usual disfigurement of a fake French accent, and he realized her small, shrewd eyes were taking in his every reaction.

As much as he wanted to reply something, nothing came to his mind. "Yes" was not quite the truth, because he was sitting here now and not on his way like he wished to be, "no" would be a lie; "as soon as you let me" was stating the obvious but rather impolite. So what could he say?

"You're not displeased with her, are you?" She focused all her attention on him.

Connor averted her searching gaze yet again, looking instead into the lead crystal glass in his hand. "No."

Madame Poivre sighed with relief. "Good. After two days that would have sounded rather unbelievable, anyway. You're probably asking yourself how she came to be here in my house?"

When she said it, Connor knew that that was part of what had been bothering him all along. But before he could react in any way, she snorted and went on, "I have this acquaintance. He is a young sailor who has chosen, might I call it a less than perfectly respectable profession? The poor boy never had anybody else to look after him but his Auntie Polly, who herself grew up in the worst part of London. But she made something of herself. She even learned a bit of French in her time, and she taught him some virtues that are so easily forgotten these days."

Connor looked up at her and she winked at him. Was she talking about herself?

"Oh, listen to me, digressing again and chattering about something that is totally beside the point. This acquaintance of mine is probably the last honorable buccaneer there is, and I have seen one or two in my time. He brought her to my doorstep." Pausing, she let out another dramatic sigh.

Connor finished the whiskey and set the empty glass on the small table next to him. He'd rather she stopped talking about Jaidyn. And he'd rather be on his way. Standing, Connor bowed to her and excused himself. "I thank you, Madame Poivre, but I'm afraid I need to leave now. I—"

"She is a rare beauty, is she not?" Speaking quickly, her eyes narrowed at him once more with a peculiar glitter.

Connor paid her no mind, though. He turned to leave the room. He'd show himself out; after years of coming here, he knew the way only too well.

"I will make a fortune with her now that she's trained, you know."

That stopped him. Slowly, he turned around and met her stare. Her lips twitched into a grin as she leaned back in the chair, obviously pleased with herself.

"I beg your pardon?" Connor didn't know why he reacted the way he had. He'd heard her perfectly well; his ears were in faultless condition. He didn't know why he cared. That was the way with whores. They sold their favors to the highest bidder. He knew that, after all. Why was it bothering him, then?

Counting off on her fingers, she began to enumerate the "benefactors" who were on the list, falling back into her fake French accent. "There is Monsieur Abeiros 'oo expressed interest in 'er. Also, Monsieur Cameron wishes to get an appointment with 'er. Viconte Maleroy 'as written 'ee would visit us in a few days—"

"Maleroy?" Connor felt his eyes bulge. "You can't be serious, madame. We both know his preferences."

Rolling her eyes, she laughed. "*Oui.* They do not exactly include women nor 'armless entertainment. But 'ee pays so well, Monsieur O'Driscole. Besides, she is very thin. She might look like a boy from be'ind if you get my meaning."

Madame Poivre was thinking about introducing Jaidyn to Maleroy? If so, she must have lost her mind. That sadistic bastard? Connor had once seen what that fat, ugly beast did to women. How could she have told him about Jaidyn?

"Then there's of course the usual clientele that 'ungers for a beauty such as 'er from the old world. And . . ."

Connor wasn't paying attention to her rambling on about who'd be next anymore. All of a sudden he was too focused on sorting through his own strange feelings. He desperately needed to leave, to find some time to sort through everything. But one thing was for sure. He didn't care at all for the idea that there'd be anybody but him next, even though right that moment he wasn't sure he ever wanted to see Jaidyn again. Not that he hadn't enjoyed himself.

Yes, he was still himself. The old Connor. Nothing had changed. He'd used her well. Jaidyn might be sore a day or two, actually. She'd been sore the last few times already, but he hadn't been able to stop himself even if she'd wanted him to—and she certainly hadn't wanted him to. No doubt about that.

"Enough!" His bellow had been sterner than he had at first intended.

Madame Poivre blinked with her mouth still open. "Monsieur?"

Connor brought his left arm up and leaned his forehead into his hand, letting his fingers massage his temples. He figured if worse came to worse, he'd be gone a week at the most. He'd think of something meanwhile. Anything was better than her meeting Maleroy. Or any of the others. Jaidyn would need time to rest. Yes, he could afford that. Much more if it came to that.

Connor owed Jaidyn that much at least. "How much for the whole week?"

Crossing her pudgy fingers and leaning them against her chin, Madame Poivre studied him a long time, her right eye a little narrower than her left. Clearly, she was adding figures in her head. With interest.

Connor sighed. With one step toward her, he fumbled for the purse in his waistcoat. Taking it out, he tossed it on the small table next to where his empty glass stood. Madame Poivre's eyes lit up with glee at the distinctive clatter of gold coins muffled by the leather of the pouch.

"Here. That should compensate you." Connor had difficulty not hissing through his clenched jaws.

She uncrossed her fingers to grab the heavy purse. Opening it to peek at its contents, she hummed her approval.

"Just make sure nobody touches her until I return."

She bowed her head and that asinine turban bobbed once. "Very well, Monsieur O'Driscole. That should suffice for . . . ten days?"

Nodding to show he'd understood, Connor left. One problem at a time. He had a prior appointment. Right now he'd focus on his friend and see whether Reinier needed his help. And then he'd think about . . . the other matter.

11

After spending the morning losing herself in her work again, inspecting the planting back in the fields, then overseeing the boiling and the rum production as well, Emiline now found herself famished having skipped breakfast. So she started toward the mansion taking the route past the harbor.

This morning she had promptly lost her appetite. There had been a note on her breakfast tray that explained why there was a breakfast tray in the first place since she usually broke her fast in the sunroom. Having read the note, she'd been nettled. Well, if one could call her unladylike growl and the emotional outburst that followed just a little piqued. She'd furiously shredded the condescending, incredibly high-handed dismissal into tiny pieces.

Merely thinking about it had her temper flare yet again. Any positive thoughts she'd had about that *man* the day before had been shredded to bits like the vile note. What had that note said? If only it were as easy to wipe the words from her memory as it had been to tear up the slip of paper and watch the confetti rain on her while she wished those specks would miraculously vanish like soap bubbles.

Dearest Lily, it had read. *Go about your day as you see fit. I have other matters to attend to that will not require your presence. I will seek you out when I have need of you again.*

Disdainful, arrogant fop. Who on earth did he think he was?

Ah, yes, of course. He was the monsieur. After all, he'd signed the note with "M" for monsieur, she supposed. Foolish title in her opinion.

Sniffy, haughty dandy! How dare he dismiss her?

What in the world could he have possibly had to do? Emiline had resisted the despicably immense urge to run to the window and see if the top of the *Sirene*'s main mast was still peaking over the green hills of Ronde.

She had passed the harbor later on her way to the fields, anyway, and the *Sirene* had still been there.

Thinking again now of that moment of weakness made Emiline halt in her angry stride. She harrumphed, almost failing to resist the contemptible need to stomp her foot.

Well, fine! If the whole point of this ridiculous exercise of his was to do as he said, then, of course, she would do as she pleased!

She resumed her walk heading down the path cut in the vine-covered slope leading to the sea, feeling very proud in her defiance only to stop short again when it dawned on her that the whole thing was rather depressing.

The saddest part of it all was that she'd gone back to work because it was the only thing she knew to do, the only thing she ever did. Well, except for reading or cooling off in her secret swimming spot, but she had much too much frustration to burn for either of those.

Emiline threw her arms up and hid her face in her hands, muffling the frustrated sound from her throat that was a mixture of a despairing shriek and a discomfited huff.

When had her life become such drudgery? She had known how to have fun once. She'd had friends, attended parties, and been invited to tea. In fact, when her parents were alive, the island was always full of visitors. It had been rare that a week went by without someone else at their dinner table.

What a horrible hermit she had become. She'd never thought to question it before, but she'd cut herself off from almost everything she'd known before her marriage. Agreed, her life might have been a teensy shallow and frivolous before, but surely there was some medium between that and the sad, boring existence she had now?

Well, not right now. Until this morning the last day and a half had made her normally lonely existence seem so very far away.

Did she really want to go back to that life in just a couple more days?

Lowering her arms and blinking into the sun, Emiline wondered, when her divorce became final, she wouldn't have to go back to . . . that. She'd be completely free then and she could do anything she wanted.

Hope blossomed in her chest as she continued to make her way toward the manor. Indeed, she thought, almost bouncing in her tracks, she could create a great scandal by throwing a lavish ball to celebrate her new-found freedom. She could even find another lover or another husband, for that matter. Or both?

Her heart missed a beat. Disgust spread in her and hope's bloom withered away in an instant. Why did thinking about someone else fill her with dread and almost paralyze her completely?

She cringed with a nearly physical sensation of bitterness. Why couldn't she imagine wanting another man but Reinier?

Chiding herself, she made her way grudgingly to the small harbor. She needed to find a rational explanation for her peculiar reluctance to think of the new, bright future and what it might entail. Maybe she couldn't imagine being in another man's arms right now, but things would change for certain after he was gone—for certain. And then she'd want to find someone else. For certain.

Emiline was almost to the middle of the wharf where a ship was loading cargo. No longer alone with her thoughts, she breathed deeply, taking in the hustle and bustle, happy to be distracted from her inward gloominess. It was comforting, all those people busy with running around and shouting commands and loading the belly of a ship.

Workers were lined up, conveying the cargo into the hold, and the mingled odor of sweet sugarcane, spicy rum, and the distinctive scent of hard manual labor filled her lungs. Seagulls were screeching over her head; people were nodding a friendly greeting in her direction.

Swallowing a sigh of relief, Emiline felt a smile creeping in. This was her life; this was a good life, and this was what she felt comfortable with. Realizing that had pride pulse in her chest, elevating her to almost where the seagulls drew their circles.

Eyes roaming the dock workers, she tried to make out the wharf captain so he could tell her where that ship they were currently loading had come from. There were a few ships due in soon that she wasn't familiar with yet.

A glimpse of sun-gold hair among the workers caught her eye.

When had she hired . . . ?

Who was . . . ?

Emiline almost heard her jaw drop to the ground with a nasty clunk when she finally understood. That man wasn't just one of the workers.

Inhaling sharply, she frantically searched for a hiding place. Emiline knew it was a ridiculous reaction. So this side of Reinier was rather unexpected, not to say astounding. Why hide? But instinct won out and she walked backward, crouching like a crab to duck out of sight behind a stack of wooden crates. Knowing how silly she must have looked, it shouldn't have surprised her when her heel caught in her skirts and she stumbled. Her calf bumped into the side of another, smaller crate that had been hidden behind the bigger ones. All she could do was throw her arms up for a fraction of a second before she tumbled and landed ungracefully in a heap on her backside while her shoulder caught most of the fall. She pressed her lips together tightly to muffle the sound of distress coming from her throat. Then she righted herself, rubbing the soreness in her shoulder blade to ease the pain a bit.

At least Emiline could be thankful she was safely hidden now since she had a feeling the earth wasn't going to kindly open to swallow her that instant.

So *that* was what he had to do this morning. He'd traded being with her for . . . sweating along with the other men on the dock as if he were just another common worker?

How pathetic she was to be . . . here. Emiline should be mortified. But curiosity had got the better of her.

Might as well make the best of the situation meanwhile, Emiline decided as reason and instinct concurred for once and she glimpsed from behind the crates to spy on Reinier.

Having removed his shirt, stockings, and shoes, he toiled side by side with the line of workers loading the ship. Barefoot and bare-chested, his torso glistened with a fine sheen of exertion. His muscular back was to her, and it rippled and bunched rhythmically as he moved.

The sight had her whole body tingle from the inside out all of a sudden, the ache in her shoulder completely forgotten. Her breath caught in her throat as her mind played tricks, picturing him not working on the wharf but . . .

Averting her eyes, Emiline mentally slapped herself. This was not the time, or the place, or was it in any way appropriate to even think of something like that.

Or was it?

Her eyes wandered back to the mesmerizing sight on their own accord and she had time enough to think that, although tanned, his back was still much lighter in color than her own, before her mouth went completely dry and she licked her lips. She suppressed a moan when the overwhelming, wanton craving to lick a salty path along that distinctive scar that crossed his back from his left shoulder to his right hip, hit her with unbridled force. Drawing in a shaky breath, she almost succeeded in scattering the yearning to run her hands over that powerful body, taste his kiss, feel what she knew was hidden in his breeches in her hands, then stretch her secret muscles . . .

Luckily for Emiline, the cargo was all safe in the belly of the ship now and she found herself able to breathe again. The line of workers broke up. Some braced themselves on their knees, others bent back, their hands massaging the small of their backs.

Reinier just stood there, back straight, his unblinking eyes fixated on the horizon. Only when a droplet of sweat sneaked over his eyebrows did he blink. He brushed it away, staring at his hands as if he saw them for the first time. Emiline fully expected Reinier to turn toward the manor now—but he didn't. Instead, he walked off in the other direction; not to her, but to a more secluded patch of beach she knew was just beyond the dock.

Scrambling up, she quickly gathered her skirts and followed. She was careful to remain hidden in the trees and undergrowth lining the shore further down the coast of Ronde. But she simply couldn't resist, never mind how pathetic her behavior must seem.

Emiline arrived just in time, stooping behind a silver button mangrove, to see him release his hair from the leather restraint and remove his breeches, stalking into the sea in that long-legged, graceful, pacing-cougar stride as naked—and as flawless—as God had created him. Her attention was immediately riveted to his male, muscular bottom. She had always thought that his narrow hips and especially his exquisitely shaped backside were . . . lovely. More like mouthwatering, she mentally corrected herself yet again and cleared her throat.

The ocean swallowed the lower half of his body as his golden mane swung and shivered and danced in the breeze as he opened his arms wide, throwing his head back to welcome the waves of cooling salt water enveloping his body.

She knew she should still feel something akin to anger, because he had abandoned her that morning preferring to work instead of entertaining her with some new scheme he'd thought up for their bargain. Alas, her treacherous body had a mind of its own. Heat streaked down her throat, into her abdomen, and coiled tightly between her legs. In that moment, she longed to become a drop in the sea to lick and lave at his body.

Throwing his arms up, he dove in, swimming until he resurfaced again farther away, tossing his head from side to side, his hair firing droplets of salt water. It was all Emiline could see from him in that distance.

She had to look away as her chest began to constrict.

How can that be? Why?

Lost in thought, she made her way back to Bougainvilla just as she'd intended before her embarrassing spying interlude.

Emiline wondered at the fact that Reinier hadn't headed back to the manor to bathe with scented soap before luncheon. Oh no, he'd run for the beach, preferring the natural scent of the sea on his skin. He might be very good at acting tame and domesticated, but there was a superior wildness in him.

A wildness that nothing could erase.

He might act the supercilious fop, but he was so much more than that. He didn't shy away from manual labor, and he didn't need perfume and powdered hair or pristine wigs to feel at ease, or tons of lace around his wrists and throat, for that matter.

She had almost made herself forget, but this encounter had woken memories she had buried. Not for the first time Emiline speculated whether his trademark expression that displayed faint amusement as much as light boredom was just a mask he wore to hide a depth to his soul that she was sure must be there.

There were just too many contradictions about him to believe otherwise.

If only he could just be that way always, she could love him. Or better yet—if he had stayed and he'd been that way all along, they could have been happy.

But he hadn't. He had made the choice to go away.

Yet, she couldn't help but wonder: Had she underestimated him?

Lounging in a brown leather chair tucked away in a corner of the study, Reinier flung one foot over its arm and let it swing idly. He lifted his hand and let his fingers play casually with the thick velvet curtain, catching a glimpse of the main mast of his ship in Ronde's harbor every once in a while.

The curtain draped him in darkness. He felt quite at ease hidden in the shadow of the otherwise sunlit study. Leaning his head against the head of the leather chair, his eyes settled on the immense bookshelf at the other side of the room.

Reinier felt much better than he had last night. A good morning's work had done him a world of good, helping to clear his head from the frustration of the night before. And now he'd come to a decision. He'd play out the game to the end, cut his losses, and be done. It was the only way.

Just as well.

He was jolted out of his thoughts when Emiline came into the study, walking straight to the bookshelf. Fortunately, she wasn't aware he was there.

She looked fresh and cool in her pale lavender day dress. It set off the warm color of her skin, making it glow. It also clung to all her enticing curves in just the right places, especially now as she leaned to one side, standing on tiptoe and reaching for a book in the upper row. Her dark chocolate hair was loosely piled high. Parts of it were still damp; Reinier could tell by the way it curled.

Why was she wearing her hair up again? Whatever the reason, Reinier made a mental note to require she always wear it down again from now on. He'd tell her to leave it loose so he could run his fingers through its welcoming softness whenever he wished.

His line of thinking was beginning to make him slightly uncomfortable in his chair, so as quietly as possible in order to remain unnoticed, he shifted to sit straight and cross his legs. Luckily, any noise he might have made was hidden by the sibilant noise of the curtain's swinging lazily in the breeze at the window closer to her.

She put back the book she'd almost taken from the shelf and was running her hands along the spines of the others. It was obvious she was quite fond of them. Her fingers stroked them adoringly, almost as if . . .

Now, there was no need for Reinier to feel jealous, was there? It was rather foolish to feel the pang of covetousness when one observed one's spouse just selecting something to read, wasn't it?

From the few glimpses he got of her profile whenever she turned it in the general direction of the window, Reinier could see her expression seemed disquieted. Yet, her touch on those beloved books was so tender. Was she trying to find some comfort and peace in her collected volumes? What dark thoughts could be plaguing her?

Her fingers flew aimlessly now, and Reinier knew when she finally took out a book that she'd selected it randomly. She began to flip through it, lifting it high enough for him to catch the gold-leafed name on the cover in the light.

The Welshman who preferred the still life of the country to the bustle of the ton, Reinier mentally mused. Emiline sighed and was immediately drawn into the words, turning more to the window to catch a better light for reading. Her lips slightly opened and closed as she mimicked silently the passage that had captured her. Reinier saw adoration and longing on her face. Instantly, the angry taste of bitter sadness was back, making him wish she could look at him with such . . . affection.

Would that be enough?

Probably. If he were a fool—and what was it they said about fools? Only fools fell in love.

Before that train of thought could continue to meddle with his mind some more, Reinier lifted himself out of the chair in one quick motion and stalked toward her, reciting aloud what she was reading. " 'Let sensual natures judge as they please, but, for my part, I shall hold it no paradox to affirm there are no pleasures in this world. Some coloured griefs and blushing woes there are, which look so clear as if they were true complexions; but it is a very sad and a tried truth that they are but painted.' "

At that Emiline jumped and slammed the book shut. With her mouth ajar, she stared at him as if he'd sprouted a fish tail and become a merman. Ignoring her bewildered look, Reinier gently placed one finger under her chin to close her luscious lips again, then lifted the book from her hands, flipping through it himself.

Reinier spoke into the pages as if he was merely thinking out loud. "Don't look so startled, Lily. I could take offense that you think me so ill read. Vaughan's a little too maudlin for my taste, though. I do think Donne's my favorite. I so love the contrasts in him."

He closed the book and turned it in his hands. After admiring the richness of the leather and the skill of the binding, he glanced at her. She opened her mouth again to reply. Nothing came out but an embarrassed gasp.

"This is an exquisite edition, Lily. Wherever did you find it?"

Reiner watched her visibly shaking herself out of her trance. She blinked, her eyes bouncing from his to the book in his hands and back. But then the question seemed to have turned on some light inside her. Her eyes now sparkled like a full moon reflecting on the tides; her whole being exuded excitement. Watching the change was truly mesmerizing.

"Isn't it, though?" Her hand brushed the unique leather binding quickly once. "It definitely took some persuasion to get it away from the mayor of Grenada. Turns out all it took was passing on the recipe for mother's 'secret ingredient'"—she curled her forefingers in the air, changing her voice to imitate the graveness of that so-called secret, and continued with a laugh—"for her famous Alsatian Chocolate Balls to his cook, although it's really only a knifepoint of cinnamon added to the vanilla, nothing out of the ordinary. The cook could have figured it out herself. Well, that and three cases of rum. That did it. It was really amazing how easily he let go of it then!"

Laughing some more, she turned to the shelf, pride glowing on her face. "But for most of the collection I have a wonderful bookseller in Grenada who is always on the lookout for things I might like.

"Oh . . . and . . ." She all but skipped to the bookshelf, bouncing on the balls of her feet, and reached for something hidden on a high shelf. "Here it is! Have you seen this edition of Chapman?"

Taking the book out, she caressed it once, front and back, then pressed it to her heart before she presented it to him. When he took the proffered book from her, she clasped her hands under her chin and continued hastily, "I've yet to authenticate it, but I have it on good authority it's from Andrew Marvell's collection from his time in Bermuda . . . Of course, it's the poetry that really matters, I suppose, not so much the binding, but . . ."

Her words trailed and she quickly looked away. Reinier suspected she felt self-conscious that she'd begun to ramble, but he could have listened to her talk of poetry all day.

He set both precious volumes in his hands back in their place. Stepping behind her, he wrapped his arms around her small waist. He enjoyed the familiar feel of her body against his.

"Do you have any idea how beautiful you are when you're enthusiastic about something?" His murmur was muffled as he pressed a soft kiss on her temple.

Turning her head to the side and away from him, she harrumphed. "I normally don't read in a crowd, no."

"Maybe you should. It's captivating. But I have an even better idea. Let's you and I find a private spot for a picnic and maybe we'll discover even more things we might have in common."

At that he felt her whole body relax and melt into his. She crossed her arms in front of her, holding his arms in hers. Turning, she beamed up at him. "I think that might be very pleasant."

12

Emiline let her arms dangle by her sides, because with every step she took hers would brush against Reinier's, who in his other hand was carrying the basket Justine had ordered to be packed for their picnic. Of course, the contact was hidden in Emiline's skirts. Nevertheless, or perhaps because they kept it covert, she liked it.

It was one more little secret they shared. Actually, Emiline found that sharing secrets with Reinier, old, new, and *very* new, was . . . nice. Not just that, it was surprising and so very exciting. And that was what she decided she would do the remaining days of the bargain. She resolved to enjoy finding out secrets and marvel at what they had in common. She'd forget about the rest and always remember the good times she'd had with Reinier.

Just as they were passing the stables, John, the groom, came around the corner with a rope in his hands.

Oh no. "Did she do it again?"

John seemed fretful that she had caught him, stepping from one foot to the other and wringing the rope in his hands. "Yes, mum. I swear I turned my back just a second and the moment I turned back, she'd bitten through the leather again!"

Reinier snickered. "That filly hasn't changed at all, has she? So haughty as a mare now, sabotaging the bridle and tack?"

Emiline snorted with contempt, not dignifying Reinier's comment with a reply. In her opinion, all the mare required was a lot of love and even more patience. "John, you have to take better care. We can't get leather here at the pace that mare is chewing it up. And she'll bite through that thin rope in no time."

The stable lad sighed, nodding in agreement and uttering something that sounded like "stubborn" beneath his breath. Emiline would have chided him some more, but something about the way Reinier was looking at the rope just now caused her to forget what she'd wanted to say.

"Reinier?"

He jolted when she spoke his name, but then his impeccable masking smile was back on his lips, although his eyes were still a little clouded.

"I believe I saw a gig in there last time I was in the stables." That grin on his face was lopsided and quite broad.

Confusion had her eyebrows wrinkle, but automatically she nodded. "I bought that chaise on a fancy a few months ago. They said it was the latest fashion, but I thought, fashion or not, it was perfect for my purpose. Sadly, though, I haven't used it yet."

"Have the gig ready, boy, will you?" His order was directed at John, who almost jumped in his tracks because he'd just been trying to steal away from them.

The groom almost hiccupped his contradiction. "Yes, but—"

"No worries, we'll take enough rope with us to ensure that mare will get us back as well, won't we?" Reinier cocked his head to Emiline and raised his eyebrows briefly.

She had to swallow and avert her eyes, realizing the stable lad was patiently waiting for her confirmation. At her minuscule nod, he ran off to do as he'd been told, but she hardly saw that. She was lost in Reinier's gaze and what it did to her.

She recognized that look. In fact, she'd never forget it. It made her shiver. Not with a peculiar coolness, but with a fresh wave of anticipation and lust. He'd had that same expression yesterday. Just before their escapade in the tack room.

Reinier's hand wrapped around hers and he brought it up to his lips. "It is perhaps wise to take the gig. We do have a long way to go, and this basket is quite heavy." His breath tickled her knuckles. "I hope you don't mind, my Lily?"

There. He only needed to say that name in that special tone, with that particular emphasis, and her toes curled while she fought against that rush of a pleasant tickle up and down her sides. "No—o," she stammered, and the left corner of Reinier's mouth kicked up.

"I thought so." He hadn't looked her in the eye when he'd said it. He'd absently brushed a loose strand of hair behind her ear. What was he thinking about?

Just as she wanted to ask, she thought better of it. He'd proven that he meant to keep their actions private so far. If there was something on his mind—without doubt there must be, because there were even unspeakable things on her relatively virginal mind—he certainly wouldn't tell. He'd show her. That knowledge added to the pleasant murmur of tingling anticipation coursing through her veins already.

In no time the chaise was outside, the horse in front of it, she was seated on the passenger side and Reinier sat next to her, reins in hand. He clucked his tongue twice, the mare jumped into motion, and they made their way up to the secluded cove where her father had constructed himself a rough-hewn shelter.

After the conversation in the study, Emiline was determined to ignore all her deep thoughts and contradicting feelings. But now as they made their way in silence, listening to the slow trample of hooves and the occasional high-pitched protest of the wheels, she found that old habits die hard, unfortunately.

Even though she'd vowed to let it be and only lose herself in enjoying his company, she still had moments, like now, trying to analyze his mind, as well as her own. But she didn't want to waste the remaining one-and-a-half days—and the night—worrying over whether her feelings were good or bad or she didn't know what else. She'd try harder from now on, she pledged to herself.

"Here we are."

Reinier's words stopped her thoughts right there and Emiline looked up, realizing that they had, indeed, arrived at her second favorite place on the island. He was walking around the gig now, holding his hand up to her to help her down. She stood and jumped down, securely caught by Reinier's arms.

Lifting her chin, she was instantly lost in the green fire in his eyes. His head dipped and he brushed his lips across hers briefly, his hands wandering up to her shoulders, squeezing gently. As pleasant as that fleeting kiss was, Emiline winced at the touch, lowering her right shoulder a bit. Reinier immediately drew back, his eyes narrowed.

"What's wrong with your shoulder? Are you hurt?"

The surprising amount of worry she saw flicker over his face made her cringe inwardly. How she'd come to hurt her shoulder was much too embarrassing to tell. "It's nothing, really."

"Lily, why does your shoulder hurt?"

The tone with which he'd spoken was stern and Emiline knew he wouldn't let it go unless she told him. With a sigh, she looked down and stepped around him. "I did nothing but what you required. I spent the morning as I wanted to."

"And that entailed hurting yourself?"

She shrugged, already busy getting the blanket open, spreading it half in the shadow of the shelter just off the beach and half in the sun. "In a way . . . yes."

Kneeling, she straightened the blanket, but Reinier was in front of her and grasped her upper arms.

"Lily." Now his tone was so tender that she bit her lip not to blurt out that she'd just bumped her shoulder spying on him.

"All right, then. I was clumsy and I fell."

"Clumsy? How? Why?"

Rolling her eyes, Emiline took an exasperated breath. "I saw you on the docks and ducked and hid to watch you. Only there was a crate in the way. So. There." Her chin was lifted in defiance.

Reinier stared at her, his face an impenetrable mask, and Emiline felt her defiance crumble pitifully.

Finally, he blinked. "You spied on me?"

"No, no! I *watched* you, and it was just a coincidence!"

"You spied on me."

"Well, look who's talking. Those who live in glass houses?"

Reinier suddenly burst into laughter, rolling from his knees to sit with one leg stretched while the other was bent. "Lily, you happened to come into the study and I revealed I was there mere moments later. You, on the other hand, spied on me."

He looked at her with his head tilted. He licked his lower lip, then briefly bit it. "What did you see me do?"

That was enough. That was definitely something he didn't need to know. It was mortifying enough as it was. Emiline jumped up to go and fetch the basket from the chaise. When she returned he was still waiting for an answer.

Opening the basket, she looked inside. "Well, I didn't see so much. Oh, look, lobster salad! You working, you bathing. Mmh, there's mango again! I love mangoes." She blinked at him, her eyes the epitome of innocence.

By the way his chest gradually started to shake, she could see he was fighting laughter. When she added the sweetest smile she could manage, he burst into fits of chuckles. She didn't think she'd ever seen a more compelling sight than him laughing that openly. There was so much warmth in his eyes, what she could see of them anyway through the tears of mirth that eventually leaked forth. His genuine laughter was intoxicating, sweeping her away. Emiline couldn't help but laugh with him.

When he sobered, he wiped the tears from his cheeks. "What else is in there?"

Emiline noticed him getting up off the ground but thought nothing of it as she peeked inside the basket. She cocked her head to see what else was there for them to eat, picking an earthenware bowl up and sniffing it. "Ah, prawns in garlic." Putting it aside, she continued searching. "Oh, there's also granadilla purée. What—"

Her shriek when she was suddenly blinded was almost ear-splitting. Immediately, her hands flew up to rid herself of the cloth that covered her eyes, but Reinier caught her wrists.

"Trust me, Lily."

He'd only whispered the words, but the tenor was so different from when he used his "command and conquer" tone on her, showing her that he knew how she felt and that he wouldn't do it if she insisted.

It had never occurred to her that he could be vulnerable as well in their games. He knew he was pushing her limits, but did she truly want him to stop?

Spellbound, Emiline brought her arms down again. She felt the knot at the back of her head and the blindfold tightened, leaving her in complete darkness.

"Since you've seen too much already today, I believe this punishment is rather fitting." His front pressed reassuringly against her back, and his lips brushed the side of her neck. Emiline thought she felt him place a fleeting kiss there as well. She yielded to his will in a heartbeat.

Gradually, she got accustomed to the unnatural blackness and felt her other senses grow more acute. She could hear the seagulls again, although she knew they were far away. The waves washed against the sand on the beach just a few yards away. Garlic and mangoes and the salty air of the sea created a symphony in her nose that was simply unique. The faint aroma of ginger tickled her nose. Her eyes were covered with silk, while she felt rougher linen on her temples. He must have covered her eyes with his silk handkerchief before he used some other cloth to secure the blindfold around her head.

"But, monsieur, how am I going to eat if I can't see?"

"I will feed you, Lily. Soon. But first things first."

Her breath pitched. She became aware of Reinier's natural scent. A green field of lilac poppies suddenly flashed through her mind, and his alluring darker note, resembling pepper, burnt in her throat. Arousal shivered through her.

Reinier's front was still pressed against her back and her head became light. The moment he touched the laces on her front, the tips of her breasts popped up without shame. His wrists brushed over them when he slowly opened her dress and she gulped air into her lungs as each seemingly casual stroke sent electrifying sizzles through her and into her belly. Moistness pulsed out of her. Her core wept so fast for him she had to suppress a moan.

Her dress fell open, allowing the warm breeze to cool the crevice between her breasts. Her sensitized skin rippled with gooseflesh. The dress fell away from her right shoulder, and his hands worked the laces some more until her other shoulder and a good part of her upper body were exposed as well.

Every inch of her skin sizzled as if set on fire. She felt his breath on her shoulder. He must be watching himself, she thought, watching his hands, his clever hands, cupping her breasts, squeezing the tips lightly. His masculine purr made her feel dizzy with wanting and she let her head fall back, resting securely against his shoulder. The humid warmth of his breath tickled her earlobe.

"Stand, Lily." His voice was rough already and even deeper than usual. His body exuded tremendous heat even through the shirt he still wore.

He helped her stand; she discovered it was not easy at all to find one's balance without one's eyesight. Then he tugged her dress down slowly as if savoring every moment when inch after inch of her body was leisurely revealed. Her overwhelmed senses spun. The tension in her immediately escalated; the lust she already felt pitched even higher. She could hear her own breath coming in shallow gasps, and she continued to remind herself not to move at all, for he'd given her no leave to do so.

Emiline felt completely at ease with her lack of clothing now. She'd always loved the feel of the sun and salty air on her skin. But, she mused, even better than that would be to feel Reinier's skin added to those.

When he wrapped his arms around her waist completely, the slight pressure downward told her he wanted her to get back down on the blanket. Reinier's arms supported her.

His breath tickled at her throat; then she felt it on her shoulder again. Next, he kissed the small hollow at the base of her neck, his hands cupping her breasts once more, but this time squeezing the tips hard. Emiline sucked in a gasp, her hands curling into fists as another wave of welcoming heat moistened the juncture of her thighs.

His lips wandered to her shoulder, then back up to her earlobe while his hands moved with easy slowness across her body.

"So much has changed about you." His husky whisper in her ear had her floating on a wave of pleasure. She never thought that she could be as aroused as she already was. She didn't want to have anything to do with the food in the basket. Right now all she wanted to have—

"You're still so beautiful, but your body is different. It's leaner, more defined." Reinier pressed his teeth against her nipple until the peak pouted up between them and was received by his twirling tongue. She couldn't suppress the moan that escaped her throat.

"Monsieur," she pleaded, helpless in her passion.

"But your skin still has that flawless, rich, tawny color." The palms of his hands now rubbed against her breasts until her nipples were caught between his fingers. Mirroring a scissoring motion, he squeezed them once more, making her shiver yet again.

"I always loved marveling in the contrast in our coloring," he continued, and Emiline panted a ragged, high-pitched "yes" just before his demanding mouth closed over her lips and kissed her breathless.

Their kiss made her forget all her ladylike demureness. In the state she was in now, her unrelenting lust demanded he take her now. Her arms snaked up and wrapped around his shoulders, diving into his soft mane while her tongue thrust deep to show him that her patience was almost at an end. She drew her thigh up and wrapped her leg around Reinier's waist, her hips gyrating instinctually.

His little treasures, those pleasure balls, would have never kept her on edge as much as feeling his body, so close to her, vibrating with lust, his hard flesh pressing into her lower belly; yet he held back, drawing the moment out until it became nearly unbearable.

Reinier broke the kiss, his hands capturing her wrists. He brought her arms down to her sides again, pressing them to her thighs. "I do believe it's time we have our little picnic now."

She harrumphed her resentment, but only got his hoarse chuckle in reply. Then he was gone, and she almost felt physical pain at his leaving. But she knew he was still near. The thick blanket under her let her feel his motions.

She heard the distinctive clinking of earthenware bowls being opened and the scent of food was even stronger now. Only then did she become aware of her growling stomach. She hadn't had anything decent to eat today, so why not enjoy the promise of being fed such excellent food?

When the delicious aroma of lemon and the faint nuance of celery ignited in her nose, she knew he was offering her a morsel of lobster salad first. Emiline opened her mouth dutifully and he fed her a small piece of bread he'd dipped into the salad. Palm oil covered her tongue before the lobster, salt, and pepper followed and added their flavors to the taste.

He hadn't been very careful, though, because a drop of salad still clung to one corner of her lips. Her tongue was still occupied, so she meant to bring one hand up to wipe her mouth clean, but Reinier stayed her arm. His warm, sweet tongue caught the stray drop straightaway, and his unique bouquet was added to the delicacy, creating the rarest specialty she'd ever had. Moaning, Emiline chewed a bit longer before she swallowed.

"Good?"

Smacking her lips, she grinned while giving him a nod. No need to stroke his ego even more by telling him that that was the best lobster salad she'd ever had. She'd much rather stroke—

Reinier paused while feeding her. Emiline supposed it was to dine as well. Then he continued, offering her another morsel, pausing again. Each time he fed her something different, mango or prawns or granadilla purée, and at each offered bite Emiline opened her lips in anticipation.

At some point it seemed he got clumsy on purpose, because he dropped granadilla purée on the tips of her breasts and slowly licked it off. Not that Emiline complained. She relished being used as his personal dining table. He even drew a wet trail with a piece of mango across her body, letting it rest in her belly button only to collect it with his lips, licking the sweet, fruity path he'd made clean.

When he held the next morsel to her mouth, she closed her lips with dutiful slowness and chewed with sensual appreciation.

"You do that very well, you know."

She felt his hand on her hip, caressing her skin. "And what is that, monsieur?"

"Take every bite as if you were savoring something else altogether." The lazy movements of his hand, from the top of her thigh to her waist, had Emiline almost forget her reply.

"It's very good." She worked to make her tone as unaffected as possible, but the words came out in a slight croak.

"I think it's you who is very good."

"Well," Emiline replied, cocking her head and trying to speak in the direction she thought he was. "One should always try one's best to be good to avoid further punishment, I should think." She couldn't help but smile at her own boldness.

"Hear, hear! Speaking of punishments . . ." She felt the blanket under her move. He lay down at her side, and to her disappointment she realized he was still fully clothed.

He put an arm around her, an endearing, possessive gesture, and brought his lips closer to her ear. Emiline wiggled, rubbing her thighs against each other. How much longer was he going to make her wait?

"Tell me how you feel about what happened yesterday."

Her good mood died quickly. She didn't want to think too deeply about what had been happening. It was too mind-boggling, too dangerous. "Must we talk about it? I'd much rather we didn't."

"I asked you a direct question, Lily, and I expect my questions to be answered without hesitation—something you've forgotten already, or so it seems."

Emiline started to protest, but Reinier nipped her objection in the bud. "It's important for me to understand what you thought of the things we did yesterday before—or if—we continue into other things." His hand grasped hers then and he brought it up, placing a kiss on the heel of it with just a hint of tongue in it. "I'd very much like to continue into other things, Lily."

Turning her head away from him, the fingers of her other hand played over the blanket, finding a thread she promptly picked at. "I don't even know where to begin, monsieur."

She sighed and his lips wandered down her wrist. Reinier centered all his attention on her pulse now and Emiline somehow felt complied to answer. "I enjoyed it, yes. And no."

"Yes and no?" He'd unexpectedly stopped his ministrations at that. He'd probably lifted his head, her answer having puzzled him.

Her cheeks heated with embarrassment. His finger under her chin raised her head a little for another kiss. That brief, silken brush of his lips against hers made her concede. "I didn't enjoy it at first. I had never even imagined doing the things we did yesterday before, never imagined I could have ever been comfortable doing them, much less enjoying them. . . . But I did."

"You looked so perfect bent over that saddle with your legs wide and your bottom thrust into the air." Reinier's voice became dreamy. "Your perfect, warm-colored skin was waiting to be marked."

"It stung, but then it felt warm, yet it still stung and it tingled and it made me dizzy and . . ." Thinking of it again now made her almost feel giddy. "And . . . it was more arousing than anything I've ever felt. It was . . . freeing . . . somehow."

Releasing her hand, his fingers caressed her jaw then. "You were wonderful in the tack room, and there are so many more pleasurable things I want to show you."

"May I ask . . . what might those entail?"

"Oh, but I find those things are so much more effective . . ." She felt the heat of his breath against the base of her neck and heard the smile in his voice. "If they come as a surprise."

"But—" Remembering she wasn't supposed to contradict, Emiline bit her tongue and fell silent.

Once more, the thick blanket under her moved. By the sound of it, he must have gotten up. She could hear his footsteps leading away from where she was. He was walking to the chaise. The mare's whinny gave him away. Silence. Then he came back, and Emiline noted his stride had changed. It was more purposeful now.

What had he gotten from the chaise? Emiline licked her lips quickly. The whip?

She was sweet and irresistible in general, but now, as she lay sprawled on the blanket like a buffet waiting to be devoured, she looked magnificent. Reinier couldn't help the grin of anticipation spreading over his face. In fact, he couldn't wait to be the one to devour her, but he needed to control his passion, at least for a little bit longer. He had plenty of discipline, just not so much around her. But he would assert his impeccable control over himself now. It was all the sweeter if the yearning got to the point where it made one almost miserable.

Her chest heaved with the quick, shallow breaths she took, emphasizing the sleek curve of her breasts. Brave Lily, so eagerly awaiting her punishment. But whether it was her being punished or he himself, Reinier wasn't quite sure. He was all too aware of the heat and scent of her body. His lust was nearly driving him out of his mind.

He had to make sure she wouldn't touch him again quite yet. He was almost to the point where he'd disgrace himself by coming in his breeches. Maybe a cooling bath in the sea before he served her would do the trick.

He noticed that even though she was burning to know what he would do, she didn't ask. She'd pressed her full lips together and her cute little fists twitched at her side. Reinier swallowed the low groan he felt watching her fighting her anticipation. Yes, part of the reason for what he was about to do was for his protection against her touch, but it was also for the pleasure he got out of playing his game.

"Kneel, Lily."

The tone in his command was soft, but it was clear—at least he hoped—that he wouldn't welcome any objection. Surprisingly, she complied without hesitation. She got up, wiggling her backside on her heels out of excited keenness or so it seemed. He helped her back into the shadow of the shelter. She'd sweat enough anyway, so there was no need to expose her to the hot afternoon sun.

"Open your knees."

Yes. That one word rumbled through his mind with a primeval growl when she afforded the best view he could ever imagine.

Tightening his grip around the length of rope, he crouched down behind her. He reached in the basket for the sharp knife he'd pilfered from the kitchen along with the other item he'd found by chance there and that he'd perhaps put to good use. He placed the blade by his right calf.

"I am going to take a swim in the sea," Reinier announced. "You're too curious to let me do that in private, so I thought I'd keep you from removing your blindfold."

"How . . . ?" She'd turned her head to the side to speak with him over her shoulder, her voice hoarse, yet uncertainty swung with it as well.

"I'm going to tie you." He said it matter-of-factly while already anchoring one elbow behind her back and wrapping one end of the rope around her upper arm just above the elbow twice.

She held her back rigid. Reinier paused.

"I won't hurt you, Lily." He accompanied his words with nibbling kisses from the back of her neck down to her shoulders, feeling her body become pliant momentarily. Her skin felt so balmy and supple under his fingers.

She let out a soft, capitulating sigh. Only then did Reinier resume his devious, but very pleasurable task.

He stuck two fingers under the rope, captured the longer end of it and pulled it through, then plucked at it until it created a nice loop. He quickly tied several links of crochet stitches until he reached her other elbow. He wrapped the rope around her arm in a loop and secured the loose end.

Looking over her shoulders, he was very pleased with the result. He'd made the knots between her elbows a bit shorter. It didn't strain her shoulders, but still Lily had no choice but to thrust those wonderful, ample globes of her breasts out.

He inhaled, drinking in the sweet, musky spice of her arousal. But he mustn't forget he wasn't finished yet; he still needed to secure her hands.

Using the knife to cut the remaining rope off, he folded the rope in half, wrapped it around her wrists, palms together, twice, bent the loose ends across each other, passed one between the hands and the other between the lower arms, and finally secured the loose ends with a plain knot.

"Perfect. I can bathe in the sea now without having to fear someone's spying on me."

She chortled. "Careful. We don't want your pale skin to get sunburned."

Was she teasing him? Because if she was, he could punish her some more for it, but he was too disciplined to rub his hands with glee.

Reinier stood and started to shed his clothes quickly, then bent to retrieve the bundle from the bottom of their picnic basket. Timing was of the utmost importance now. Knife and bundle safely by his calf again, he knelt in front of her this time. One hand captured her chin, holding her neck arched, while the other went directly to her core. She was heavenly moist already. He loved that sensuality about her. She'd always become wet so easily.

"Audacious Lily. And here I thought you wanted to always be good, not to be punished any more than was necessary." Chuckling menacingly, his fingers found her folds and parted them. He delighted in her high-pitched moan when he touched her and that even louder gasp as he thrust two fingers deep into her. She pushed back, riding his hand and sobbing for more.

Her head grew heavy in his hand; but he wouldn't let it fall back, not now. He needed to see her every reaction as he stroked and teased her. Her juices were already trickling onto his hand and creaming his palm. She sighed with pleasure.

He left her, dragging his drenched fingers farther back to wet the tight opening there.

When one finger entered her taut hole, she caught her breath, her mouth slightly agape. Reinier was slow and very careful now. He wouldn't want to hurt her in any way and certainly not in that way. He pushed into her a little more, retreated, then thrust forward. Her muscles fluttered around him just before they loosened for him. He stuck his thumb into her wet cunny and pumped into her, his middle finger farther back.

Again her head fell back and her breaths came in shallow gasps. Soon she groaned breathlessly, the sound moving slowly through his bloodstream and licking at his skin. Her hips ground against his hand. Her breasts swayed in time with the seductive movement of her hips. God, she was stunning in her passion. There was nothing more beautiful than Lily's natural response.

Just when he wasn't paying attention, she threw her head to the side until she caught his thumb between her lips and sucked at it with unmatched greed.

Reinier felt his cock twitch and saw the drop of anxious anticipation it wept. He had to stop now before he lost the last shred of control over his own body. So he retreated, unwrapped the bundle, and dried his hand in the linen that held the ginger root. Knife in hand, he quickly carved a plug, measuring the length and width of it by his finger.

He'd have just a few minutes to cool off in the sea, but he hoped that would be enough for him.

Emiline found it a bit strange that he'd kiss her just once again, the gentle, intimate caress of his fingers at her center notwithstanding. When she heard him run toward the sea and a quick splash after that, she knew he was in the water, while something was still . . . well, stuck in her. Not that she minded, it was a very delicious feeling, knowing that he'd again placed something in her, never mind that it was not where he'd put those "treasures" the day before. It was rather delicious to know that he made sure she thought of him while he was gone. Although she'd have thought of him enough, being blindfolded and tied on top of that, kneeling there and waiting for his return. Even though—

Holy mother of . . . What had he done to her! She was suddenly on fire, burning up from the inside out. Her rectum seemed to tighten and expand all at the same time, to escape and to snuggle closer to that . . . that *thing* in her.

Merciful . . . Her sensitive nub was throbbing as well. She remembered he'd brushed his fingers over it just before he told her not to move and then had run off.

175

She wanted to wiggle, to get more comfortable, but each motion brought on the sensations even more. What was happening to her? She shouldn't move, she knew, he'd told her not to move, but she couldn't help it, it was . . . she was . . .

Then the stinging, burning sensation changed and it tickled through her body. Emiline had to suppress a moan as that terrible, wonderful feeling spread through her. Her whole body was suddenly pulsating with it, as if her skin, her muscles, her bones had become one big throbbing organ. She still burned, but with passion now, hot and fiery and so strong she thought she was going to drown in it. And she'd willingly drown; it was the most exquisite feeling she'd ever experienced.

Her breath came in ragged gasps, and joy burst through her with the force of a hurricane. That hot, pulsing fire left her body screaming for release, only she knew she wouldn't find any. Not yet. Not just because her arms were bound and she was not supposed to move, but because . . .

Pleasure is not yours to take but mine to give. His words rang in her ears as she fought against wave after wave of the purest, most sublime state of lust she'd ever been in.

She heard herself moan at the fierce gush of arousal that pumped angrily out of her. She knew she was so hot, so ready, so primed that she'd just need a brush or maybe two and she'd find a short, temporary relief, but she mustn't . . . mustn't move . . . he'd know . . . he'd probably see . . .

Her ability to think coherently started to dissolve. But she hung on to her sanity by a thread. Soon he'd be back, she knew . . . she hoped . . . Another moan and she licked her lips, breathing heavily now . . .

"Are you wet for me, Lily?"

She groaned but couldn't reply. Not with words, anyway.

His knees pressed against the inside of her thighs. The feel, the taste, the scent of him mingled with the salty breath of the sea on his body. Her famished senses soaked it all up. His arms wrapped around her. He was cool and wet. He rubbed salt water on her with his body. The droplets would probably evaporate in seconds as hot as she felt.

He bent her back in his arms and buried his face between her breasts as he cupped her backside. His fingers dug deep. Sucking at the tip of one breast, he shoved her up his thighs until her core was flush with his pulsating hard flesh. Her entire body responded, recognizing him, reacting with unmitigated need.

He found her drenched core, his fingers gliding over her folds in the smoothest, lightest touch. The shriek she let out instantly changed into a low moan from deep in her throat.

"Yes." He almost hissed the word. "You are wet. Goodness, how wet you are." His voice had degenerated. It was barely more than a sensual rasp now. She gasped at the anticipation in his voice. She could hear the triumph in it also.

"Now I'm going to take you, and you are going to come. With every long, hard thrust you'll come. I'll make you fly, Lily." She moaned at his outspokenness but couldn't wait for him to slake her burning need.

He shoved his rigid flesh into her fast. His arms slung around her, between her sides and elbows, then over her shoulder blades. The soreness in her shoulder she'd felt before was but a silent tingle now. His fingers dug deep into her shoulders from behind, while her secret muscles worked at him, tried to accommodate being stretched so unexpectedly.

Emiline could feel her nether muscles flutter and constrict around him some more. It was just as he'd said. Golden sparks flew before her eyes, blinding her in the artificial, complete darkness she was in. Her orgasm hit hard, and all she could do was give herself up to it, up to him.

She sobbed when he retreated, but he was in her again, and she saw lightning cut her mind to pieces. Her bones became jelly; she felt as if she were floating in a cocoon of thick, sticky syrup.

Another hammering climax racked her body. She didn't think that unrelenting passion he'd created could ever diminish. She still wanted more. She couldn't get enough.

With his next thrust, her whole body caught fire. The sparks singed her skin and danced before her inner eye. Like a shell shot out of a cannon she flew, up, up, high into the sky toward the blinding, golden disk of the sun.

His word was good. He'd delivered promptly.

That was the first thought Emiline could actually grasp when she had floated back into her body.

She lay on her side, her head higher than the rest of her body. She was no longer restrained. She blinked her eyes open with deliberate slowness. She didn't think she could do anything quick at this point, anyway.

Emiline saw her hand. Fingers splayed on his naked chest. Her head rested on his shoulder.

Even though his skin was tanned, it was still somewhat lighter than hers. The contrast was striking. What had he said? She'd been incapable of replying then. He'd always loved marveling in the contrast in their coloring. She'd always loved that too.

Long fingers ran through her hair, gently massaging her scalp. She'd always loved when he did that. He'd loosened it, probably when he'd removed the blindfold and ties.

His hand left her scalp and came to lie on the small of her back. He brought his other arm up and captured a few curly strands in his hand. He splayed them over his stomach.

He'd always had a penchant for her hair, for her wild curls that no one could tame. She'd been unhappy with her hair—until she'd met him. Already the way he looked at her chocolate-golden mane was enchanting. His playing with separate strands of it was enthralling. He'd take a mass of her hair, bring it up to his nose, and inhale deeply; she remembered that also. He'd always been completely captivated by her hair. Now that she thought about it, she'd loved that too.

The fingers of his other hand caressed the small of her back with idle, languid movements. He didn't speak, just petted and caressed her, placing soft, tender kisses on the crown of her head.

Drawing her leg up, she let it rest on his thighs. It was too much effort to disentangle the other one from his legs. She felt a smile flit across her face and get stuck there. Snuggling closer to him, she sighed. She felt indolent. And very contented.

Bending her neck, she looked up at him. He'd been watching her, and now that she'd made eye contact with him, he smiled too. It emphasized his delicately curved cheekbones. She saw her reflection in his eyes, those eyes the color of translucent, crystalline lime green draped around amber in the center. Full lips. Straight, elegant nose. Delicate cheekbones. Soft chin. He'd always looked much too *beautiful* for a man.

His lids lowered and he bent his head to her, stroking his tongue between her lips with exquisite gentleness. Emiline opened for him, welcoming him. Their kiss was unhurried but thorough. His tongue slipped between her lips, swirling around her own, tempting her to pursue it back between his teeth. His hand was moving with easy slowness across her back.

"How do you feel?" His breath tickled her still-wet lips.

"Lazy," she replied, wincing at hearing her voice as strained as it was. But the next moment she felt proud of it. It was a reminder of the ecstasy he'd given her.

She brought her mouth closer to his again for another one of those wonderful, languorous kisses. Emiline had always loved his kisses, no matter what kind. Heated and famished or slow and deliberate, they were all superb.

But his hand cupped her cheek and he broke their kiss much too soon. "Really?"

She nodded, snuggling even closer, burying her nose between his neck and shoulder, inhaling deep. Lilac poppies and pepper—she'd always loved that contradiction in his natural scent—with the faint trace of salt. Not sea salt but his sweat. Something deeply savage in her responded to that scent, and her tongue snaked out to taste him. She moaned, his fragrance sending a shivering echo of what she'd just experienced through her.

Finally, she found the strength to brace herself on her elbow, head resting against her fist, and brought her other hand up to let her fingers trace the contours of his chin, the outline of his lips. One corner of his mouth kicked up and his eyes sparkled. That grin was probably mirrored on her lips.

"Don't look so smug, Reinier. It was nice, I grant you that."

"Nice, was it?" He guffawed. "Well, it took you long enough to come down again."

"Very well, then. If you take offense at that word, how about 'surprising'? Is that more to your taste?"

Turning his head a little more to the side, Reinier looked straight into her eyes. "I still don't think it covers it completely, but I like it better."

She sighed. "I have to say the last two days have been nothing but surprises."

Emiline had said it absently, almost in jest, but something in that statement brought a tiny bit of the past with it. It must have for Reinier also, because his expression changed. His eyebrows drew together and the corners of his mouth turned down slightly.

"It's incredible how well you've done. How strong you are."

Why couldn't she fight the feeling that he hadn't referred to their encounter just now? Spitefulness roared in her and she wanted to respond once again that she'd had no choice. But she decided to let it go.

She knew she should want to talk about it, try to make him confront what he'd done and how they'd gotten here. But as it was, she didn't want to. She didn't want to think of the past or the estate. She just wanted to let go and feel. She wished they could just enjoy their bodies again. But the look in his eyes . . . It was so far away, maybe even a little unguarded.

"Your father taught you well."

Emiline wished that he could let it go also. With a sigh, she nodded. "In the time that he had, yes."

Averting his eyes, he lifted his upper body. She crawled up, and as soon as he was free of her weight, he turned away, watching the ocean. Emiline remained sitting behind him. "My father always said only a petty tyrant rules by fear. A true leader rules by loyalty and care." She refrained from running her fingers along the scar on his back. "He ran the estate like he ran his ship."

"Would that he'd been my first captain."

Reinier's murmur had a strange shudder run down her body. "Father had retired well before you took to the sea."

What an odd comment. Maybe she'd heard him wrong, because his words had been barely audible. But maybe she hadn't?

"Never mind." He turned fully to face her. "I was being maudlin, and we have no time for that, do we, Lily?"

Emiline let herself hope it was regret she saw in his grassy, pale eyes just before that familiar, despicable veil closed over them.

On the other hand, it was better this way. She smiled with genuine relief in the change of subject. No need for her to know something she'd have to make herself forget when—

"No." She interrupted her own train of thought right there. "No time for that, monsieur."

Her lids lowered as she let her eyes wander wantonly over his glorious, naked body. She reached for the golden patch of wiry hair between his legs but stopped in midmotion.

Blinking up, she asked before she proceeded, "May I?"

A wily grin spread over his face. He stretched his legs, leaning back and bracing himself on his forearms, waving one arm in invitation. "By all means."

Emiline leaned forward, her lips just a whisper away from his tight, male nipple. "You've been so generous before, monsieur. I'd very much like to return some of it."

His gaze filled with heat and mirth. "How noble of you to strive toward such a high goal."

The tip of his tongue traced his full lips and she opened her mouth, her tongue darting out to lick his nipple. "Oh, I'm very ambitious. You'll see."

His whole body twitched and his lids lowered as he let out a low, soft groan. Emiline had always admired that he was so sensitive there. Come to think of it, she remembered now he was sensitive all over. Time to use that information for her own purposes.

She let her mouth wander over him, tasting and licking the salt from his skin, her fingers fondling the hard peaks and grooves of his magnificent, muscled body. Her teeth nipped at his skin, and with every kiss and lick and soft bite, his body twitched and gooseflesh drizzled over him. With her mouth open, she kissed his chest; then her tongue traced the intriguing pattern of muscles at his sides while her fingers splayed and followed the path she drew down his body. He was growing harder with every touch.

Emiline thrust her tongue into his belly button, while her fingers ran over his hard flesh in a tantalizing, slow caress. Reinier arched under her.

"Oh. I see. Now." His words were jerky and distorted by

his gasps of pleasure. She would have given in to the silly titter she felt in her chest if she hadn't been already occupied with the pleasurable task of licking over the tiny slit in his erection, savoring the salty drop that had leaked forth.

Her eyelids drooped and she let out a low moan as his taste spread over her tongue and immediately seemed to permeate every fiber of her body. She laid her head on his lower belly and let only her tongue run around the tip several times, her fingers cupping his sack and playing with the balls inside, feeling their weight, joggling them.

His breath pitched and she let her lips close over just his tip for now, sucking it slowly while her tongue continued to tease him. She heard him groan and she almost lost her strong hold on him. Bracing herself on her forearms, she saw he now lay there like an offering. He'd let his upper body drop to the ground, closed his eyes, arms at his sides.

Emiline quickly crawled up and straddled his calves, bending forward to resume licking and sucking him, worshipping all his length, distributing her kisses and nibbling with her lips at the soft skin spread tight over his hardness.

His breath came in shallow gasps and his hands twisted at his side, curling to fists and opening again. He'd always been so responsive to her ministrations, but he was even more sensitive today.

Her one hand found his sack again, and pulled and pushed and squeezed it gently while her other hand wrapped around the base of his erection, pumping him once before her mouth engulfed him and she immediately swallowed two thirds of him. Her tongue continued its teasing game as her lips and teeth ran over him, up and down . . .

She'd deliberately chosen a quick pace right from the start, hoping she could drive him insane with wanting, just as she'd desperately clung to her sanity before. It worked; his hips rolled up in frantic, choppy motions, seeking to sink even deeper into her mouth while his whole body tensed. He pressed his head into the ground, swallowing tiny gulps of air through his open mouth.

Emiline released him with a soft plopping sound and sat up. Instantly, his head snapped up and their gazes met. Hunger darkened his eyes.

Straightening her thighs and bracing herself on her hands, she crawled up his body, her eyes never leaving his. She lowered her hips over his just as she lowered her mouth over his. Grinding her core against his hard flesh, she thrust her tongue deep into his mouth, reaching down with one hand to lift him skyward.

Never breaking the kiss, she slowly sank down, moaning into his mouth when she felt his thickness impaling her. Simultaneously, he rolled his hips upward to drive his shaft deeper into her slickness.

At first, her hips moved in a slow, circling pace until he bucked against her. His teeth locked on her lower lip, biting down. She closed her eyes briefly as the pinprick pleasure in her lip went straight to her groin and had her gasp long and loud.

Opening her eyes again, she saw his calculating grin. He might have allowed her to take charge, but she couldn't fool him, nor could she fool herself. She was doing what he wanted her to do, his gaze said, and realizing that changed something in her. All the gentle playfulness was forgotten. Like a volcano, passion erupted in her and had streams of molten lava run through her veins. His gaze and the message it conveyed had been the incentive she hadn't known she'd needed to once again turn into a lust-crazed wanton.

She ground hard on his thick shaft, increasing the rhythm, and he responded, lifting his hips to meet her every stroke.

Emiline went wild with the heat building up inside her and threw her head back, moaning her pleasure out loud.

His hands snaked up and fisted in her hair, urging her head back down for a smoldering kiss that sent her into a delicious frenzy. She was pumping hard against him, and harder still, wanting, craving, yearning for more.

He rolled her off him and effortlessly turned her on her side so quickly she didn't realize it at first. His hands spread her thighs wide and he entered her with a quick, relentless thrust until his thighs pressed against the back of her legs. His fingers found her nub and rubbed it tenderly while he pumped into her harshly. The contradiction snatched a piece of her mind away with each stroke.

But then his motions slowed down more and more until he didn't move at all. Emiline was twisting in his arms, one hand fisted in the blanket, one in his hair. Wild and crazy with passion, she didn't want it to stop; she wanted more, so much more, and she wanted it to go on forever and ever.

"Relax and open for me." His whisper didn't make sense. She had already opened, she thought, sobbing as she felt him retreat completely.

Then his fingers were buried deep inside her for the fraction of an instant before she felt one of them pushing into her farther back again. She remembered what it was like. She remembered how delicious it felt, how intimate the touch was, and she welcomed the sensation once more, sticking her backside out for him and pushing against his hand. His finger was entering her slowly, and now she knew what he'd meant. She wanted more. With a groan, she twisted her upper body, bringing her lips closer to his. Her tongue snaked out to brush over his lips before she moaned, "More."

She'd barely spoken the word when she saw that spark

darken his eyes and she felt him spreading her wider, entering her with two fingers now. Emiline sucked in a ragged gasp of air when she felt him stretching her. She was so sensitive there. The sensation was delectable, tearing a low groan from her throat.

"More?"

His question was superfluous, she thought while pumping into his hand. Her body was asking, pleading, begging for more still and she was in no state of mind to think about it. Her breath pitched when she was being broadened even wider and she almost grunted in disappointment when he left her. But even though the feeling had been extraordinarily delicious, feeling his thickness in her core again made up for it.

But then he was gone again and his thick, rounded head pressed against her back there. Emiline's eyes flew open as she fully understood what he'd meant earlier. It was too much, she thought, he was too thick, he'd hurt her. Did she really want this?

"Shh," Reinier breathed soothingly into her ear. "Relax, Lily."

His arm wrapped around her and his hand went straight to her core. Opening her folds, his clever fingers strummed her clit, and that was all she needed to let herself fall. Pleasure rippled through her body at the touch of his fingers; passion peaked as he slowly sank inside with seemingly no effort at all. He stopped there and didn't move. Only his fingers tirelessly played with her sensitive button.

The soft pressure she felt against her tender walls as they stretched and loosened to take him in felt marvelous. He rolled his hips slowly to let her adjust to him, she supposed. Heat, thickness, and strength spread her. The sensation was unbelievable, the pleasure in his thorough conquest barring words.

She could hear his soft groans with every move he made, and those were the sexiest sounds she'd ever heard. They spiked her passion, heightened her ardor. She felt so close to him, connected in the most intimate way. It was breathtaking. A very special bond formed between them; Emiline could feel it. With each thrust she experienced, with each moan she uttered, with each groan she heard, that special bond grew more intense. They fed each other's lust with heat and ecstasy.

His torso rolled against her back, his strong arm was still around her, his fingers strumming her center. It was so delighting; she shivered at each new, deep penetration.

"Feel me in you, Lily."

His voice was a low purr, almost as erotic as the silken strokes of his cock. She obeyed, bringing her hand down, shoving two fingers deep into her sex. His hand left her, clamped down on her hip to hold her in place, but it didn't matter. The heel of her own hand provided the pressure she needed just now, and her moans pitched as she felt him move in her through the soft tissue of her dam.

His thrusts became more urgent and Emiline felt her consciousness splinter—the fierce strokes of his big cock, his lips moving on the side of her neck, his teeth clamping down, pleasure spiraling through her, down to her center. Too much.

All too much.

She felt her secret muscles grip and convulse around her own fingers even tighter. Her fierce orgasm shook her, wrenching a sharp, ecstatic bellow from him as he also crested.

He rolled his hips some more, rocking gently against her while her body continued to ripple with ecstasy.

Then she went limp. And her mind went numb.

13

"No, don't." Reinier grasped Emiline's hands, stopping her from piling her dark chocolate curls back up on her head. "Let it loose." His tone was softly pleading. Her golden highlights were more intense when her hair was an untamed cascade down her back. Any restraints were, in Reinier's opinion, absolutely unnecessary.

Turning around, Emiline blinked. "But it's still wet."

And, Reinier added to himself, recalling their recent bath in the sea, probably dotted with little bits of sand as well. Had their skins not started to shrivel like apples left in the sun, they'd still be there in the water doing what they'd been so reluctant to interrupt—or rather finish, yes, by now they would . . .

Clearing his throat, Reinier tried harder to close the fly of his breeches. When he was in his trousers, his shirt still untucked, he took a step closer to her to run his fingers through her glorious mane. "I like the way it curls even more when it's still damp."

He saw she mirrored his loving gaze and fell into his arms.

While they clung to each other, he pressed the softest of kisses on the crown of her head. Her fingers dug deep into his back as if she desperately held on. Her head was on his shoulders, just where it always should be. He could stay like this forever.

"When did the sun begin to set?" Her words were muffled against his shirt.

With a heartfelt sigh, Reinier broke their embrace. "I don't remember, but we should probably head back before people think I've done something unspeakable to you."

Cheeks blushing, she tried to hide a giggle in her hands. "Reinier, you have done unspeakable things to me."

At her mock reproach he gave a brief chuckle, fingers capturing her chin to lift her head. "We've done wonderful things together."

Her answering nod was a little shy. Reinier kissed the tip of her nose and, leaning back, he fell into the depths of her aquamarine eyes, drinking in all the tender emotions and feelings they conveyed.

She was so beautiful, she robbed him of speech. He could look at her like that always and he'd never tire of it.

And if she always looked at him the way she did now, he could stay. Forever.

At the thought, the smile on his face crumbled and he quickly turned away to hide the change from her. He couldn't go on like this. He couldn't go on with this heinous ruse he'd concocted. He'd stay if she let him.

But now was not the time for talking about any of that. They should talk over dinner. It was only fitting; it had all started at dinner, after all.

Thus resolved, Reinier tucked in his shirt and made himself presentable so the servants had no reason to gossip. Then he helped Emiline gather the ceramic bowls from the picnic and placed them back into the basket. They folded the blanket together. When they walked toward the gig, they didn't just walk hand in hand but with their arms wrapped around each other.

Reinier became aware that it had been a very long time since he'd felt this kind of stillness in him. It had been a long time since he'd last felt this free. It had also been a long time since he'd felt this loved and could return that love from the bottom of his heart.

Helping her up into the gig, he quickly walked around it to take his seat, thankful that contrary to what the groom had predicted, the mare hadn't bitten through the reins. Taking them in his hands, he clucked his tongue twice and they rocked into motion. Reinier put his arm around Emiline and she snuggled close. He let his chin rest on her head as they trotted back to the manor.

Her happy sigh made his heart jump. How would he begin? How could he make her talk about it at all? Should he wait until the main course was served? Which would be the right moment?

Suddenly, she wiggled out of his embrace. "Stop the chaise."

Reinier gave her a look that must have shown all his bewilderment, because her eyes pleaded with him, yet the tone in her voice remained determined. "Stop the chaise, Reinier. Please."

He did as she'd asked, tucking the reins under his thigh just as she grabbed his hands. She brought them up, raining kisses on them. Reinier could only watch as if he were merely an onlooker to his own body.

Straightening, she swallowed and licked her lips. "Reinier, we need to talk." Her words were low. She lifted her head and they locked eyes. "This is . . . We . . . I mean . . ." She laughed and shook her head, then took a deep breath.

Her eyes radiated so much warmth; Reinier couldn't help but smile back, although he must have looked very much like the besotted simpleton he felt at that moment. Was it possible? His heart beat heavy in his chest and hope had him thinking that maybe she felt the same, maybe she didn't want to wait until dinner.

"Reinier, I l—"

Whatever she'd meant to say died on her lips and she leaned to the side, eyes narrowing past him at something in the direction of the harbor. Her face suddenly sobered like a slap had wiped her smile away. With a nerve-wracking slowness, she turned back to face him. Tipping her chin up, her hands left his.

"Whose ship is that?" Emiline's voice was totally devoid of emotion.

Perplexed, Reinier drew his eyebrows together. There was his ship, the *Sirene*, but—

At the dark, callous glare in her eyes now, Reinier turned in his seat to see what she was talking about. He inhaled sharply. The cold, foul breath of doom skittered along Reinier's back and something in him exploded with a deafening shatter until he could almost taste the bitter shards in his throat.

"The *Coraal*." His whisper sounded loud to him in the quiet as his heart missed a beat. Molars grinding, he looked down. A sudden silence spread in him, like a snake coiling and waiting to strike. "That's Connor's ship."

Emiline gasped and turned from him. Folding her arms around her body, she hunched, hiding her face in her hair.

Helpless at the unexpected change in her demeanor, Reinier could only stare at her, preoccupied with his own inner turmoil. When he finally showed the presence of mind to try and soothe her by placing his hand gently on her shoulder, she jolted as if a scorpion had stung her. Throwing her arms before her body like she wanted to ward him off, she hissed, "Don't touch me. Don't you dare."

Something hideous and dangerous formed in his gut at her rejection, a swirling black mass that rattled with a revolting snarl. Without another word, Reinier took the reins in his hand

and let them crack, the sound splitting the warmth of the evening and causing sleepy birds to rise out of a nearby tree with indignant twitter. The mare spurred into motion again with a contemptuous whicker.

Reinier tried to find an explanation for her sudden change, for why at Connor's arrival she'd turn from a playful, warm lover to . . . well, back to being his wife.

With a mental snort of derision, he stopped searching his mind for what made the fickle woman do what she did and tried to work out how he himself felt about Connor's arrival. That at least promised to be a much more fruitful exercise than brooding over his wife's moods.

Honestly, he'd forgotten all about Connor. He'd forgotten he'd made arrangements for him to come and assist in teaching his cuckolding wife a lesson or two.

In a way, he was glad to know Connor was here now. Reinier could slap himself for his tremendous stupidity. Not once or twice but a thousand times. How often had he told himself not to let himself feel something for her again? What had made him throw all his well-formed caution to the wind? He'd known he needed to pay close attention around her to save himself from another broken heart. The old scars were still too tender to survive another blow.

Now Reinier was certain he couldn't wait to get off this rotten island. Connor's presence helped him confirm that. He'd also help him with whatever disturbing contradictions churned in his belly.

His affection for Connor, Reinier knew, went beyond what was sane or sensible, but at least it was mutual. Reinier had never questioned it, nor had he ever had reason to. Connor was his friend, his only, best friend.

He was so much more than that if Reinier were completely honest with himself.

If Reinier were completely honest with himself now, was he truly happy that Connor was here?

The mare must have known the way instinctively because she halted right outside the mansion and stopped Reinier's contemplation. Reinier jumped from the gig and held his hand up to help Emiline down without looking at her.

She walked into the manor ahead of him, not dignifying him with a look either. It seemed things had returned to the way they'd always been.

When Reinier entered the open foyer by his wife's side, he saw Justine waiting for them. Apparently, she was just as unhappy about Connor' arrival as her mistress, though she tried to conceal it. That was more than Reinier could say for his wife. Well, at least the maid had some manners.

"You have another guest, mistress," Justine spoke without acknowledging him. "I've escorted him to the sunroom and asked Cook to prepare a light tea service. The next tide is before dinner, so I assume he won't be staying past tea."

Forget about the maid having any manners, Reinier thought, his eyes narrowing.

Emiline's answering smile of approval didn't sit well either. "Thank you, Justine," she drawled smoothly. "I'm sure you did the right thing."

Reinier began to feel ganged up on. He'd be damned if he let these two vipers just run Connor off without having a say in it. Clenching his jaw, Reinier grasped Emiline's arm and guided her into the sunroom in silence.

Before he could stop it, a tight smile flitted over his face when he spotted Connor looking completely relaxed and at ease, almost like a visit to Bougainvilla for tea was a common occurrence. Reinier's jaw muscles jumped when he clenched his teeth even harder. Connor was, Thank God, oblivious to the tension his visit was causing between them. He was gazing out the window. To Reinier, it appeared that Connor's mind was enraptured in the far distance that reached beyond the horizon, but then Connor blinked and turned to them, his typical easy smile in place.

Reinier felt the corners of his lips curl down. Connor had seen it, Reinier judged from the way his naturally dark eyes sparkled for a short moment. The Irishman acted as if he hadn't noticed, though, and rose from his chair.

Keeping his own expression blank, Reinier firmly shook Connor's proffered hand. "How nice of you to come, Connor. I hope you can stay for dinner at least."

When he felt Emiline tense by his side, Reinier took irrationally devilish delight in it, letting his expression ease with the satisfaction he felt.

"I would be more than honored, of course," Connor replied. Bowing to Emiline, he took her hand.

For an absurd moment, Reinier was almost shocked that she'd let him take her hand and brush a kiss to her knuckles, but just as quickly as she'd acquiesced, Emiline pulled away. She turned her back on them both and walked toward the window.

The knowing expression on Connor's face made Reinier feel uncomfortable, and his teasing wink was even worse, but before he could scold the Irishman with a look of disapproval, Connor retrieved a small chest from beside the table and walked to Emiline.

Made from stained and polished cherrywood, it was adorned with vines bearing stylized roses and gold inlay in the form of leaves. The box was exquisite, a truly lavish gift, and Connor offered it to her with the words, "Madam, I hope you'll accept this small gift as an apology for my intrusion on your hospitality."

Without replying, without one small crack in her distant manner, Emiline took the chest and set it on the wide windowsill. When she opened it, Reinier saw that Connor's superb taste and the lucrative nature of their business ventures were evident in the contents: finest silks in rich hues of aquamarine and gold, the former matching her eyes, the latter setting off her skin and emphasizing the light tresses in her hair, as well as the best and whitest of Belgian laces. It was, Reinier thought, a gift worthy of a queen. As regal as any empress, Emiline examined the silks and laces in great detail.

When she turned back to Connor, her eyes were filled with a frosty shimmer. "How wonderful! Really, it was very thoughtful of you." Her smile and the peculiar pitch in her voice was too exaggerated to be genuine. "Thank you. Next time one of the servants needs a cap or an apron I'll be sure to put these to good use."

She shut the lid on the box with a loud snap, hooked it under her elbow, and looked Reinier straight in the eyes, daring him to comment. Her glare was full of disdain.

She'd dismissed Connor so rudely that Reinier was appalled and ashamed at the same time, but just as he took a deep breath to utter a reproach, she walked purposely toward the door. "Now, if you'll excuse me, the sun has given me quite a headache. I'm afraid you gentlemen will have to enjoy your tea alone, but I'm certain that won't be a problem for either of you."

She was almost at the door when Reinier's fury snapped. That spiteful, overbearing woman, he roared mentally, restricting himself to bellowing, "Madam!" Stalking after her, he continued, "You will not—"

Connor was suddenly at his side, gripping his upper arm. Emiline was through the door, her skirts swishing aggressively against the frame.

"Come back here at once!" Reinier growled from between his teeth, struggling against Connor's tightening grip.

"Reinier." Connor's forceful tone registered through the haze of his ire, and momentarily Reinier's attempts to shake off the hand that held him back ceased. "Let her go. Come on, let's enjoy our tea."

With his eyes still narrowed at the top of the stairs where Emiline had just disappeared into her rooms, Reinier took a few calming breaths. Eventually, he felt he had himself under control again, and wrenching his arm free, he harrumphed and stalked back into the sunroom.

Emiline bolted the door shut to drown out Reinier's angry bark. Stalking, she threw the tainted gift across the room, brushing a priceless Grand Siècle vase in the process. Breath held in horror, she watched the china depicting Louis XIV amidst nymphs and satyrs feeding him and groveling at his red-heeled shoes sway slightly. Round and round it rocked until it finally tipped and fell to the floor where it crashed into tiny bits of merely unremarkable colored porcelain.

In her mind she snorted and reprimanded herself to not pace the floor and wear down the carpet. He wasn't worth ruining another unique heirloom.

In the silence that followed she wasn't sure what to do with herself. A gale of feelings swamped her; she felt foolish and furious, and Lord only knew what else.

The catalyst had been the bright flag at the top of the main mast of the *Coraal*, full of mirth dancing and vividly waving at her.

She hadn't really needed to ask Reinier whose ship it was. She'd known. *L'Île de Ronde* had been part of Connor's regular shipping route ever since they had started their company and Reinier had left. But there had just been that split second when she'd held out hope that her eyes had somehow failed her.

Every time Emiline had begun to forget that she'd ever had a husband, every time the pain would lessen for just a bit, the merry sails of the damned *Coraal* would appear on the horizon and force those haunting memories back to the surface.

They'd never spoken during his visits; they'd never even seen each other but from a distance—Emiline in her study anxiously awaiting his departure; Connor at the docks and then back on his ship. He'd never made any attempt to call on her at Bougainvilla, and Emiline had always made sure Captain Blanc or the dock foreman was available to conduct business with him.

Time and again she'd tried to find an excuse to stop him from coming, but how could she prevent what technically amounted to the master of the estate's shipping fleet doing business with himself? So she'd endured those cruel jabs her heart suffered with each visit.

Why was Connor here now? He wasn't scheduled to pick up another shipment of goods for two months yet. He had to be up to something.

Suddenly, Justine's words chimed like hysteric bells in her head. They were known, she'd said, for entertaining women together.

Fighting not to lose control of her breathing, Emiline shook her head from side to side. Her hands balled into fists and her body went rigid.

No, she thought. No, no. The word repeated itself in her mind with each gasp for breath she took. That can't be it, she moaned inwardly. Reinier would never do that to her. He couldn't possibly ask that—demand that of her.

The man she'd been with this afternoon would never do that. He'd cared for her, put her best interest above all else. He'd looked at her with so much affection. When she'd started to tell him how she felt in the chaise, she'd been positive he returned her feelings.

But that left her once again with no explanation why Connor was here now.

Had he followed Reinier here to take him away from her again? Was he that much of a scoundrel that he would show up here just to prove that he could?

Upon seeing Connor's ship, Reinier had completely shut her out again. She had seen the curtain veil his eyes that exact moment. Being left outside once more, especially after the wonderful time they'd just spent together, had hurt her so deeply there hadn't seemed an end to it.

Did she really need any of this?

Fine! Connor won. He could just bloody well take Reinier and be gone! She didn't need either of them.

Emiline sank to the floor and covered her face in her hands in a futile attempt to stop the tears from forming.

Who was she trying to fool? True, she didn't need Reinier. She wanted him. And—damn that Irish bastard—they'd made a bargain! She wasn't going to just let his intrusion interfere with that or the fact that on top of everything, she'd promised herself she'd enjoy every minute of their time. She and Reinier had another day and a half, and Connor could just go back to where he came from until her time was up.

She was no coward. She was a fighter. Her unique heritage didn't permit her to give up, certainly not so easily. She was Emiline du Ronde, daughter of a pirate and a noble woman, and not just some simpering sap!

Wiping her cheeks dry, she hiccuped a sigh and brushed a fold out of the rumpled skirts on her thighs.

It wasn't just that bargain that had her taking such offense at Connor's showing up. There was more to it. Much more.

This wasn't about some silly pact, not anymore. She loved Reinier—even more now than when they'd married. Then it had been a childish attraction, but now what she felt was much deeper. It was richer and finer. It was all-encompassing, influencing every aspect of her existence, making her experience life with much more intensity, making her feel whole. Her love for Reinier wasn't infatuation. It wasn't just physical attraction. Her love for Reinier had matured despite her fit of petulance earlier—never mind that she'd been right . . .

Her breathing slowed and a calmness washed over her. What if she'd made a mistake?

Maybe she had, indeed, been wrong to react so badly. She hadn't trusted Reinier; she'd doubted him, although he hadn't failed her thus far. Maybe he wouldn't now either.

The Reinier on the beach today wouldn't be so easily swayed. He wouldn't choose another over her, wouldn't share her with another. He'd continue to be with her and look out for her, and he'd never let Connor come between them.

But Emiline hadn't given him a chance to prove any of that.

Shaking her head, she wiggled her nose, disgusted at her preposterous behavior. She felt so ridiculous now for letting past fears and jealousies cloud her judgment so profoundly.

What would she do in his stead? She would send Connor on his way as soon as possible, not wanting to waste any more of the time they had left. And perhaps that was exactly what Reinier would do.

He just needed a nudge in the right direction. That's why she needed to look her best at dinner. For Reinier.

And after dinner she'd find a way to apologize thoroughly for her rashness, something very . . . special that she was sure Reinier might like. Oh yes, now that was something she could enjoy contemplating while setting the perfect scene.

Emiline sprang to her feet and rushed to call for Justine, who came up the stairs and into her room a blink of an eye later.

"Have my bath drawn as quickly as you can. And fetch a bar of the French-milled scented soap."

Justine gave her a look that clearly conveyed she believed Emiline had lost her mind completely. She mumbled something under her breath but did as she'd been told.

Particular arrangements needed to be made for dinner also. "And tell Cook to make something with ginger." It would remind Reinier of their delicious little secret this afternoon.

Justine, already on her way out the door again, turned on her heel and stepped back into the room. "Yes? Anything else?"

"None I can think of now."

"Very well." Nodding, Justine turned to leave again.

"Perhaps the scented candles, along with the special china for the table. Tell the maids that."

Justine halted in her tracks, pivoted, and stepped back into the room, remaining by the door and not moving at all.

Emiline fumbled at the laces of her dress. What would she wear? Perhaps the blue one? No, that was too somber.

She saw Justine was still there despite the hurry, the wrinkly corners of her mouth pointing downward. "My bath, Justine?"

"Yes, I heard you the first time already. I'm just waiting if there's anything else you want. In my age it's not considered prudent to take too many unnecessary steps."

Emiline's shoulders slumped. Walking up to Justine, she grasped her upper arms. The maid had always been her dearest friend, her closest ally, and all she'd ever wanted was to save Emiline from harm. Her rigorous stance right now was a warning, but Emiline knew exactly what she was doing. "Justine, trust me in this. I need to make things right. Everything will turn out just fine, I'm sure."

"Well, at least one of us is." With a sigh, the strict expression on the maid's face softened. "I don't think I can bear seeing you hurt again, girl."

Emiline cupped the old woman's cheek. "I know."

Justine petted Emiline's hand, leaning into the caress.

"Thank you," Emiline breathed.

They hugged, then Justine broke away. "I'll be a minute, don't you worry. Can't work miracles, but I'm trying very hard to."

As the door closed behind her lady's maid, Emiline walked straight to her wardrobe. Even within the best of Caribbean society, things were much less formal and relaxed than in Europe, but being half French, Emiline was well adept at looking her very best when she chose to. One glance at her dresses and Emiline knew which one would be perfect for the evening.

Lastly, she rummaged in the top drawer of her vanity table to retrieve the flacon containing that special fragrance she'd ordered but never worn.

A man should never underestimate the devices of a determined, half-French woman with seduction on her mind.

All went smoothly and quickly until she and Justine encountered a large obstacle. The trouble was her hair; it wouldn't bend to their will. Almost no one ever wore wigs in the West Indies. It was simply too hot for that extravagance. Poor Justine had become quite frustrated around the third or fourth style she tried that Emiline didn't think was quite right. Reinier loved her hair loose, but completely loose didn't fit with the intricate beauty of the dress and feast she'd planned. Justine huffed and Emiline tugged impatiently at her hoopskirt while trying to find a solution. Finally, she and Justine settled on sweeping the front up and away from her face into a complex weave of curls while the rest of her hair was left down, falling over her shoulder to her waist just as Reinier liked it.

Emiline then dabbed a little of the perfume, a light combina-

tion of fresh bergamot with a discreet layer of violets underneath the lush sweetness of wood strawberries, behind her ear-
lobes, on her wrists, between her breasts, and between her
thighs before she stepped into her dress.

She couldn't remember the last time she'd taken so much
care in her dressing, and she'd forgotten how much fun it could
be. Emiline looked at herself in the mirror, her fingers smooth-
ing the shimmering coppery silk of her stomacher and dress
that were highlighted with silver flowers and bows. The same
flowers trimmed the three rows of silvery lace flounces on her
sleeves that ended just above the elbows. The lace ruff around
her neck held small, silvery flowers as well and complemented
the six silver bows in graduated sizes on her bodice. Silvery
satin shoes completed the ensemble.

When she made her way down the main stairs, she felt both
confident and excited. She was so eager to show Reinier how
she looked, she had to force herself to stop and take deep, calming breaths before she opened the doors to the study to—

She needn't have bothered. They weren't waiting in the
study.

Was she late? Hadn't she rushed enough? Emiline tried the
dining room next, but the only people in there were the maids
setting out the china. Taking a moment to double-check the
preparations and finding everything to her satisfaction, she resumed her search for her husband and their guest.

When she didn't find them in the main sitting room either,
Emiline started to worry. They were nowhere to be found. Her
choker seemed to leap with each forceful thrum of her pulse.

Rushing to the sunroom, she checked what she could see of
the harbor, holding her hand over her heart as if that would stop
it from jumping out of her bodice. She could see both the *Sirene*
and the *Coraal* were still anchored, only their captains were—

A small movement on the south lawn caught her eye. It was

a nervous blinking at first until it eventually captured the last rays of the dying sun and blinded her. Emiline held her hand up to shield her eyes and saw two figures.

She hesitated for a moment, reluctant to soil her shoes, but curiosity got the better of her. Out of the open doors that led from the sunroom into the garden, she ventured toward that blinding little object. Finally, she realized it was one of those stupid iron balls she'd hidden in a shed.

Standing at the entrance of the naturally grown archway of vast, wild oleander shrubs, Emiline heard laughter. Focusing in the direction where she'd heard the merriment, she spotted Reinier and Connor. They were playing lawn bowls, both in just their breeches and shirts with their sleeves rolled up over their elbows.

She pressed her lips together. Obviously neither one was worried at all about taking care to dress for dinner or to even be on time for that matter. Her heart sank more with every passing moment.

It was Connor's turn. The black ball rolled directly at the silver ball closest to the smaller, white jack, knocking Reinier's ball out of play. Connor, having won the game, thus raised both his hands over his head. They didn't just shake hands like gentlemen, they fell into a warm hug. Reinier said something Emiline couldn't make out; then they were roughhousing with each other while retrieving the bowls, pushing and laughing at each other all the while.

Her thoughts went still.

So, her husband and his friend were having a grand time enjoying each other's company and not sparing a single thought on her.

How could she have been so wrong about Reinier? She now saw quite plainly that it all had been nothing but a game for him. He'd fooled her into giving in to his every whim right from the start, and it had always been a way to fill idle time away until Connor showed up again, then he'd leave.

What a deceitful bastard!

Connor looked in her direction and remained still as if he'd seen her. Reinier followed the Irishman's gaze, then walked to the small fountain close by.

Emiline would show them both what she was made of. Nothing they did could hurt her. This had only ever been a means to an end and her freedom. Remembering that helped her shut down her feelings. She made her way back to the manor, her chin inched higher and her shoulders squared.

14

"I don't know what's gotten into her." Reinier sighed, crouching next to Connor to pick up the silver ball while he gathered his. He avoided the Irishman's gaze on purpose. It hadn't been easy to reveal there were problems with Emiline, not that Connor couldn't have guessed from her behavior earlier. But perhaps he had a clue that would help. Maybe something that Reinier had somehow missed.

Connor laughed, still jesting. "Or gotten into you? Your aim is way off. Are you letting me win?" But then he paused and Reinier could feel his contemplating gaze on him. "You needn't worry, Reinier. She's just angry."

He was at his wit's end at the moment. "I wonder if marrying her was worth all the trouble."

Getting up, Connor nodded in understanding. "In my opinion that's the real drawback about marriage—once you're in, you're in."

That was a little hypocritical. "I'm not as fortunate as you,"

Reinier snapped. Unlike Connor, he didn't have prospering warehouses to bank on. "You know why I married her. I do believe it was on your suggestion that I did."

Tossing the jack into Reinier's hands, Connor quirked an indignant eyebrow. "Yes, I know why you married her. But do you?" He took a deep breath and his demeanor softened. "Reinier, I also know why you left."

Pursing his lips, Reinier headed back to the end of the green. He heard Connor's breathy laugh at his side the next instant. "She probably just needs a good whipping."

Reinier couldn't stop the smug grin from blossoming.

"Ahh." Connor chuckled. "You already did that."

Nodding, Reinier shrugged and harrumphed. "So much good it did. She's developed into a termagant."

Connor stopped in his tracks and burst into grunts of laughter. "You mean there is finally a woman you can't manage with your customary sense of detachment?"

Reinier snorted. He wanted to contradict him, but Connor was right, and as irksome as it was, they both knew it.

"Well, if you ask me, I think it's perfectly understandable."

"What is?" Reinier rolled the jack to the other end of the green.

"Her reaction." Connor spoke low, carefully watching where the jack came to lie. "You sailed away from her and didn't return for four years. I'd say she's entitled to a little hostility."

Time and again, Connor had chided him on his decision to stay away from her, but Connor would never understand why Reinier had to do it. He wasn't in the mood to hear it again. "Are you on her side now?"

"Side?" Connor sputtered the word with a half snort, half gasp. "This isn't about sides, Reinier. It's about marriage." Holding his hand up in an appeasing gesture, he cut off Reinier's reply before he could even take a breath to utter it. "Of course she's brushed me and my gifts off. Who is it that you've been spending your time with the last four years instead of her?"

"Still, I see no reason for her to—"

"Love has got nothing to do with reason." Connor placed his hand on Reinier's shoulder, his gaze a trifle too observant for Reinier's taste.

"This isn't about love and well you know it," Reinier growled. Connor had no idea what he was talking about. He'd been a fool to think the Irishman could impart some kind of insight. Connor was as far off the mark about Emiline as he himself was with his lawn bowling aim.

"It isn't about love?" Connor raised a cynical eyebrow.

"No." Reinier heard the irritation in his own voice. "It's about divorce. She wants to divorce me." He spat the words out with all the disdain they created in him.

"Oh." Connor lifted his reassuring hand off Reinier's shoulder, turned, took aim, and tossed the first bowl. "Really?" Connor's tone dripped with sarcasm. "I can't imagine why."

His bowl came to lie right next to the jack, and when he turned to face Reinier, his eyes glinted with triumph. "Well? What's keeping you?"

Taking aim, Reinier swallowed his reply. He cared for Emiline more than was good for him, but her distant manner earlier was beyond his grasp. Why couldn't he let her go?

Reinier heard Connor's knowing snicker. The Irishman had just made his point. Damn Connor's cleverness, but he was right. If Reinier didn't love her, he could have divorced her without a second thought.

"Irish bastard. Why can't I be mad at you?"

Connor shrugged, let out an exaggerated sigh, and flicked his wrist in an airy gesture. "It's my charming smile. It has a devastating effect on the ladies as well." He winked, drawling, "Gets them every time. . . ."

Bursting into laughter, Reinier elbowed Connor in the ribs. "Conceited fop!"

Bending forward, Connor clutched his chest and mimicked great pain, stumbling with the pretended impact. He might have been about to reply, but his gaze was suddenly drawn to the flower-covered archway leading back to Bougainvilla and his whole demeanor changed. He straightened and the playful smirk on his lips sobered into a polite, welcoming smile.

Reinier followed his gaze and saw Emiline standing there, looking like a goddess in a copper gown lavishly embellished with silver. She wore her hair down, just as he'd asked.

But by the way she held her back so perfectly straight and her hands balled into fists at her sides, there was no mistaking that this was his wife as he knew her, the veritable epitome of cold perfection.

Reinier went to the small fountain where a fat little cupid spit water. Washing his hands in jerky motions, he splashed more water around than was necessary but didn't notice until Connor cleared his throat loudly by his side, wiping a few drops off his shirt deliberately.

When Connor had cleaned up as well, Reinier handed him the linen towel in silence. Looking toward the manor, he saw that his wife was no longer on the lawn. They were late for dinner, he assumed, and she'd come looking. He waited for Connor and they walked back to the house to freshen up and change as quickly as they could.

On entering the dining room, Emiline stood by the table with her eyes down. Her surprising compliancy upset Reinier even more. She acted the humble, demure hostess too perfectly for it to be genuine, which raised his suspicions anew.

Connor's barely audible sigh disrupted the emotionally charged silence. The Irishman walked toward her and bowed over her hand. "Madame, you look splendid if I may say so."

He waved his hand, an exuberant, inviting gesture for Reinier to have a closer look himself, which he ignored. "You are aware that your lady is the most beautiful woman on either side of the ocean?"

Snorting, Reinier rolled his eyes. "Appearances are deceiving, especially in this case, believe me." Staring down his nose at her, his tone was deliberately cool. "I think it's time to apologize to Connor."

With a smile that didn't reach her eyes—or the corners of her mouth, for that matter—Emiline bowed gracefully in turn. "Please forgive my contemptible behavior earlier, Monsieur O'Driscoll."

Of course she'd given the perfect apology. Anything else would have been beneath her. Connor seemed happily unaware of all that and flicked his wrist as if to say he thought nothing of it.

The next moment, Justine's forceful stride interrupted them. With her gaze fixated on Emiline, she announced, "Dinner is served."

Reinier's reaction to Emiline hiding behind the mask of the ideal wife after what they'd shared was fiercer than ever before. He was furious; he wanted to hiss and spit his contempt but thought better of it. If she could uphold her detached façade, then so could he. He just went around the table to sit down, his eyes flicking to his wife every once in a while, watchful to catch any sign of when or if that façade might crack.

Connor took his seat as well, but Emiline remained standing. "May I sit down with you, messieurs?"

"No," Reinier answered quickly, his eyes narrowing on her. "Kindly stay where you are in case we require anything." The corner of his lip twitched into a devious smile at the unspeakable, vicious satisfaction he felt at the moment. Not even Connor's condemning glare could taint his joy.

"Really, Reinier. Come now." His words were full of reproach. "The lady was unwell earlier. You should take more care with something so precious." Connor stood and walked to Emiline, offering his arm for her to accompany him to the table. "Come, madame, and sit close to me."

Emiline took his hand, her eyes widening for a moment, before a devious glitter highlighted them. She slung her arm around Connor's and, with her other hand on his upper arm, leaned into him a little more than was proper.

"Thank you, Monsieur O'Driscoll," she breathed. "You're too kind." Her sideward glance to Reinier didn't go unnoticed.

Laughing, Connor shook his head as he righted her seat. "Don't call me that, please. If you say that name, I believe my brother is standing right behind me." Connor gave a theatrical shudder and leaned closer. "It's Connor only for you, milady."

He gave Emiline his best "devastatingly charming" smile, as he'd called it. Reinier was anything but amused. He supposed he might find the whole situation hilarious if this weren't his wife and his best friend. But right now Reinier found it all rather alarming, especially when Emiline leaned in closer to Connor, her chin resting on her hand with her elbow braced on the table.

"Your older brother?" she asked, her voice low and slightly husky.

Good Lord! Was she flirting? Reinier staked his conch as if it were still alive and not just merrily swimming in lime juice and chilies.

An exaggerated sigh preceded Connor's reply. "My younger brother, unfortunately. We were told that he was born two minutes after me."

Reinier watched in growing aggravation as Connor reached for Emiline's plate and served her some of the snapper with onions and peppers. Reinier's dinner tasted very bitter all of a sudden.

"Upon my father's death he assumed his place chiding my waywardness," Connor continued, helping himself to some snapper as well.

"Your wayward . . . ?" Emiline asked, prodding him to elaborate.

"Yes," Connor nodded. "Preferring the sea to running one or more of the warehouses and"—he made a circular gesture with the knife he held to emphasize a vague description of his "waywardness"—"all that."

"And all that . . . wildness, I presume?"

Connor seemed a little jolted at that. Reinier was quite astonished himself.

Again, she laughed. "I may be secluded on this island, but I'm not completely shut off from the world here. Sailors tend to . . . tattle."

"Ah." Connor's eyes flicked to Reinier briefly. "I see."

"It's a pity we haven't met all those times your ship was anchored here. You could have called on me at least once." She pouted her lips slightly, silently chiding Connor.

Reinier had never seen her like this. Was this coquettish behavior something all women were born with? Reinier wondered. Was this the way she behaved with all the guests she entertained? Did she entertain a lot of male guests? Somehow his appetite was dwindling.

"A pity I never called, indeed," Connor concurred. "It seems the occasion never arose."

Reinier snorted with contempt. Connor always rose, quite quickly actually, when the situation called for it. . . .

"So, Connor, you have a younger brother—a twin?" Emiline continued, ignoring Reinier's slip.

"Yes?"

"Is he as good-looking as you?" She batted her flirtatious lashes.

Putting his fork aside, Connor placed his hand over his heart and bowed. "Milady, you are too kind. We do look very much alike, although Kier wears his hair much longer. Unfashionably so, I'm afraid. Once or twice we have been told that his eyes were brighter. In general, he's a bore—although he wasn't always like that. But now you wouldn't like him at all."

"No?"

"No." Connor shook his head to emphasize his point. "He is too serious. He wouldn't match your spirit or your playfulness, believe me." He winked.

That was quite enough. Their banter had used up all the patience Reinier had left, which after this afternoon hadn't been much to begin with. He pushed his plate away and leaned back in his chair, his eyes narrowing on both of them. "When you two are finished, I'd appreciate it—" Turning his anger fully on Emiline, he continued, "If you could get me some more wine."

"Of course. I'd be delighted to." She rose and passed Reinier without so much as a sideward glance. Who on earth did she think she was?

Just when she bent over his glass to refill it, Reinier was slowly losing his inner struggle not to let his ire show. He did his best to hold on to his outward detachment with everything he had, but when she stood and stared at him as if daring him with eyes void of any emotion, he felt his fury snap.

"The perfect hostess. The perfect wife," Reinier drawled. Reaching for her bodice, he pulled it down with one quick motion. Her eyes, suddenly wide as a doe's, conveyed her shock for just the fraction of a second.

Taking his time, Reinier exposed her breasts one after the other. When he was finished, Reinier took a deep breath and let it out with relief. "There now. That's much better. Now you're not quite so perfect anymore."

She pressed her lips together tightly. Despite that, Reinier saw nothing in her demeanor that betrayed any reaction except for a faint blush on her cheeks for the blink of an eye. His frustration knew no bounds. How far did he have to go to see her mask of indifference crack?

Emiline set the decanter down with a soft thump and attempted to cover herself, but Reinier stayed her hand. "No, leave it. I do believe you're even more perfect now, Lily."

Slowly and reverently, he caressed her breasts lightly, pinching one until her nipple puckered and stood invitingly; then he teased her other breast, rubbing the tip lightly and tweaking it in tiny, playful motions until that nipple popped up too. He tore his attention away from her breasts until his eyes met hers.

"They really are wonderful." He even surprised himself with how cold he'd delivered the line. "Wouldn't you agree, Connor?"

It was three heartbeats until Reinier finally heard Connor's answering rumble. "Yes, very beautiful."

Only then did he lower his gaze once again and let his fingernails graze the satiny skin around her areolas. "The color, the shape, the softness," Reinier uttered, a thin, smoky layer covering his throat as he flicked those hard peaks. "The way the tips perk up so easily . . ."

This time Connor didn't hesitate to affirm Reinier's observation. "Extraordinary, truly."

Something changed in Reinier. Gone was the hissing, venomous growl in his head. Instead, a low, purring sound filled his mind and spread through his whole body.

"You chose the perfect dress tonight, Lily, wrapping them in bows like the gifts they are." His arm went around her waist and Reinier pulled her closer to him. His one hand grabbed his freshly filled glass of wine, while the other smoothed down her body, cupping her cheeks through her skirts. He took a deep sip of wine into his mouth. Then his lips closed around one nipple. He suckled her while savoring the wine, and when he finally swallowed, her tip stretched until he felt her shudder in his arms. Reinier repeated the same action with her other breast, only this time he let his tongue snake out for a final taste before he loosened his grip on her.

"Delightful. Come, sit between us and we'll feed you," he offered, patting her bottom.

From the corner of his eye he watched Connor get up from his seat and position the empty chair between them. Reinier guided her to it and when she sat, he reached for a piece of the conch in lime juice on his plate and fed her from his fingers. She only hesitated for a brief moment before licking his fingers clean with a few strokes of her tongue.

Connor cut some of the snapper on his plate into tiny pieces and, piling it on a spoon, offered it to Emiline. "That snapper is wonderful." He brought the spoon even closer to her lips. An encouraging smile from him and a gentle nudge on her lower lip made her open for the morsel he presented.

Reinier pulled the dinner plate with the curried cabrito closer to him. It was accented with hearts of palm and callaloo artistically strewn around it. He took a small piece of the young goat meat and put it between Emiline's teeth, then, closing his lips over it, he sampled it, placing a soft kiss on her lips in the end. He repeated the action, only this time he didn't take it.

"Connor, taste the cabrito. That is the best I've ever had."

Slowly, Connor leaned close, and with his eyes not leaving hers until the last second, he closed his lips over the morsel. Reinier smiled when he watched Connor's gentle lips working over Emiline's, saw him bite just a tiny part off the cabrito, and only when she accepted his lips on hers did he sample the rest.

By now her chest was heaving so fast it drew Reinier's attention. Peering over the table, his gaze fell on the dish that held the plantain gratin. Checking that it wasn't too hot, he took a spoonful and dropped a dollop on each of her breasts. It crept down the peaks inch by inch. "Here"—Reinier turned to Connor—"taste this. I'm sure it's to die for."

Both heads lowered to her at exactly the same time. Reinier and Connor licked and laved the gratin off her slowly.

He heard Connor's approving hum. "It is superb."

"How about dessert now?" Reinier asked, raising an eyebrow in question at Connor.

"That would be absolutely wonderful."

"We'll move to the study," Reinier declared. "Why don't you serve dessert there, Lily? I'm sure you can attend us even better in a more . . . intimate setting."

15

Emiline tried to clear the shock from her voice, but her automatic "of course" still came out as a half whisper, half croak. She sent an irritated glare Reinier's way when they left. Once she was alone, though, she let her mask fall completely. Had her husband really just flippantly exposed her, touched her in front of Connor, and even allowed another man to use her chest as if it were a dinner plate?

She rose quickly while righting her bodice, then moved to the sideboard to prepare dessert. Her brain refused to process the last hour, so she was happy to have something to busy herself with.

Her mind reeled and her hands began to shake. Emiline wasn't sure if she shook with ire or shame, disappointment or resignation, or—God forbid—arousal . . . or maybe all of it rolled into one horrible, unwanted emotion. She forced herself to resist the urge to fling everything on the cabinet to the floor. Taking several deep breaths, she tried her best to compose herself.

Reinier would not see that he had shaken her resolve. He

would never have the pleasure of knowing just how shattered she felt.

She placed a stack of plates, forks, spiced ginger cake, and rum sauce on a silver tray but suddenly froze. Reinier had moved them into a smaller room, one where he could shut the door and they wouldn't be disturbed.

And what would happen then?

Emiline willed her fingers to still, took the tray, and walked toward the study. When she opened the door, the loaded silence wafted toward her. The chandelier illuminated the room, making hulky shadows dance in the corners. Reinier was sitting in one of the two wing chairs, staring up at her without blinking.

Pursing her lips, she moved to the table with great deliberation, her head high, her shoulders squared. She set out the plates and served the cake on the small table between the two chairs but remained standing by the table perfectly still like a statue, unsure of what would happen next.

Out of the corner of her eye, she saw Connor was seated in the chair facing her husband. Strangely, the image of light-hearted pleasantry was gone from his features and was replaced by a blank mask. Presentiment had a cool shudder run down her spine.

Emiline turned when Reinier cleared his throat. He moistened his lips with a small flick of his tongue and motioned her to him. She wasn't surprised in the least when he had her sit on the rug he'd placed by his feet, once again exposing her breasts as if her dishabille was the most natural thing on earth. She knew she shouldn't allow him to touch her at all, but she'd agreed to the damned bargain. If only she'd known.

Emiline bit the inside of her cheek, her fingers crossed and tightly entwined on her lap. Whatever the case, she vowed to endure it with her head held high.

Reinier reached for his plate. "Ahh. Ginger sponge cake. Don't you just love the aroma of ginger?"

At his mention of ginger, Emiline went cold. She'd thought herself so clever earlier when she'd asked Cook to make something with ginger, hoping to remind her loving husband of their day. How life could change in the blink of an eye. Now all she wanted was to forget the pleasures of the afternoon, and she certainly didn't want them to be spoken of in public.

"Wonderfully unique," Connor replied. "I've been told that in Asia they make soup of it." His words gave Emiline hope that the conversation would take a different turn. She relaxed a tiny bit, unclenching her fingers a little.

"They do?" Reinier seemed fascinated by the fact.

"Yes, but mostly they use the root to add flavor to seafood I've heard. A fresh ginger root is the best. It's sweet and yet it burns you alive, and even if you think you can't take any more, you wouldn't want to miss those contradictory sensations brought on by it."

Her heart sped up its rhythm. What a very astute description.

"Ginger is definitely very versatile. Wouldn't you agree, Lily?"

A gentleman didn't tell—but surely Reinier would. Damning Reinier for asking, Emiline refused to respond.

"So you showed your wife the sweetest use of all, I take it?"

"I did. This afternoon, in fact."

"Oh?" Connor uncrossed his legs, leaning toward her. Emiline's eyes widened a fraction. "And how did you like it?"

That impudent scoundrel! Damn them both to hell, Emiline thought, still not speaking.

"Ah." Reinier flicked his wrist. "She loved it. Came so hard and so many times I lost count."

With a smile that didn't quite reach his eyes, Connor turned back to her husband. "I'm sure she did. How did you apply it?"

Reinier's snicker was downright brazen. "Well, there aren't that many ways—"

"No, I mean, did you use the whip with it?"

"No." Reinier shook his head. "The tack room was too far away for that."

Connor let out a theatrical sigh. "I know you prefer the riding crop, but I still think that ginger with the cat is the best combination."

"You and your cat-o'-nine-tails." Reinier laughed low at Connor's feigned melancholy. Emiline fumed at the affection in it.

"It's not just a personal preference, Reinier. It's in the woman's best interest as well. Instead of one mark per stroke, you get so many softer marks. And if you're very careful on the inside of the thighs—provided you conditioned her thoroughly to enjoy it beforehand—you get very much the same result as you did this afternoon. She will crest again and again with each blow, and her pussy is then so drenched the juices will run down her thighs."

Closing her eyes, Emiline wished herself far away. The vivid pictures Connor's words provoked made the tips of her breasts sizzle and tingle all of a sudden; tight threads of arousal ran to the hammering pulse between her legs. Her breath pitched, and instantly her eyes flew open to vanquish those images and the mindless heat they brought.

With a broad grin, Connor added, "When the ginger's effect has diminished, you can take her as hard as you want, as often as you want, where you want—and she will still cry and beg for more."

"Very interesting, Connor." Reinier's hand unexpectedly began to caress Emiline's hair and she stiffened. Leaning in, his breath tickled the sensitized skin right below her earlobe. "Lily, tell me. Are you aroused by our conversation?"

Emiline only offered an infinitesimal shake of her head telling him no.

"Come now. Admit it." She could feel that knowing, devious smile in his voice. "You have a penchant for the crop. Just thinking of it makes you delirious with desire."

Her lips thinned and she held her breath. It was true, Emiline had felt every word they'd said pulsing through her, but she hated them for speaking of it so bluntly. She despised herself even more for enjoying it as much as she did.

Was there some way to stop her body's response? She didn't want to feel what she did. Why couldn't she stop it? He wasn't worth it.

"Show him." Emiline had to struggle not to jump at Reinier's firm command.

She hesitated. She knew she should stand and slap the arrogance from his face and walk out. She should go and leave them to their ... "friendship." But she'd be damned if she let him force her to end the bargain. Emiline would show him—show them both that there was nothing she wouldn't do to be rid of him for good.

Standing, her eyes locked with Connor's. There was a startling warmth in the entreating gaze he gave her that helped her muster the last bit of courage she needed to lift her skirts for him.

"Is she moist, Connor?"

He glanced down for only a small moment. "I don't know. I think she may be."

"Spread your legs a bit more, Lily, so Connor can see you better." Reinier's voice sounded tight with barely leashed emotion.

Emiline took two steps closer to Connor. At his supportive

nod, she felt emboldened enough to place one foot on the arm of Connor's chair, tilting her hips forward slightly.

"Can you see it now?"

Lowering his gaze to linger for a bit longer this time, Connor's face went blank—as if he was careful not to show any emotion. But then the moment was gone, and in the next instant his dark blue eyes met hers in an encouraging way yet again. "She's beautiful. And glistening."

"Have a go at those lovely breasts, then. She's particularly sensitive there."

Connor obliged, leaning forward and stretching his body. At first he touched her with the tips of his fingers only. He played over her soft skin in a light, gentle caress, teasing it to goose bumps; then his thumb brushed against the sensitive peak of a nipple once. He straightened some more until his lips reached the puckered tip of her other breast.

His mouth was warm with rum, circling around it with deliberate kisses. Connor took her nipple between his teeth and his lips closed around her areola. His hand was kneading her other breast, faster and harder just when his teeth nipped her.

Emiline felt her eyelids lower at the sting. He'd found the perfect balance of pleasure and ache. A quiver trembled through her. Connor's teeth now scraped the protruding nipple and Emiline almost stumbled, her hands fisting into her skirts.

"Is she wetter now, do you think?" Reinier's question was clipped and tense.

"Mhh," Connor let out a teasing hum in reply, all the while continuing to play with her breasts lazily. "Perhaps."

"You're not sure? Touch her, then."

Connor's eyes flicked up to hers with concern. He, too, must have noticed the low growl in Reinier's words. His hand left her breast and traveled down her body until he reached the junction of her thighs. Fingers caressing her moist labia, Connor played over her, found her entrance, and with agonizing slowness thrust into her. Emiline's breath pitched.

His mouth ceased its caress on her breast and, eyes still locked on hers, he croaked, "She's deliciously creamy, Reinier."

"Good. Now come here, Lily."

Both relieved and wary, Emiline placed her foot back on the floor. Connor's supporting grip on her waist helped her not to sway. She straightened but didn't release her skirts from her clenched fists. Then she turned to Reinier as he'd asked her.

As soon as she was within his grasp, he reached out and thrust two fingers into her, hooking them to drag her closer to him. Instantly, her secret muscles gripped him in a tight embrace. That inexplicable thrill she always experienced when he touched her had her pulsing core meet his hand with a thunderous primal rhythm.

She gave up on a reasonable explanation for her body's susceptibility to his touch and just let herself be drawn into the eroticism of the moment. Anxiously, Emiline settled onto his lap, her legs spread wide. His gaze was focused exclusively on her. She wasn't afraid of that dark, calculating glitter in his gaze; she wasn't even concerned about what must have shown in her eyes. She was beyond worrying now.

Reinier's arm wrapped around her waist to hold her captive. His lips touched hers, brushed against them once just before he nipped her lower lip. Tongue flicking over the tiny soreness, he then closed his mouth fully over hers. Arching her back in his embrace, he punished her with hard, domineering kisses. Her arms drifted around his shoulders.

The two fingers seated in her slid in and out. Ruthless in his attempt to arouse her more, he opened them and began rotating his hand. He concentrated on her sensitive peak, rubbing and stroking it with his thumb.

The hot, pulsing fire he created within her had her body

quake with shivers down her spine. Connor's caress had been pleasant, but Reinier's lips and tongue and fingers worked their magic on her like only he knew how.

Damn the bastard.

"Ahh. Good girl." His voice was nothing but a hoarse croak when he dipped his head to nuzzle the underside of her jaw. "You like that, don't you? You like it when I touch you. Here . . ." His tongue licked roughly along her neck. "And here . . ." he whispered just before his teeth bit lightly into her galloping pulse.

Reinier rolled and pinched her nipple with his free hand. Hunger and desire rode over her in a wave high enough to drown in.

"And most definitely here . . ." He chuckled, hooking his fingers inside her once again, causing her muscles there to jump with unfulfilled longing.

Emiline tried hard to ban the low sounds of bliss from her lips, but her body's violent response and the fresh gush of moistness pooling out of her must have told Reinier everything.

"Now you're dripping." His hiss was cunning and self-assured, his eyes dilated, scintillating in hues of gold and bright green. "Like a wanton."

His wanton. He hadn't said it, but Emiline understood.

The shame of it!

Bringing his hand up, he painted her moistness over her breasts, licking them clean while his questing fingers pressed into her once again. Thankfully, his lips sealed her mouth before he could kiss his name off her lips.

He stroked her in delicate, deft thrusts. Her reason dissolved entirely in the frenzy of her arousal. Her hands gripped his shoulders, touched and scraped the fabric, craving the feel of his skin instead. Emiline whimpered. Rapacious passion surged through her veins, numbing her mind. Her instinct begged her to urge him deeper, faster, harder, to bring an end to the bitter-sweet torment.

Reinier stopped suddenly and met her gaze straight on. "Do I make you crazy with lust? Tell me."

At first, Emiline could only gasp for breath through a shaky moan. Then her mind was slapped into wakefulness. She braced her palms against his chest, barring him from moving any farther. Emiline was mortified by her desire for his touch, shamed by her wanton response to his kisses.

"I hate you."

Chuckling, Reinier began stroking her again, his tongue wandering over her neck down to the vee of her breasts. "Doesn't feel like it to me."

Everywhere his mouth touched her, she blazed. Her core pulsed and throbbed with pitiable desire. Through the haze of her desire and the turmoil of her despair, Emiline understood what she would do.

"I hate you for making me do this," she growled at him through clenched teeth.

"What? This?" He thrust one more sensually torturing finger into her core and, helpless to withstand her body's craving, Emiline let out another low moan.

The triumphant undertone in that despicable, confident snicker was the final straw. Emiline drew in a ragged breath and steeled her spine. Her head snapped up and she gave him a level stare, allowing her eyes to gradually fill with every bit of loathing that surged through her. A slight frown formed on his face.

"No, this." She tore herself away from him, stood, and turned. Walking deliberately toward Connor, she placed her hands on his knees to spread his legs farther apart. She sank to the floor and began working the buttons of his breeches. In the blink of an eye his shaft was free of its confines and her fingers trailed over him.

She'd spent so long feeling jealous of their friendship. Now it was Reinier's turn to be the one left out. Time to show him she didn't need him, that any man would do just as well—even one she disliked.

Emiline took her time, determined to learn every inch of Connor's member. He was darker and thicker and not quite as long as Reinier, but his skin was just as soft and warm in her hand when she wrapped it around the base. His scent was pleasant and she licked along the head first, savoring the poignancy of the slightly salty tang under her tongue.

Every touch of her fingers, her lips, and her tongue had Connor's breath change, and each gentle gasp from his lips flashed through her mind with a blaze of iniquitous enjoyment in its wake.

His body rose to her suckling lips. He gasped when she ran her tongue from base to tip several times, hissed when she engulfed just the tip, her tongue circling it with rapid flicks. Connor hummed a low moan when she took him deep and sucked hard; he held his breath when she opened her mouth and laved him with her tongue and teeth. Looking up, she saw his lids lowered over dilated eyes.

Then she dared a glance at Reinier. His jaw was set tight and his eyes narrowed at her, a dangerous fire burning in them. When his gaze moved higher, she knew he witnessed Connor's bliss and the pleasure he took in her talented mouth.

Oh yes, any man would do.

Feeling like she'd made her point, she put all her concentration into her task—suckling, laving, licking Connor like Reinier had once taught her.

She never saw Reinier move, but just as her mouth loosened so that only her tongue could flick the small slit on the tip, she suddenly sensed him behind her. In one swift, rough motion, his arm went around her waist to position her higher on her knees. The next instant she heard a rip in the precious fabric of her beautiful skirts. The cooling air of the room whispered over her backside.

He thrust into her, stretched and filled her with more force that she'd ever felt.

Emiline moaned. Her mind was ravaged by desire for him and only him, her blood boiling, the lust reeling and hissing like a venomous snake in her veins. Her hands gripped Connor's thighs, blindly searching for stability under Reinier's rough and hard thrusts. She knew she'd be lost in no time as she was pushed closer and closer toward something she wasn't even sure she wanted.

Connor's commanding hands closed around her head, taking her away from her task, but Emiline barely noticed. As soon as his hard length was freed from her lips, Connor nudged her away from him, stood, and moved her hands to the arms of the chair. He was leaving them, she thought, but she was in no condition to wonder about that now. Her arms moved farther into the chair, stretching her upper body completely as she opened herself wider for Reinier's assault.

His hips jolted her, his violent strokes hard and ruthless. He drove into her again and again with a ferocity unseen before. His fingers dug into her cheeks, spreading her flesh even more. Each stroke was fiercer than the last; each one felt like it would tear her apart.

Emiline didn't care. She wanted it, needed it. Her wrath was out of control, out of boundaries. She wasn't afraid of his rage; she had her own and it fed from his. She was burning—bright and strong, with fury, with lust, and with despair as well.

Her closed eyelashes were dotted with moisture. All her frustration, all her rage flowed into her answering thrusts. She swayed back, taking all of him in, impatient to feel him, hating herself for that irrepressible craving. She detested and reveled in their rough, driving passion.

When her orgasm hit, Emiline threw her head back with a mindless scream. It shocked her with its intensity, ripped through her like a violent torrent, and crested in a blinding explosion blending with Reinier's hoarse, climactic bellow.

In the ensuing stillness, she felt his hot seed dripping down her backside just like the silent tears that rolled down her cheeks.

Her shame, will, and reason were all hushed.

That disgraceful passion, that humiliating affection she felt for him . . . it would never stop, no matter what. No matter if she had her divorce—which she would. No matter how long he stayed away—which she hoped would be forever.

She hated him so much; hated him because she could never be free of him.

She was doomed.

She was his.

16

Emiline's mind hadn't let her find more than a fitful slumber. Walking through the harbor now, she felt numb. She scarcely remembered Justine waking her or when she'd gotten dressed. She couldn't even remember if she'd eaten that morning. She only knew she needed to get away, and there was only one place she could think to go. It was the one place where she might be able to sort through it all, where she could be alone with her thoughts and those haunting images that taunted her.

The island was still asleep but gradually coming awake with birds lazily twittering their morning prayer, accompanied by the soft hymn of the gentle waves washing against the pilings of Ronde's harbor. Emiline's gaze was drawn to the mesmerizing sight of the golden sun slowly rising from where the sea met the sky.

It seemed as if she were the only person alive. Only the rhythmical cracking sound of the *Sirene*'s and the *Coraal*'s hulls bid her a good morrow. The *Sea Gull* was anchored farther away simply because Ronde's harbor was a small one.

Sighing, she kicked a pebble out of her way before she stumbled over it. Instead of the soft sound of the pebble tumbling over the planks as she expected, the sound of splintering wood nearly frightened her out of her skin. The deep timbre of a man's voice soon followed.

"Why do I feel so awful? Dammit!"

Another crack sounded, followed by a frustrated growl. Suddenly, Emiline saw Connor's black hair flash into sight, then vanish behind a crate again.

"I didn't even come. Damn it all to hell and back! I didn't cheat on her. I didn't!"

Emiline's eyes widened as an almost empty flask came flying toward her, rotating in the air and spilling its contents merrily all over the place. If she hadn't stepped aside in time, it would have hit her and not shattered next to her on the wharf, drenching the wooden planks. By the smell of it, it was some of her finest rum.

Another loud curse came from Connor's direction. Thank goodness being mistress of the island had gotten her used to sailors and their excessive and expressive swearing, or Emiline's ears might have fallen off.

Looking around, she debated what to do. Emiline had her own problems and she should leave him to his. The sound of splintering wood caught her attention and she turned to see Connor punching an empty, defenseless crate.

"There's no such thing as cheating on a . . . a . . . wh—"— Connor stepped from behind the crates and Emiline saw him gape at her just like she goggled at him—"*hóigh* is what I meant to say." He bowed awkwardly, slightly swaying as his head was almost down to his knees.

"Connor?" Emiline gasped. He'd shed his coat. The shirt he wore was torn in some places, streaked with dirty smudges in others, and halfway untucked. The collar was partly ripped open.

232

His jet-black hair wasn't shiny as silk like it had been the evening before and it stood awkwardly in places, waving wildly, part in, part out of the braid. "Dear Lord, what's happened to you?"

When he straightened again, he lost his balance and his shoulders hit the man-high stack of wooden crates behind him just before the back of his head connected with an evil thump. He gave up struggling and let his body just slide down the crates that had escaped his wrath until he was sprawled on the dock.

"Nothing," Connor mumbled, shaking his head to emphasize his point while rubbing the back of his neck.

Emiline approached him with caution. She stood over him, giving him an austere scowl. "Are you drunk?"

His laugh was filled with despair when he examined the small cuts on his knuckles. "Wish I were. I only had a glass of your excellent rum. A glass or two maybe. No more." His eyes flicked around; he seemed to have difficulty focusing. "Wouldn't want to fall into one of my dark moods. Not here, anyway."

His murmur was probably not meant to be heard. "Dark mood?"

All of a sudden, more images of the previous evening sprang up and she caught her breath. "It . . . it isn't because . . . I mean . . . it doesn't have anything to do with—"

"No, no, milady." Connor's face puckered and he waved her concerns off as negligible.

She exhaled with relief. Heedless to the damage to her dress, Emiline plopped down onto the dock beside him. Leaning forward, she placed a soothing hand on his shoulder. "Connor, I do believe that after last night you have every right to call me by my given name."

His shoulders slumped. When he looked up at her, his eyes were bloodshot with dark circles under them. He really did look awful. Had he slept at all? The expression on his face was enormously gloomy. His misery was almost palpable.

He sighed. "Emiline, you do not want to burden yourself with my poor state of mind, believe me."

"Oh, you have no idea about the burden on my mind, so by all means, distract me with yours."

With a slight hesitation, Connor stared at her as if he was making up his mind. "Very well, then. I'm cursed."

Emiline gave him a look that was more curious than anything else. "Cursed, you say?"

"Yes," Connor nodded, a doleful expression on his face. "I'm bewitched by an Irish goddess with emerald eyes and flaming hair."

Emiline suppressed the understanding smile she felt. Love could, indeed, feel very much like a curse when it took you unawares. Poor Connor. He wasn't aware that he'd fallen in love.

To a certain extent, the two of them were in the same boat. It felt good to push her own deep concerns aside for the moment.

"Do you love this woman?"

Again, Connor shook his head. "That's not the point—"

Emiline snorted with a cheerless laugh hinting at her heartbroken state of mind. "It's the only thing that really matters. Unfortunately, love is the only thing that can make us utterly miserable or entirely happy."

She held her breath. Hopefully, he was still too drunk to see how closely her statement hit home.

His mouth twitched into the parody of a smile. "And lust is but a fleeting moment. Fickle passion!"

Shaking her head, Emiline contradicted, "Not if love's got her hands in it."

Something akin to understanding flittered over his face, making his deep blue eyes glitter for an instant. She asked herself if he was really as drunk as she'd assumed at first. His gaze was too sober, too intense to mistake it for a drunkard's delirium.

"Like you love Reinier?" Connor cocked his head.

Emiline looked down, crossing the fingers on her lap.

"Did he ever tell you how we met?"

She glanced up just long enough to harrumph as a sign Reinier hadn't.

"In a way, this is all my fault," Connor started out with an apologetic shrug. "You see, I found him in a tavern in St. George's. He was in bad shape and his mood was even worse. When I'd watched him sipping at his watered-down ale for an hour, staring into nothing but his tumbler and ignoring the rest of the world, I sat down next to him and poured him a glass of rum."

He shrugged, letting his head fall back against the crate, and stared up into the sky with a distant look in his eyes. "I knew he'd been there for the first time. His skin was pale, like white linen. Nobody who'd been at sea for long and in the Caribbean for longer would have had that light coloring. With his complexion, he would have suffered a sunburn at least."

Connor chuckled and Emiline smiled with him. She'd never heard that part of their story and strangely, she didn't mind hearing it. He'd known Reinier longer—and better—than Emiline had. Ever would, she mentally corrected herself.

Looking straight into her eyes now, Connor continued, "I insisted he have a taste of the finest rum in all the Caribbean. It came, I told him, from a tiny island just north of there, owned by a wealthy African pirate who'd bought the whole bloody island with its stunning villa and lush green hills for his lovely French wife.

"He was so intrigued by that story that as soon as he got the chance, he came here. To a ball. Where he met you."

What did he mean? Did he insinuate if it weren't for her, they'd still be happily whoring around the Seven Seas? Or was this his way to say he felt responsible for the way things had turned out and what she was going through right now? It would entail that Connor had more of a conscience than she gave him credit for.

On seeing the sadness tainting his expression, it occurred to her that perhaps Connor wasn't the total villain she'd made him out to be.

Leaning his head to the side, his gaze felt very much as if he was reading her like an open book. "You cannot understand him unless you comprehend how he came to be that way. It's hard to love him, Emiline. The call of the sea will always tear at him."

Caught unawares, she felt defensive and didn't try to hide the frustration. "What is it about the bloody ocean that draws men like cattle to hay?"

Connor's smile was indulgent. "It not about the sea itself. It's about freedom, Emiline. And for Reinier, part of that freedom is to love on his own terms."

Emiline crossed her arms and glanced sideways at the Irishman. To her, love was feeling some responsibility for the other person, and that meant you weren't free to have everything on your own terms. You had someone else's needs to consider. There had been times in the last few days when she felt they were doing just that. But if there was always something or someone that he wanted more . . .

Connor interrupted her rambling thoughts. "Give him something that he feels stronger about than his most precious freedom, and his heart and mind will follow."

He of all people offered her advice on how to love Reinier? That was way too hard to believe. And how could she ever trust that there wouldn't come a day when Reinier's feelings changed like they had before and he'd be gone again?

No, she couldn't take that chance. She'd had divorce papers drawn up. There was no turning back. Not at this point. "That's a challenge I'm not sure I'm prepared for, Connor."

Shrugging, he smiled secretively. "Maybe. But it would be worth it in the end. Don't you think?"

Frankly, her mind was too overloaded with everything that

had happened since Reinier's return. This new bit of information only added to her confusion.

Did she really have the means to make things right, to have a happy marriage with Reinier?

A horse's whinny made her look up, and she followed Connor's gaze to see her mare galloping happily in the direction of the fields. John, the groom, followed her, swinging some rope frantically as he ran.

"Hmm." At that contemplative harrumph, Emiline's attention snapped back to Connor. He pursed his lips in thought. "Perhaps you should find another groom." He pointed his hand to the boy chasing the horse, his palm up, stating without words the obvious.

"I know." Emiline let out a grave sigh. "John is a sweet boy, but he has no hand for horses." She'd had that thought once or twice already, but she would have never believed she'd admit it. Funny how easily the words had now tumbled out of her.

"My brother's neighbor breeds horses. The finest horseflesh far and wide. I'll take the liberty of sending you some."

"No, there's no need to—" She waved her hands in protest, but Connor cut her off.

"Please. I insist, Emiline."

Surprisingly agile for his supposed hungover, sleep-deprived state, he scrambled up and held his hand to help her stand also. "Now, if you'll excuse me, I'll try to get some sleep. I must look like the devil incarnate." After an apologetic smile, he bowed over her hand, turned, and walked toward his ship.

Emiline's gaze followed him as he strolled away. She couldn't help but concur. He did look very much like the devil already on his knees but still desperately fighting a goddess's lure. It was no secret what happened to those who got involved with the gods. They always got burned.

* * *

Someone was building a ship inside Reinier's head. The pounding of hammers, the gnarling whine of saws, and the shouting of commands were never ending. Even the willow bark tea he'd choked down with his toast for breakfast had done nothing to stop that awful clamor.

Normally, he prided himself on the amount of spirits he could consume, still have his wits about him through the night, and feel relatively normal in the morning, but the copious amounts of rum it had taken for him to find sleep after the nightmare of the evening before was somewhat ridiculous—even for him. And now there was a booming shipyard in his brain, along with all the same emotions he'd wanted the rum to wash away.

Reinier was furious at them all: at himself for pushing her, at Emiline for driving him to do it, and at Connor for his horrible timing at daring to show up—never mind that Reinier had asked him to. His guilt for all those things made the anger that much sharper.

His frustration and pain grew even worse the longer he searched the manor for his wife and didn't find her. She wasn't anywhere in the house now, and Reinier knew for a fact Connor hadn't spent the night there. He'd seen the lantern light from the captain's stateroom on the *Coraal* glowing toward him like a beacon as he walked the docks, bottle in hand. But its call had held little appeal compared to that of the dark windows to the mistress's suite.

Images of Emiline and Connor together the night before flashed in his mind: Connor's mouth locked on her dark nipple as she moaned, his blissful expression as Emiline's succulent mouth engulfed his cock. The pain in Reinier's chest now made the pounding ache in his head seem like cotton bouncing on fluffy clouds.

What if the light bobbing on the water had been for her?

What if his stupidity and rage had driven them both away from him and to each other?

Reinier was almost crippled by his roaring emotions when he finally found Justine picking lavender in the kitchen garden. "Where the devil is your mistress?"

A small, flat basket hanging on her arm, Justine continued at her task, not even bothering to greet him after his stern, commanding question. "I'm sure I don't know."

"And I am sure you do."

The maid flinched at his obvious temper but stood her ground as she turned to face him, chin high and her free hand on her ample hip. "Why would I tell you?"

Reinier couldn't quite believe what he was hearing. He took a step closer. "I beg your pardon, you overstep."

"I overstep? I overstep? Ha!" Reinier couldn't hide a slight recoil at the volume of her voice. "You overstepped the moment you used that girl to build that silly ship of yours and sail off without even a by-your-leave!"

This conversation was preposterous and the very last thing he needed this horrible morning. The last thread of Reinier's sanity was wearing perilously thin. "Oh, please. I'm sure she barely even noticed I had gone."

Casting the basket off her arm, Justine stepped closer, dangerously waving her cutting shears as she spoke. "Barely noticed? You can't be serious! Don't you have any idea what you did to that poor girl? She sat staring out at that damned harbor for months and months crying herself to sleep at night for a man that will never deserve the heart he stole." She took a deep breath, her nostrils flaring, her hand trembling with the wrathful daggers her words and her eyes spat at him. "Why would I tell you where she is? Huh? So you can rip her poor heart out again and sail away with that blackguard you call a partner to go and do God knows what with every woman in every port between here and the Carolinas?"

Reinier took a step back more out of shear confusion from her words than any threat from the sharp implement she was holding in front of him. "How dare you! Sully my name if you must, but leave Connor out."

Justine glanced at the blades in her hand as if she realized just now what she'd done, tossed them onto the basket of lavender, and gave a low grunt. "How dare I?" She rolled her eyes and, arms akimbo, stomped her foot. "How dare you? Always choosing that reprobate Irishman over your own wife. That poor child never wanted anything but your love, and what do you do? Toss her away as if she were nothing but a fleeting fancy, and give your time and affection to that . . . that . . . scoundrel. You, sir, are the worst kind of villain." Thrusting her chin up, she looked down her nose at him.

Reinier could literally feel the last thread of his temper fraying and then snapping in his head. "Woman! Have the fumes from the distillery soaked your brain? I'm the one whose heart was ripped out. I'm the one that was a prize she could brag to friends about, something to laud over them and check off her list of ingredients for the perfect marriage."

Stepping forward, Reinier loomed over the impertinent maid, beating his chest with his own fist. "She never loved me. It was all about bragging rights to her. I am the one that was lucky to get out with my pride and my soul still intact before she had me so blinded I wouldn't have been able to recognize myself any longer! Thank goodness I did have one true friend to rely on."

Breath heavy, Reinier stood his ground, his eyes daring the maid to rebuke him. She looked as if she was about to do just that, refusing to back away, one hand on her hip and the other with an accusing finger pointed at him. Her mouth stood slightly ajar. Clearly, she was ready to rail at him once more.

But then she stopped and took a deep breath. Her expression changed and she tilted her head in thought. Reinier wasn't sure why, but her sudden change in demeanor worried him even more than her righteous fury.

Letting the air out of her lungs slowly, Justine put her hand down, bent her head, and shook it. When she straightened, there was a look of pity in her eyes.

"Listen to me." Her pleading tone was as evident as the hands she held up, palms out, as if calling for peace. "I know Emiline better than anyone left on this earth, and believe me when I tell you she loved you—loves you still."

Reinier only shook his head in doubt and confusion.

"Although it's hard to believe, girls—and, yes, even ones as beautiful as our Emiline—sometimes greatly doubt themselves when they shouldn't. I'm sure whatever it is you think she might have said to those silly tarts that once called themselves her friends was said out of uncertainty and in the heat of the moment to silence their stupid gossip. That wasn't how she truly felt."

Reinier still didn't speak but gave a slight nod, trying to, wanting to believe her.

Justine took another deep, slightly wheezing breath, and her eyes bore into him. "No matter her mother's nobility, no matter her father's wealth, no matter how much they worked to make her feel loved and included in society, Emiline never completely forgot she wasn't like them, and that some would always think less of her because of the color of her skin."

My God, he thought, covering his eyes more for the light of understanding than the piercing rays of the sun. He'd never seen her that way, never once thought any less of her in any way because of her father's heritage.

Money forgave many things in the Caribbean that couldn't be overlooked in Europe. But he'd never cared about that. He'd always seen her unique parentage as what made her more beautiful and something better, more rare and precious than all the others.

It was hard for him to fathom that she wouldn't see herself that way too. But he did know what it was like to be made to feel inferior. His mother had often told him how low he was compared to his older brother, her one greatest accomplishment. His father barely noticed him at all, much less noticed how his mother treated him. He'd escaped his childhood only to step into a world aboard a trading ship that wasn't much better.

What had he done? He'd made a horrible mistake. He'd projected his own stupid insecurities about himself onto Emiline and had completely misunderstood the situation—her feelings and his own.

Reinier ran his hands through his hair. Eventually, he looked back to Justine with a sad sigh. The look on his face must have conveyed how completely defeated he felt. "I've been a complete fool. Please tell me where she is."

Justine stepped forward and placed a hand on his sleeve. "I saw her walking toward the harbor early this morning. There is a cove off the beach on the other side, just past the palm grove. In the cove there is a short swim through a cave that comes out into a pool with a waterfall. That's where she always goes when she needs to be alone. My bet is that she'll be there."

Reinier placed his other hand over Justine's in thanks and took off, sprinting toward the harbor.

17

The cool spring water, flowing over the flat rock cliff into the shallow end of a small pool, splashed over Emiline's whole body before it found its way through the caves to the sea. She'd always loved that it was so secluded here she could cast off all her clothing, most of which was left safely tucked in an oiled sack inside a hollow palm on the other side of the cave. Emiline had shed her shift as soon as she'd emerged into the pool.

The water felt wonderful as she ran her hands over her face and hair. The crystalline pearls tickled her skin. The loud noise of the crashing water drowned out the outside world. Emiline sighed with bliss. This was her sanctuary. Besides being entranced in one of her favorite poems, there was no place on earth that made her feel better than here.

Until today.

Today, she just wanted to wash it all away. Everything. Her love, her hate, her hurt, her guilt, her confusion.

At first she'd been glad she'd run into Connor on her way here, but in the end it had only added to the disorder in her mind. And now even the solitude and beauty of her private pond couldn't help her.

She loved Reinier even though she hated what he'd done last night. She understood now that she had never stopped loving him, but that didn't really change anything. The fact that she still loved him didn't stop the hurt he'd caused or the pain she felt when she thought of how alone she'd been for so long—or how she'd focused all the blame and all the jealousy at Connor. Even if she could one day believe that Reinier might truly care for her, how could she ever be sure that he wouldn't again choose Connor one day?

To make an oh-so-horrible situation even worse, there was guilt as well. Regret that she'd pushed him so far last night. Remorse that she'd been weak enough to let him goad her to it. But the overwhelming amount of her contrition came from the fact that even through her anger and shock, there was a small part of her that had been aroused at the same time.

And not one bit of all that changed the fact the she wanted a divorce, which Reinier was graciously willing to let her have once the price was paid.

Emiline swatted impotently at the steams of water, wanting to hit something, anything. She'd been in charge of the estate, the one in control and responsible for so long that it was crippling to feel so confused and not knowing which way to turn. Salty tears of frustration mixed with spring water on her cheeks. She couldn't feel them on her skin, but she knew they were there. Wrapping her arms around her shoulders, Emiline hugged herself.

She thought she'd heard her name. It was only a faint moan over the roar of the waterfall. There. She heard it and began to rapidly blink the water from her eyes, straining her ears to hear.

Emiline caught her breath when she saw Reinier standing on a rock at the other end of the pool trying to get her attention.

He cupped his hands around his mouth shouting her name once more, but she still only heard it as little more than a whisper.

For a long moment she didn't move, only stared at him. His feet were bare, his soaking-wet buckskin breeches stuck to his thighs, and his white shirt had become transparent and clung to his chest and shoulders. His golden mane was slicked down to his scalp.

Snapping to her senses, Emiline fumed. For crying out loud, could the man not give her a moment's peace? She jumped back through the fall of water to disappear into the small alcove behind the spray, hoping he'd understand that she didn't want to talk to him.

Good Lord, how long had he been standing there calling to her, watching her? And how on earth had he been able to find her?

She paced, in as much as she could pace in the small, shallow, misty cavern behind the waterfall. The plan was to wait here long enough so he'd go away. But, of course, she had no such luck. She saw a shadow move and a tall shape looming on the other side of the wall of water.

Stepping through, Reinier looked like a river god from ancient mythology. Emiline shivered. With a determined expression, he shook the water from his hair, then slicked it back.

How dare he invade her private place? Emiline turned her back to her intrusive husband, crossing her arms over her chest. "Go away!" she shouted over the din of the crashing water.

"Will you not talk to me?"

"No, you know, I just knew there was going to be trouble the minute I saw Connor at Monsieur Améliore's office. I knew he'd run and tell, and you'd come here to confuse and hurt me again." And make me fall in love with you anew, she added to herself.

"Pardon? Emiline, I can't hear you over the roar."

She felt his hand on her shoulder and she jerked away. "I prefer to be alone. This is my place and I said leave!"

She sensed him taking a step closer to her, but he had enough common sense not to try to touch her again.

"Emiline."

It dawned on her that twice now he'd called her Emiline and not Lily. Was his devilish game over now? Good. She was done with playing games. Maybe he was here to say he'd signed the papers and he was leaving?

"What do you want?" They still needed to shout to be heard, but he was even closer now.

"Turn around and talk to me." A hand touched her back. This time she couldn't make herself move away.

"I'm sorry."

A little confused, Emiline looked over her shoulder but kept her pride. "Too little, too late."

His eyes rounded and it seemed some color left his face, but he just stared blandly at her, hesitating as if he were debating what to do. She turned away again, her chin thrust up in triumph.

"Emiline . . . please." His voice boomed over everything else. She felt the dampness of his shirt pressed to her back now as both his arms wrapped around her waist and his lips were close to her ear. "Just come and sit with me in the sun so I don't have to keep shouting. Listen to what I have to say."

Emiline bent her head, still thinking. As always, he was making everything harder for her. She didn't yet know her own feelings, so how was she to respond to his? Everything was still so painfully raw on the surface.

Hoping he'd go as soon as he'd said his piece, she nodded and let him guide her through the rushing curtain and around the mossy bank to a large flat rock shaded by palms. Her shift, now dry, hung from a branch nearby, and she quickly reached for it and slipped it on, donning it more for emotional armor than for modesty. They were way past modesty between them.

Emiline sat beside him on the warm stone with her knees bent and her feet flat on the rock, looking at him as he played with a piece of palm frond.

"Well?" She was eager to get their conversation over with.

"When we married I might not have been thinking as clearly as I should have been." He was still staring at the palm frond in his hand, playing with it as if testing its weight.

"That much has become quite obvious to everyone by now, Reinier." Emiline pursed her lips and stared him down.

Jerking his shoulders, he twirled his wrist. "Perhaps that wasn't the best way to put it. I'm not quite sure where to start."

Really? That was a first. Biting the inside of her cheek, Emiline tried to swallow her sarcasm. She failed. "The charming Dutchman at a loss for words? That's highly unusual."

"You know not everyone has led the sheltered life you have, darling."

"Do tell."

Reinier tossed the palm branch into the pool with more vigor than was remotely necessary. It was apparent he was getting frustrated at both his own inelegance and her impatience. Since he seemed to be here to get everything out in the open, she decided to ask him something she always wanted to know. Something that might be easier for him because it didn't have anything to do with the issue at hand. "Tell me about your scar. I know it happened when you were second-in-command of a merchant ship, but you never told me anything beyond that."

"It's not a pretty story."

Good Lord, this wasn't going anywhere. "I wouldn't suspect so. It's not a pretty scar, either." To be honest, that was a blatant lie. That scar was what elevated his outward flawless-ness to perfection. What a pity it wasn't his scar that was so un-sightly, but rather his character. "I still want to know."

Biting his lower lip, Reinier gave her a long, contemplating stare. Finally, he seemed to back down. "If you insist."

He turned and blinked up through the lush canopy of palm trees into the sun. Emiline frowned. Was he afraid he could hurt her delicate senses? For heaven's sake, she was the daughter of a pirate!

"It was very clear from the beginning that the private com-mission my parents secured for me wasn't going to be an easy one. Not that I ever had any illusions that it would be, but Cap-tain Asmussen was an autocratic man. His ship did a good busi-ness and he made good money, but his crew paid a high price. Disciplined perfection doesn't even begin to describe what he expected from his crew, and he rarely received it, at least in his eyes. When I assumed my place as chief mate, I took my duties seriously. To me, that included looking out for the crew as well. So, over time, the captain and I came to an understanding: I'd do my work and most of his, then let him take all the credit. In exchange, I'd take the brunt of his anger for the whole crew."

Emiline had never really understood what Reinier's life had been like before they married. Connor had hinted at something like that earlier. . . . Reinier had such natural charm. He could make people believe that life for him was always dazzling par-ties and fabulous adventures—but now she understood that it wasn't. "So the scar came from him, your captain?"

At first Emiline thought he hadn't heard her, but with a slow nod, Reinier conceded. "Yes, one night we had almost made it into Grenada before a bad storm hit. Almost, but not quite. During the wind and rain, lashing waves crashed on deck and rattled the *Galatea* as if trying to swallow the ship whole. During all the confusion that ensued, the cargo wasn't anchored down properly. We lost a good bit due to the damage. It was blamed on the newest deckhand, a skinny, jumpy lad that couldn't have been more than thirteen. Asmussen was livid and he got to him before I knew what was happening. When I saw the boy strapped to the mast, I stepped into the path of the whip before it could strike. I was only in my shirtsleeves and much closer to the whip than the boy was, so it was worse than a normal lashing would have been. There weren't the means to treat the wound properly. I regarded it as a souvenir when I left the ship soon after."

Reinier's lips twitched in a half smile. Blinking, he bowed his head and stared at his toes. His whole body seemed to convey that the tale was told.

It occurred to Emiline that after all this time they were finally having an open conversation without the usual jests or evasiveness. "Why did you not tell me this when we married? I was—am your wife. Why did I get cavalier jokes about some boyhood adventure gone wrong instead of the truth?"

Reinier shrugged, looking into the quiet pool. "Because I wasn't looking for your sympathies and I was sure you'd never want to hear it."

"What do you mean?"

"I didn't think there was a place for such harsh realities in your charmingly innocent life."

"How can you say that?" Squaring her shoulders, Emiline turned away from him. "I've never done anything to make you think such a thing."

"You might not know it, but you did." He touched her elbow and brought her attention back to him. "Do you remember that party at Lord Pearson's to honor your dear friend Becca's return from England?"

Emiline's mouth opened and closed like a fish. "Of course I do," she sputtered. "It was one of the first big events we attended together."

"Do you remember talking with Marietta, Paulette, and Sheralyn? The three of you were alone in the lady's salon."

Emiline tried to think back, but the specific event wouldn't come to her. She shrugged and shook her head no. "Not specifically. We were all so close then. Silly young girls eager to gossip, that's all."

"I'd been looking for you everywhere. I missed the beginning of the conversation, but when I found you I heard you saying something that amounted to a list of why I would make the perfect husband for this perfect plan you had. The way you talked about me was like how Connor talked about his favorite breeding horses. It made it seem like you had no real feelings for me—that it was all business. And that wasn't how I was coming to feel for you at the time at all. It hurt, Emiline. As a consequence, I was determined to not let you get the better of me."

Emiline's cheeks flushed with anger. "Is that why you left me? Because of some overheard conversation I knew nothing about and was never given the opportunity to defend myself or contradict it?" Fickle, silly man!

"I am a fool, but not quite that much of one. It wasn't just that, although that was very ill timed. Before we married I needed money. You had it all . . . beauty and grace and . . . and even if the money might have been my initial motivation, it soon was surpassed by my feelings for you—feelings I never ever expected to have."

By and large she got the picture. Yes, Emiline was beginning to put all the clues together in her head, but she wasn't quite there yet. There were still some holes that could easily accommodate the *Sea Gull*. "You developed feelings for me you didn't want while beginning to doubt mine for you. So you ran?"

"It's a bit more complicated than that. I had a good reason not to trust an ambitious woman."

Emiline felt her eyes widen. She'd already known Reinier was a complex man with all the contradictions he seemed to combine, but she'd had no idea he was that convoluted. "Oh, really?"

"You don't know why I was so eager to leave home, do you?"

Once again she was baffled by the relevance of his question, not to mention frustrated that she didn't know. "I assume it was a yearning for adventure to show the rest of the world the allure that up until then only Holland had seen. Did you leave here for the same reasons?"

Reinier shook his head and ran his hands through his hair once again. "That allure seems to be failing me now."

He could say that again. "Well, at least it's all coming out somehow—and that's good, I suppose." She sighed. "Go on. Why did you leave home?"

Reinier turned from her, watching the flow of the water in the pool again. "I know how much your parents loved you, and it might be difficult to understand. Not every childhood is as blessed as yours was. From my earliest memory my father chose not to deal with my mother's overbearing ways, and that meant not dealing with my older brother and me either. He left that totally up to my mother, who was only ever concerned with my brother, the heir."

That certain emphasis on the last word made Emiline frown. He was so charming and likable when he wanted to be, she couldn't imagine his mother not loving him as many others did. "I'm sure you were a beautiful, amiable child. How could she have ignored you?"

"My mother always hated me for having more pleasing looks and manners than my brother. She all but forbade me from excelling above him in any way. If I ever did better with our studies or ran faster or acted with better comportment in public, I was scolded for my arrogance and for not knowing my lower place in this world. As I got older, I found I could charm the servants into going against her wishes.

"My brother was to be betrothed to a distant cousin of the Danish royal family. It was on our trip to Møn when I stood on top of the cliffs and marveled at the deep emerald waves crashing against the Møns Klint hundreds of feet below. I was wondering aloud if the water looked like that everywhere in the world. Mother realized my strong attraction to the mysteries of the sea. That was when she found a way to be rid of me for her and my brother's sake. She shipped me off as quickly as she could."

If Emiline had known this, she could have at the very least understood him a little more. "You never told me."

"It didn't matter. I was past it." His nonchalant shrug couldn't fool her one bit.

It was one more piece in the puzzle that was Reinier, yet it still didn't answer the bigger question burning in her chest. "That doesn't explain why you left me."

"Is it so hard to see? The more time we spent together and the more I cared for you, the more I was convinced it could never work. I knew nothing of estates, knew nothing of how to be a good husband or father. I felt I could either stay and disappoint you and watch your feelings grow colder and wither away when I wasn't the perfect man for your perfect plan, or I could walk away before it ever came to that."

Emiline gasped. It was as if a curtain had been pushed open wider and she saw the whole stage now. Reinier had always been at the mercy of another holding him back—first his mother, then his captain. She understood what a responsibility Bougainvilla was; to him it must have felt like any choice was taken away and replaced by someone else's plans once more.

And Reinier had loved her, he'd admitted as much, yet he'd feared for his own heart. As much as it still hurt, she could see his side now—see the man he truly was and what had made him that way. She knew now that as much as she loved him, he would never be happy if he stayed here on Ronde.

But there was still something else she had to know before the papers were signed and he'd set sail once again. "I think I can see now what might have led you to think you couldn't be happy here but . . . what about Connor?"

"Yes? What about him?"

Emiline hesitated but then softly spoke the one question that had been burning brightest at her for four years. "What did he have that made you stay with him instead of me?"

The idea of words as weapons suddenly became extremely clear to Reinier. Her question felt as if it flayed him. Had she spent all those years wondering what she lacked, doubting herself when the truth was she was more than he deserved?

Reinier turned to her and took her face in both his hands. For the first time he let all his emotions show in his eyes while he gazed into the sea-colored depths of hers. "There is nothing Connor has or had that can ever compare to you."

"Then why?"

Reinier saw her lower lip begin to shake. He leaned in and gave it a quick, gentle kiss. Taking her into his arms, he held her to him tightly while stroking her hair and running a soothing hand up and down her back. "Because I was a coward and it was the easy way out. Connor is my truest friend. We ask nothing of each other outside of business matters. I could have as disappointing a character as possible and Connor would still have me, but you . . . you deserve so much more than that. I was afraid that you didn't return my love, true, but most of all I was afraid I'd never be able to be the man you ought to have."

Emiline pulled back, bracing her hands on his arms to look into his eyes again. "But you were the man I cared for. I didn't need you to be anything more than that."

Reinier shook his head with a sad laugh, reaching for her hands and taking them in his. "Oh, I know you didn't. You've done a wonderful job with the estate. I see now that you didn't need me for that at all."

She looked down at their joined hands before she spoke again. "I did need you. I wanted you, but I managed. I managed because I was left no choice." She looked up, searching his face. "People are often capable of much more than they give themselves credit for, Reinier."

After all he'd done to her, she still believed in him. Another bit of his heart was lashed open. "You're not just capable, you're amazing. You haven't just kept things going, you've improved on them in ways I don't think a man would have ever thought of. You were born to rule Bougainvilla, Emiline, better than anyone else ever could."

She beamed a little at his praise, and he couldn't help but smile back. "Reinier, all that doesn't mean I couldn't have used a partner to share that with. But despite everything, I do love it here, the place and the people and the business part of it. It's become more precious to me than anything."

Her words thundered in his head. He'd come to this island meaning to torment her just like she'd made him suffer all those years ago and he'd proposed that bargain for his own self-centered purposes. Pride had made him believe he could elude her charms. What an enormous fool he'd been. It was his own feelings he couldn't escape.

Although his heart would be in shreds once again, Reinier knew what he had to do. He must sign the papers.

"Then you should have it. It will all be rightfully yours alone so no one can ever take that away from you."

"Thank you," she whispered.

Reinier leaned in and kissed her, exploring every inch of her mouth with his own, memorizing every nuance and texture. He would give her anything she wanted and walk away. He had no right to be here.

18

Reinier had only been here for three days, but it seemed much longer. He waved an inquisitive mosquito off his right ear, listening to the excited bustle of waves washing against the piles underneath his feet as they rose to the evening tide. Behind a few feathery clouds the sun was beginning to set, glimmering in shades of magenta and purple. Countless times he'd watched dusk settle, yet sunset still took his breath away.

Heels clicked on the rough planks of the wharf and Reinier turned to see Connor walking slowly up to him. He looked very much like a rugged pirate in his black breeches and black linen shirt. Connor always preferred dark colors where Reinier enjoyed lighter tones. What a pair they'd made, Reinier thought, and his lips twitched into a brief smile at the fleeting melancholy. He didn't move, though. He just stood at the wharf, his eyes back on the horizon, and let Connor come to him.

From the corner of his eye, Reinier saw that he, too, watched in silence as the sun was slowly swallowed up by the sea.

"You're not coming with me, I suppose." Connor spoke low, his words a whisper on the brackish evening breeze.

Reinier shook his head, then turned fully to him. A heavy silence stretched between them.

"There has never been a lover." Reinier was just stating facts; there was no accusation.

Connor pressed his lips together to hide the grin that was clearly sparkling in his eyes. "No, I admit I deliberately misled you. Otherwise, you'd have never come back here."

The Irishman had known what had been unsettling his soul even before Reinier himself had. Even so, the future was still uncertain. Still, Reinier was thankful for both his friend's boldness and prudence, but above all for his honesty now.

"There's somewhere you should go. Someone you should see again."

Connor raised his eyebrows in confusion and Reinier smirked. He'd seen the longing on the Irishman's face. Connor was thinking of her and he wasn't sure whether he should welcome it. But the Irishman and the Irishwoman belonged together.

"She'll be waiting for you."

Connor huffed. "I don't think it's a good idea."

"Although you're thinking of her all the time and yearn to see her again?"

Connor kicked the jagged remains of a lonely shell over the brink of the wharf back into the sea.

"If you're so reluctant to go back to her, I wonder what it would take to make you see her again." Reinier raised an eyebrow as the thought struck him. An eye for an eye. It was just a very little white lie . . . "Perhaps if I told you that you were her first . . . would that be enough incentive?"

At that, Connor's head snapped up. His brows furrowed, the muscles in his cheeks jumped, and a fuming inferno was burning in his midnight blue eyes. "That is a damn lie and we both know it," Connor pressed out between clenched teeth.

Licking his lips, Reinier suppressed the bark of laughter. "Well, technically," he reminded him, "you lied to me, while I simply hid the truth from you."

"What the hell are you talking about?"

Reinier gave a casual shrug and held his right hand up, palm out, fingers closed. He looked at it, studying it as if he'd never seen it before. Then he parted his index and middle fingers only, looked at Connor, and asked with mock innocence in his voice, "Do you think my hand is big enough to cover such a secret?"

He saw the memory flash in Connor's eyes. It made his sapphire eyes burn even brighter. Taking a step toward Reinier, who only grinned broadly and raised his hands in surrender, Connor hissed, "You devious—"

"Now, now. No need to get nasty with me. Technically speaking, you were her first. I saw her half-torn hymen. But her honor hadn't really been ruined before . . . an impertinent Irishman seduced her."

Connor let out a very irritated growl. "Just me, was it?"

Reinier shrugged with one shoulder only, wicked delight on his face. "Maybe I had a small hand in it as well—no pun intended, of course."

The full impact of this news hit and Reinier watched all color drain from Connor's face. His mouth went slack, his jaw almost dropping.

"What you make of this piece of information is up to you," he murmured just loud enough that Connor heard him.

The possible consequences—honor and the lack thereof or losing it—were probably rolling around in Connor's mind. In a way, Reinier was glad he wouldn't be around when the Irishman came to a decision. His mood would be one he didn't want to witness, not even from afar.

To ensure he was on the right island when that happened, Reinier nudged him a little more in the right direction. "The breeze has pitched. I assume you'll have a quick passage back to Grenada." Reinier held out his hand for Connor to shake it. "Godspeed, my friend."

Their eyes met and more than unspoken words passed between them. When they parted, Connor bowed to him one last time.

"Supper will commence momentarily," the young maid told Reinier on entering the mansion. "The mistress asked me to tell you she will join you soon."

Reinier absentmindedly waved his hand in her direction. "I find myself not very hungry this evening. Will you tell her I'll be waiting for her in the study?"

"Very well, sir." The maid's quick curtsy was accompanied by a timid nod.

Reinier walked straight into the study. Closing the door behind him and leaning against it, he shut his eyes and inhaled deeply. Here he was again at Bougainvilla, making the hardest decision in his life. He'd thought leaving her had been awful already, but this was even worse.

All his attempts to bind her to him stemmed from loving her, but he knew now that truly loving her meant giving her her heart's desire. And if that meant breaking his own heart, then so be it. He'd carry on like he always had.

Instead of strolling aimlessly around the chamber like he had a few nights before in search for clues what it would take to make good on his promise to seduce her, he went directly to the mahogany secretary. Lowering the writing surface and working the locks of the drawer, he took out the divorce papers. He opened them and, still standing, read them once more. But soon the letters blurred before his eyes and all he saw were images of the past few days.

Emiline's demeanor spitting hatred at him. Emiline's body quivering as she climaxed again in his arms. Emiline's breathtaking, contagious smile. Emiline's indifference. And finally, when he let her see inside his soul and she let him have a glimpse of hers . . .

Those deep wounds he'd inflicted would never heal. Emiline's defeat squeezed his heart so much it robbed him of breath.

What was done couldn't be undone. He was past lamenting his tortured heart. He was over trying to punish her for what she'd done to him. She couldn't be blamed. It was him and him alone who had done this to her, to him—to them.

For once, he wouldn't act selfishly. He'd end this here and now. Tonight, not tomorrow morning, he'd sign the papers, and should she wish it, he'd leave for good.

Reinier could continue to try and convince himself he could carry on as he had before, but deep down he knew his heart would never recover if she expected him to disappear and never come back again.

"Reinier."

He almost failed to hear her when she spoke. Emiline had come into the study so silently he hadn't been aware of it. Carefully ridding his face of any treacherous emotions, he put the parchment in his hands down and looked up.

Her white dress was so magnificent it made her bright eyes shine. She looked as if she wore angelic light itself.

"The maid said you were waiting for me here." Her voice was flat, belying her squared shoulders and thrust-up chin. "So, here I am."

"Yes." Swallowing a sigh, Reinier reached for the small box that contained the quill and inkpot. "I have decided that this farce has gone on long enough."

He took out the quill and inspected its point. Judging it too worn down for a clear signature, he grabbed the penknife and began to lengthen the quill's split and the open tube. "If Bougain-villa and this divorce is everything you want, then you shall have it." Reshaping the tines and the tip, Reinier continued, "I'm going to end this bargain here and now. I'll sign the papers."

The penknife was back in the box and he twirled the quill briefly, thinking. Taking the sharp implement to scrape the parchment, he erased the generous sum she'd suggested. "I won't accept the money you offer, though. I've got plenty of my own."

Reinier then opened the papers to the last page, grasped the quill, and flipped the lid of the inkpot open with the tip of his middle finger.

Finally, he looked up at her. She was blanching and her chest heaving with quick breaths, her eyes round and liquid. She was probably worried he could change his mind or that this would be another devious scheme he'd thought up. But she'd be wrong in her assumptions.

"No need to panic, Emiline. I won't reconsider this. Your well-being is what matters to me, and if that entails being rid of me, then so be it." He attempted an awkward smile, then stared at the inkpot before him and hesitated.

He loved her. But it didn't change where they were now. He had to set her free; it was the only possible solution to their failed marriage. How could he make her see he truly loved her otherwise?

Life would never be the same for him. It would be poor and petty. He'd be an empty shell in a waking nightmare, because each and every day he'd know what he'd lost. But knowing she was better off without him gave him the courage to grab the quill harder, bringing it closer to the ink bottle.

Emiline leaped forward. The sudden commotion stunned him. She reached for the inkpot and closed it with a swift flick of her wrist.

Bewildered, Reinier glanced up at her. Her breath had pitched even more and she moistened her lips with a small flick of her tongue.

"Don't."

"I'm sorry?" Reinier was too numb and too puzzled to understand.

"Don't sign the papers, Reinier."

"But—"

Emiline wasn't aware she'd been holding her breath until the very moment when her lungs began to burn, doubling the fierce, rapid staccato of her heart beating in her chest.

"I thought you wanted me to sign them. I thought you wanted to be rid of me? Isn't . . . isn't that what you wanted?"

Much to her chagrin she didn't know the answer to Reinier's perplexed outburst; she didn't even know if there was just one answer.

"Yes." She meant it, she did, but she didn't want it to end like this. "No," she corrected herself, frowning at her own puzzling reply.

"Yes? No? Which is it?"

Reinier's befuddlement wasn't supportive. The pungent aftertaste of resentment in his words made it even harder. The situation now was even more awkward than it had been before.

What had she done? An independent woman for so long now, she'd relied on reason as her sole guide; but suddenly she'd let go of all that common sense and logic, thrown her precious practicality to the wind, and stayed his hand.

How could she explain what wasn't even clear to her?

Letting the quill drop, Reinier crossed his arms on his chest and stared at her, the cream silk of his frock tightening around his shoulders despite its immaculate tailoring. His face was blank but for one eyebrow slightly raised.

Emiline caressed the stomacher she wore just where it met the rim of her dress, the knobs of the flowery pattern wobbling in her palm. The ache didn't dull and the aggravated blows of her heart didn't stop either.

"I don't know. In the beginning I did, but . . . now I'm not so certain. I mean—" With a crestfallen sigh, Emiline turned away from him.

"You have no idea what it's like, what it feels like—" She curled the hand over her heart into a fist. "Here. Inside. When I see you looking out at the sea with so much affection . . . Like it's the most important thing in your life—a position I thought I'd petitioned for when we married."

"Emiline, I—"

"No, please. Do not interrupt me." She wouldn't hide, not now. This moment was too important to waste it behind pretense.

Turning, she faced him. "You are brusque and arrogant with your exalted airs and your fancy clothes, Reinier, but you're also caring and brilliant and ever charming."

His mouth went rigid and he thrust his chin up a little. Despair had her voice diminish to a weak whisper. "I understand now. I do. We'll never have the kind of marriage my parents had. You will never be a man to stay in one place for long. It's not in you. You need your freedom."

"But—"

This time, Emiline raised her hand, palm out, to silence his objection. "I know it's unreasonable and illogical and against everything I know is good or right for me, but—God help me— I love you, Reinier. I love you with all my heart. Despite your flaws."

Walking around him, Emiline grabbed the divorce papers and carried them to the cold fireplace. She held one corner of the parchment into the flame of a flickering candle on the mantel and knelt down by the grate, watching what she'd imagined to be a bright and independent future sputter and curl until it blackened under the hissing fire's assault.

Looking back at Reinier, she saw him standing as if rooted to the rug, his spine rigid like the trunk of a tree, his amazing lime and golden eyes blinking with leashed emotions she couldn't decipher.

Was this where he'd wanted her all along?

It didn't matter. Not anymore. She'd bared her soul to him and she'd made her decision final. The fuming cackle of the papers being reduced to soot before her proved it.

Bracing herself on her knees, she got up and walked toward him. "Please go and come back whenever you choose to. Know that you'll always be welcome here. This is your home. Our home. Just . . ." Her voice broke.

Even though he made her feel alive like she'd never before thought was possible, Emiline had to give him freedom or else he would never return at all. She would never have what it took to hold him.

Averting her eyes, Emiline half turned, ready to walk out of the study, ready to give him the kind of freedom he craved whether it broke her heart or not. "Just don't let it be too long until the next time you return. That's all I ask."

She grabbed the doorknob, although more for physical support than to open the door. Her knees had turned to wobbly pudding. The weight of tears filled her eyes. Closing them, she leaned her forehead against the cool wood of the door.

She had to be sensible, had to be resolute in spite of that deep sadness that filled her now. It felt like she was breaking apart, shattering into so many pieces she'd probably never be able to put them back together again.

"I don't know what to say."

A cold shudder ran down her spine. What if she'd just made a complete fool of herself?

It didn't matter anymore. She stood by her decision.

"I believe 'until we meet again' is customary under the circumstances." Emiline swallowed the heartfelt sob that constricted her throat. "You're free, Reinier. Free to go wherever you want. Just think of me every once in a while."

His hand wrapped around her upper arm and urged her to release the doorknob and turn to him, but she kept her eyes down, much too embarrassed to let him see the well of tears in them.

"You understand, you say?"

She nodded once, certain that if she spoke now, she'd completely break down.

"I'm sorry, but you don't."

Astonished at the haughty tone in his words, Emiline looked up. "What?"

Seeing that austere frown on his face, she gasped, fearing he was about to deliver the final blow to her wounded and bleeding heart.

But then the corners of his eyes crinkled with the minuscule smile on his lips, and her heart missed a beat.

"If you really understood, Emiline, you'd realize that all I ever needed was to know that you loved me."

"But I do!" she spluttered.

"Yes, I know that—now." His other arm wrapped around her other upper arm and he lowered his head with a sigh.

"Emiline, can't you see?"

"See what?" She didn't know what to make of this. Her

mind was numb. She curled her clammy hands into fists at her hips to stop them from trembling.

"I want to be a part of you, your life, not just some fine-looking face you can show around. I want to fall asleep with you in my arms. I want to wake up beside you. I don't want to leave. I want to remain here, by your side."

Nothing he said made any sense. What was he babbling? "But you are!" Emiline exclaimed, stepping up to him. "You are a part of me. You have my heart, Reinier."

That disconcerting, level stare on his face softened into a strange, somewhat fatuous smile. "And you have mine," he said. "Be more careful with it from now on, will you?"

"What?" She didn't care that bafflement had her voice pitch into a shrieking gasp. This situation was beyond her grasp. Was he saying that—

"I'm nothing without you, Emiline."

"You're . . . ?" Like a demented half-wit she was about to parrot what he'd just said. She hadn't thought it possible, but her heart beat even heavier in her chest.

"Will you let me stay—as your husband?"

Slowly, the torrent of gibberish in her mind abated and his words reached through the fog. "Why, what kind of wife would I be to forbid it? If that is your wish . . . stay as long as you want."

Reinier's whole demeanor seemed touched with a warm glow from within. "I should give you fair warning, though. It could be quite long."

"Really?" Emiline had difficulties coping with the happiness suddenly blooming and pulsing, threatening to burst out of her. "How long are we talking about? A fortnight? A month?"

Tilting his head, Reinier pursed his truly superb lips and finally suggested, "How about 'indefinitely'?"

Time suddenly stopped. Emiline felt like she was falling, no, flying, elation carrying her one step closer to heaven.

Taking a step back, she tapped her forefinger against her chin, pretending to consider what he'd just said like they were engaged in bargaining over a barrel of her island's rum.

"That could mean years. Decades even." Her tone was deliberately stern.

He searched her face for a moment, then expanded his perusal over her whole body. Emiline felt stirred by that glance, his eyes darkening with that wonderful mixture of playful wickedness and sensual promise. Her gown was too tight in too many places all of a sudden.

"It does not fit your plans?" Reinier walked around her, his heated gaze wandering all over her. "I wonder why. Do you have a prior appointment?"

With a blasé shrug, Emiline asked over her shoulder, "In general or tonight?"

"Both." She shivered as his whisper tickled her earlobe and sweet curls of gooseflesh were bouncing up and down her back.

"None I can think of. Why?" She brought her lips closer to his. "What do you have in mind?"

"Oh, nothing too strenuous." He brushed his lips over hers.

"Is that so?" Her words were low and disrupted by gasps of yearning. "How disappointing, Reinier."

He gave a low chuckle and stood right in front of her again. The fingers of his one hand played along her spine. Her awareness of the soft pressure was so acute it was as if she didn't wear anything at all. His hand came to rest at the small of her back, pressing her body close until she felt the prominent bulge of his arousal against her belly. A quiver of yearning shot through her body, and velvety moistness settled between her legs.

He brought his free hand up between their bodies, his fingers playing over the low rim of her dress where her stomacher was held in place. He squeezed her breast through the gown's material; then his fingers sneaked in, teasing the hungry flesh right above her erect nipple. Emiline bit back a moan.

"Well." His voice was reduced to a croak drenched with desire. "I suppose it will be strenuous, but only for me since I intend to do all the work."

"Do you now?" Arousal sent her heart into a frantic drum southward.

"Uh-hm," he nodded, bringing his mouth closer.

Emiline took quick, shallow breaths through her slightly open mouth. "And what—"

His lips sealed hers. Her eyes fluttered closed and she answered him, yielding to the frenzied desire stirring in her; her tongue chasing his, her hands roaming his arms, shoulders, and back.

His kiss was delicious—feverish, yet slow; possessive, yet tender; fervent, yet oh-so-skilled. Her head spun even more than it already had.

Reinier swept her up in his arms, and when she felt her knee softly bump into the door, one hand, trembling and reluctant to let go of him, groped blindly for the doorknob.

His lips never left her. He began to nibble down her neck. She laughed with all the joy and longing that filled her.

19

Upstairs in her room, Emiline grasped his frock coat impatiently. She felt reckless and wild, and tore at his garments, her legs wrapped around his waist, her hips instinctually seeking the hardness in his breeches with gyrating movements.

Lips bruised in the kiss that had turned frantic in yearning. She felt him pulling at her stomacher hard; then his fingers got tangled in the laces of her dress, which loosened only after a tiny ripping sound.

"No!"

Despite the devouring fire burning in his eyes, Reinier drew back. "No?"

This was taking too long. She wanted him. Now. Hard. Fast. She wanted to feel him claiming her. "I mean, don't bother. I need to feel you in me."

He fumbled at his breeches.

"Now, Reinier." Another tearing sound. "Now would be—"

She cried out with relief as he filled her and stretched her wide. Lifting her hips even farther off the bed, her muscles contracted to grip him and guide him in.

"As my lady wishes," Reinier groaned, rolling his hips in a rhythm that was too slow and too steady.

Her skin was tingling and tight, and the soft fabric of her dress was scratchy and intolerable, but she held him cradled both in her arms and her core, moaned when he thrust into her, gasped as he retreated.

She tasted his lips and they tumbled deeper into the kiss. Emiline shuddered at the feel of his body covering hers. Pleasure coursed through her, making her head light and her hands clench, bunching the silk of his frock and the shirt underneath.

She blazed, she melted. She saw the passion in his look, reveled in it, and let him see how deep pleasure ran through her.

The coil in her belly tightened until the pressure became almost unbearable. It twisted closer and closer with each thrust he delivered.

"More." She moaned, urging him on. "More, Reinier, please."

He obliged, pumping harder and faster into her. His hands found hers and opened the death grip she had on his shoulders. Fingers entwined, he guided her arms up over her head, pressing her hands into the mattress with the weight of his body as he braced himself on them. Opening his legs, he forced her to spread her legs wider with his thighs. Stretched like this, she felt him slide even deeper.

Long, roughened, and relentless strokes shocked her body and blinded her mind. His hunger steamed through her, and she burned brighter and surged higher. She was heading toward the edge, only remotely aware of his soft, low groans of pleasure echoing her own loud, deep moans.

The coil in her belly finally sprang, sending her pulse hammering to where he was sheathed tight. Tremors washed through her whole body like a thousand silky tongues and a thousand feathery kisses crawling over her.

He quickly brought one hand down and left her. Gasping

for breath in the overwhelming bliss she'd just found, she watched him shiver as he climaxed too.

Reinier threw his head back, his eyes wide open. He groaned as release found him, and his mind exploded in the gigantic wave of ecstasy washing over him. Totally spent, he fell down on the soft cushion of her body, his breath coming in long and deep gasps.

He braced himself on one arm only to rid her of most of his weight. His hand came up to wipe a curly chocolate strand off her face and tuck it behind her ear.

The flickering light of the lonesome candle on her dressing table illuminated her ethereal beauty. She was so stunning, especially now in the aftermath, that his heart leaped once. He leaned closer, brushing his lips against hers. His tongue flicked over their fullness to taste her once again. The image of strawberries flashed in his mind for a moment.

The soft caress had her shiver under him. Her brilliant turquoise eyes shone for him only. Everything around him ceased to exist. What was important was to touch her, to feel her, to drink in her sweet taste, to take in her delicious fragrance in the aftermath when musk had her natural scent become deeper and richer.

Reinier smiled softly at the stillness in him. When had it happened? That absolute peacefulness that filled him in her arms only. Had it been there from the start?

Blockhead. How had he managed to overlook it? How had he been able to breathe without it all the time?

Lying on his back, he wrapped his arm around her, dragging her to him. His hands wandered up and down her back to press her against him. He reveled in the feel of her, soft and oh-so-sweet. Her body was where it belonged, close to his, wrapped around him, halfway covering him.

"I swear . . . if you tear another one of my gowns, I will kick you out."

Her words were slurred. Yes, he had done that. He had made her speech blurry, and he had torn her dress in his haste to bury himself in her and claim her.

His woman. His wife.

At her muffled giggle, pride pulsed in his chest and made his head light. "It will be my pleasure to employ a dozen modistes to have a whole new wardrobe made for you for the sole purpose of ripping those dresses apart while you wear them." His fingers took hold of the delicate back of her neck, his thumb caressing her cheek. "Until then, I promise to behave."

"Behave?" Emiline's eyes widened. "Reinier, we both know you've never been good at that."

He burst into laughter. "Very well, then. I promise to peel you out of those garments before I ravish you until your new wardrobe is ready."

His fingers started to fiddle with the laces of her gown, loosening them and brushing the garment down her shoulder so that he could reach the laced shift underneath.

"Stop that." Emiline playfully slapped his hands away. "You'll ruin it completely."

She shoved him back, swung her leg over his hip, and straddled him. "Let me do that."

Her voice was low and alluring. She straightened on his thighs, her hands reaching up to hook her fingers into the rim of her dress. She dragged it down along with the chemise, exposing her immaculate upper body to him inch after agonizingly slow inch.

His little seductress, so wonderful in her teasing.

Desire swamped him, making his head spin, his senses reel. He thought he might go out of his mind. Her dark nipples were hard and erect. Reinier licked his lips.

Her tapered hands moved farther down. He was under her spell. Mesmerized, he only watched as she bunched the skirts of her dress in her hands and dragged them up, exposing her thighs. But his little vixen stopped right before Reinier could get a glimpse of her mons.

In response, his cock hardened again, so much so he had to hold his breath not to whimper. He yearned to feel her hot moistness clamp around him like a creamy, tight fist that milked every last drop from him. The need to be in her again, that mindless craze she induced, undid him.

Reinier fumbled at his shirt, but his hands were too shaky to take care. He ripped the collar open and pulled the shirt over his head, throwing it to the floor. Hands grabbing her upper arms, he threw her off his thighs to lay her down on the bed, ignoring her surprised gasp and mirthful laugh that followed. He got up to shed his breeches and stockings before he bent down again. His hands pulled impatiently at her dress, and his teeth aided him in his effort to undress her completely.

Lifting her up in his arms, Reinier carried her to the head of the bed and laid her down. She lay naked and sprawled on the coverlet, rolling like a cat lazing in the sun with her arms stretched over her head and her thighs rubbing against each other.

Heat raged through his bloodstream. Longing, sexual and possessive, pulsed in his body. Reinier didn't swallow the purring growl. He crawled onto the bed, like a predator stalking its prey. If she kept up that teasing, he'd make her pay—dearly. And he knew she'd love every moment of it.

His heel bumped against the bedside table catching the corner of the book that had been lying on it and sending it flying. Emiline ducked out of the way, but Reinier grabbed hold of it before it hit the pillow. He turned it in his hands, wondering what reading she enjoyed before falling asleep.

When he saw the title, his eyes widened. Poems by John Donne. Tilting the book to the side, Reinier gazed into her wide-open, loving eyes and the idea struck him like lightning. He settled in next to her and immediately began looking through the pages. When he found his favorite elegy, the fingertips of his left hand caressed the page in an intimate gesture; then he leaned back against the head of the bed and silently started to read.

He wasn't aware that Emiline had been studying him until she spoke. "Would you read to me?"

Biting his lower lip, Reinier nodded and began to read aloud. " 'Come, Madam, come, all rest my powers defy,/Until I labour, I in labour lie./The foe oft-times, having the foe in sight,/Is tired with standing though they never fight.' "

Emiline blinked, her lips moving into an O of surprise. Closing the book and laying it aside, Reinier bent down to kiss her, his lips sliding against hers before his tongue flicked over them. She opened them with a willing sigh and he deepened the kiss, his body pressing against hers.

Reinier ran his hand into that wonderful mass of hair, massaging her scalp. " 'Off with that girdle, like heaven's zone glistering, /But a far fairer world encompassing./Unpin that spangled breastplate which you wear,/That th' eyes of busy fools may be stopped there.' " Rolling his hips, his cock cradled against her soft belly, his tongue slipped between her lips, tasting her, swirling around hers, tempting and teasing her.

" 'Unlace yourself, for that harmonious chime/Tells me from you, that now 'tis bed time.' " Nuzzling her chin, his hand left her hair and wandered down, beneath the cover, to cup her backside and press it against his rigid cock. She lifted her leg with a blissful sigh, wrapping it around his waist.

" 'Off with that happy busk, which I envy,/That still can be, and still can stand so nigh.' " Reinier rained tiny kisses down her neck and up her shoulder, his hand caressing the silken skin of her backside.

Drawing back, Reinier pursed his lips, his exploring fingers frozen in place down the crevice of her cheeks. "I'd say we've done all that already. I could have skipped that part entirely."

Emiline blinked, bewildered.

"To save time."

Her exasperated sigh was not very convincing. "When have you become so impatient?"

Reinier playfully bit her chin. "It's a new trait I acquired." His fingers down her crevice wandered a bit lower, so they played at her entrance without ever penetrating. "You do not approve of it?"

Her whole body arched into his touch, and a low, quivering moan escaped her lips. "No—o. I mean, yes. Oh!" She let out a frustrated huff then, her face puckering in a funny way. "Don't force me to think now. Just—"

He let the tip of his middle finger enter. She moaned and her hips bucked.

"Go on?" Reinier helped out.

At Emiline's enthusiastic nod, he let his hand travel over her hip to the jet-black curls between her legs, his fingers curling into her pubic hair. " 'Off with your wiry coronet and show/The hairy diadem which on you doth grow.' "

Her eyes fluttered closed and she rolled her hips into his touch, tempting his fingers to travel farther down. When Reinier didn't, she scowled a little.

"I believe you forgot a line or two."

Reinier gave a noncommittal shrug. "I'm shortening it a little, adapting so it fits."

His hand straightened and his fingers played over her erect, sensitive peak in the softest of touches. Emiline shuddered in his arms, her eyelids at half-mast. Her trembling echoed through him, increasing the tingling anticipation that vibrated through every fiber of his body.

"I see." A breathy laugh swung in her words. "Well, then. I'm sorry I interrupted you."

" 'Thou angel bring'st with thee/A heaven like Mahomet's paradise; and though/Ill spirits walk in white, we easily know/ By this these angels from an evil sprite./Those set our hairs, but these our flesh upright.' "

Emiline caught her breath and she pressed her lips together so tight they were nothing more but a fine, pale line. Her cheeks puffed and she blinked, her body shaking with the giggle she obviously tried to swallow.

"What amuses you?"

The whole bed shook with the force of her mirth. "I'm sorry. I don't mean to be fanciful, but . . ."

"But what?"

Emiline took a deep breath. "Knowing you, I can't imagine there's anything that would not . . . uhm . . . 'set your flesh upright.' "

Reinier hummed, nodding in thought. "I agree it has never happened before. Still, there's a first time for everything, although I can't imagine it would happen in your arms."

That bright, carefree side she'd just let him see disappeared completely and she blushed, her eyes narrowed to dangerous slits. "Oh," she huffed. "Oh! You! Rascal! Scoundrel, you!" Her small fist hammered against his shoulder with little punches.

Reinier ignored her and slid two fingers deep into her core. Instantly, she stilled, threw her head back, and gasped, her hand falling limply down, her hips gyrating against his hand.

"I'm sorry, but did you say something?"

"Oh, please—" Again Emiline moaned, a little louder this time. "Don't stop."

" 'License my roving hands, and let them go/Before, behind, between, above, below,' " he whispered in her ear, pressing a soft kiss on her earlobe. " 'My mine of precious stones, my em-

278

pery,/How blessed I am in this discovering thee!/To enter in these bonds, is to be free;/Then where my hand is set, my seal shall be.' "

His kisses traveled down the side of her neck until his lips circled her nipple. Her skin was warm and soft. Teeth grazing, his tongue soothed and his lips closed over her to gently suckle one breast, all the while the fingers of his other hand never ceased to pump slowly in and out of her.

He broke away to repeat the teasing game on her other breast, whispering against her skin, " 'Gems which you women use/ Are like Atlanta's balls cast in men's views,/That when a fool's eye lighteth on a gem,/His earthly soul may covet theirs, not them.' "

Goose bumps raced over her deliciously dewy skin and Reinier wanted to kiss every one of them. He almost succeeded as his lips wandered farther down her body. When he reached her belly button, his tongue snaked out to tickle it just before he nipped her lower belly. " 'Then since I may know,/As liberally, as to a midwife, show/Thyself: cast all, yea, this white linen hence.' "

Wandering down her body, his hands cupped her hips and tilted them slightly. Farther down, he dipped his head, his tongue stroking the inside of her thighs with lazy flicks. The more she spread her thighs, the more Reinier moved upward. When she opened up for him completely and parted her legs, he took in her scent that whispered like silk over his skin, felt its balminess on his lips, its taste a rich syrup on his tongue.

Burying his face against her, his tongue flicked over her once, twice, savoring that unique, musky fragrance. His grip tightened to hold her in place the instant before he closed his mouth fully over her. He suckled gently and felt her shiver against his lips. Slowly, he lapped her creamy folds with the flat of his tongue, nibbled and nipped at her, teased the tight nub at the top of her sex with the tip of his tongue with gentle but rapid flicks.

Every soft gasp from her when he suckled, every quiver of

her body, every breathy moan sent the building desire faster and faster through his veins. Her hips' response became violent and he knew he'd bring her any moment now.

She arced, then her body came off the bed and she cried his name. Reinier closed his eyes while he drank her sweet honey, kissing and lapping at her just a little longer until her ecstasy abated.

He pulled away and wandered up her luscious body, dragging his tongue with hungry licks up, flicking over the elongated pebbles of her nipples. Then he settled in between her legs, which promptly wrapped around his waist. He felt her arch under him to increase the pressure of his cock against her wet core, but he remained still.

" 'Why then,' " Reinier hissed the last line of the poem. " 'What need'st thou have more covering than a man.' " He drew his hips upward and entered her in a slow thrust.

Again, a delicious shiver tickled down his spine as he felt himself slide in, sheathed to the hilt in her moist heat, each one of her muscles gripping him.

His pulse pitched when he heard her whisper his name again and again. He felt stunned, yet his head spun. Bliss exploded throughout his body and mind.

Before he started to move, his mouth took hers again in a heated kiss. Then their lips parted.

He saw the fire of ecstasy in the turquoise blue depths of her eyes, saw flames of passion, but above all, he saw the bright blaze of her love for him.

A tender smile grew on his face. That moment he knew that nothing could ever wipe that smile away again. At long last, he was no longer alone, no longer running from something he'd never really understood. Finally, he was truly free; free to love and to cherish her like she deserved—and to be loved in return.

"I love you, Emiline," Reinier said with a happy sigh.